DRY BRIDGE OF VENGEANCE

BAER CHARLTON

Cover photography: Keven Lokey
Cover model: Jolie Richardson
Cover art: Roslyn McFarland
Rogena Mitchell-Jones, Literary Editor
www.rogenamitchell.com

Published by Mordant Media, Portland, Oregon

10 9 8 7 6 5 4 3 2 1

CONTENTS

OUT

In rodeo, anything in the arena and no longer confined
in a chute or behind a gate is "out."

The loud buzzer rang down the cell block. All conversations stopped or were hushed.

The loudspeaker echoed in the three tiers and ricocheted off the metal toilets and sinks in the cells. "Prisoner four-eight-two-seven-three-one… stand at your door."

She looked over to her cellmate of seven years. They mouthed their goodbyes.

The rolling bell rattled as it buzzed—three heartbeats and then the hard silence.

Every prisoner listened for the cold steel latch back and the metal roll of the wheels. Every ear waited, every heart skipped half a beat, every head lifted as the faces all wore looks of mixed emotions. The dull muted sound of the smaller buzzer on the processing door hummed through the steel and armored glass.

The lock clicked, and the lower hinge complained softly. The foot wearing a size eighteen boot stepped out onto the steel decking. The man's voice was more tired than soft.

"Come ahead, Rocket."

She stepped out of the cell. She carried the tan jumpsuit, bedding, and the last of her toiletries on her two outstretched forearms. As she looked straightforward out through the high windows, her eyes slowly closed with a sigh. As her eyes opened, she finished with the dust-grayed scene of the wall outside. Cell block C had a nickname of *cruel*. The upper deck looked out and down at the front gate—the gate to freedom, covered by a dry bridge and two battle turrets. Two thousand, five hundred, fifty-six days—and the next hour would be the longest.

One hundred and sixty-eight spoons, lightly tapping, chimed each of her steps on the cell doors.

Seventeen steps brought her to within arm's reach of the big man's throat. A half step more, and he would be within shiv range. He never moved. She stopped. Her arms outstretched from the elbows. Her hands held the jumpsuit folded and flat, just the way they had seven years before.

"Jeb."

His voice was soft but dispassionate. "Is this the last time I'm going to see you, Rocket?"

Her lower lip rolled as she thought. "I hope so... but probably—"

He shook his head in resolution as he turned. The buzzer sounded in the door as it began to roll open.

He had first met the woman the week he returned from the first Iraq war—the short one. Every village, town, or small city had been scrambling to find something for their hometown heroes to do. They saw it as extravagant recognition for winning a war. Every returning service person recognized it for the same political bull manure the mass assault on the tiny country had been.

Sergeant Jubal Johnson sat in the stands with his mother and her third husband, their three heads buried in worn Stetson hats. The rodeo was in their blood. The bull and bareback riders were short rides—for the most part—par for a local rodeo using almost pro stock for rides. The barrel racing was barely more exciting.

Jeb wasn't alone when he sat up for the first round of the tie-down roping. There was only one category for a rider, calf, and horse. There was only one young gal competing against twenty-three men. Nobody came close to her. Her lasso was in the first pass over her head when her body broke the chute. One more loop around and the rope shot out and hit the calf. Nobody could tell if she had leaped over her horse's head or was already running. Her horse never needed a jerk-line to get him to back up to apply the tension—they were a longtime team.

The judges had to look it up, but she had set a record. The new nickname of 'Rocket' followed her the next night onto the stage.

Jeb was the honorary judge of five for the Rodeo Queen. They had asked he be in uniform. All the voting tallies went through him to the secretary. His math was fast enough to see the second runner-up wasn't even in the hunt. Even the four-inch scar on the side of Rocket's face, where a wild pig had nailed her while her long knife sliced the boar's heart, had been more of an asset than a disfigurement. All the locals knew the boar was her first kill. She had asked her father to take her hunting for her sixteenth birthday.

The day the other county beauty queens gathered for the state beauty pageant; she had told the officials she had other plans. While the other young women were parading the stage in evening gowns at the Miss California pageant, Rocket was shoulder-to-shoulder with her father—skinning and boning a large sow and its two suckling piglets. The two hunters were stripped to the waist and covered with steaming hot pig blood. A soaked shirt and jacket in the night's frigid air could kill a person. Blood washed off. Death was permanent.

She knew they would have to pack out the two hundred pounds of meat that night and return in the morning with the burro to pack out the rest. The burro had balked at the heavy load but soon followed as the two hunters packed out their own weight in meat.

More scars would come later.

She stood at the counter as Jeb handed her the yellow envelope of her personal effects. She opened the flap and poured out the few items. She knew the keys were useless. The apartment and truck would be long gone. She flipped open the thin men's wallet.

"Where's my ID?"

The man settled his weight on his left leg. "They took your driver's license and security card shortly after you got here. I don't think they are going to let you back in at the DOJ again. And, just so you know, I checked this morning—you're still on the no-fly list."

She looked up at him through her eyebrows. Her shadowed eyes were like flinted steel. "What time does the bus get here?"

"I can run you into town…"

Her head never moved. "What time for the bus?"

He ground his head around to look at the large clock. The longhand clicked right. He looked back. "About twenty minutes."

She studied his perfectly pressed uniform. She guessed the badge was placed exactly where it was supposed to be. *He probably even uses a ruler.*

She looked up. "If I was Mary or Ogre, would you still be offering the ride?"

The man was silent. His cheek twitched only once.

"I thought so. I'll take the bus."

PAPERWORK

Before you can ride, walk into the arena, or risk getting hurt, there is always paperwork. Everybody hates it, but eventually, everybody needs it.

Jolie had always hated the interiors of large buildings. Her anxiety increased with every floor level away from the ground. The offices of Macklin, Thomas, and Williams on the seventh floor were no exception. Even the leather on the overstuffed lounge chairs in the waiting room did nothing to make her feel comfortable.

The original Jacob Macklin and Jedediah Thomas had been principals in the Union Pacific Railroad. When the final rails were laid between Pueblo de Los Angeles and Monterey, they had seen hundreds of homesteads, no longer along the new rail line, become valueless in most minds. Some of the mile square homesteads, they bought for less than a handful of Golden Eagles. Year-round water could double or triple the price. Those were bought by men more interested in ranching and getting dirty. Some men only wanted to possess and have others get dirty. Still others wanted to own, get dirty, and have someone else take care of the money and other concerns such holdings could irritatingly produce. So the two men quit running the business of the railroad and formed a partnership to run the business of landholdings.

When Thomas's daughter, who was sent back east to a proper girl's school, returned to California married to a young accountant, knowledgeable in the ways of the land, they hired the young Williams. By the end of his second year of association, he had produced two heirs and doubled the business. The firm, feeling secure about the nature of the continuation for at least a second if not a third generation, tendered the young man an offer of a partner.

The only original family left were all Williams. The other two produced no other heirs.

"Ms. Richards?"

Jolie looked up. The woman's hair was snow-white, and since Jolie was a child, she had never seen a smile on the woman's face that seemed genuine.

"Mr. Williams will see you now." As Jolie rose and approached, the woman swung the door open. She never offered to fetch anything so menial as coffee or water.

The man at the desk glanced up but never rose. Jolie had initially thought it was out of rudeness until her father pointed out the tips of two canes protruding from under the desk.

"Good morning, Mike. You're in early. I would have thought you would take the opportunity and put in more time catching hard curls off Trestles or down off Rincon Point." She dropped into the chair facing the desk as he finished signing some last documents. The smile to one side proved he was listening.

Mike threw the few folders into the out basket and leaned back. Jolie felt his eyes examining her—her physical condition as well as how she was carrying herself. If nothing else, the man was highly perceptive. One year during high school, she had worked hard to draw a number for the state rodeo in Sacramento. She had a great horse named Launchpad. He was a sleek stallion cross between a Montana mustang and an Arabian. There was more chestnut than blond, but when they broke the trip wire at the end of the chute, the horse looked like flames rippling over the muscles. They had broken the trip wire more than a hundred times a day, every day, for over a month. Their time was a consistent winning single digit to the throw and not much more to the tie. They were primed and ready. Except, eight days before the rodeo, the man had looked her over and said she wasn't ready. He had been right. Her times were some of the worst she had ever scored in competition. The next year, she practiced even harder. Their times were even faster. They went to every roundup, branding and small rodeo in four states.

Nine days before the rodeo, she went to see him. She sat and said nothing. Finally, he swung his chair around and looked out the large window at the breakwater a mile away. When he turned back around, he told her to turn Launchpad out to pasture and for her to check into the spa by the sea for four or five days. He told her to get a massage in the morning and again in the evening. Eat on the patio overlooking the ocean. Go swimming, fall in love, and lie in the warm sand and get tan. She took his advice. On the drive up to Sacramento, she and Launchpad were both calm and relaxed. Even in the first chute, she could feel his calm. Primed and ready, but without the usual sidestepping or grinding of the bit. The calf released, and neither of them flinched until the millisecond before the trip line released them. They were the third fastest to hit the wire and the time to beat the rest of the rodeo.

She studied the gray sweeps over his ears. When she last saw him, they had been only a fingerprint on each side. There as darkness lining around his eyes. He was only a couple of decades older than she was but now looked more like forty years older.

"It doesn't look like you got much surfing in these last seven years, Mike."

His eyes were slow to blink as he leaned back and steepled his fingers. "Other than the chemo and radiation, not much time for anything else."

Jolie felt foolish for joking. Hoping to get back on top, she tried at the positive. "At least you kept your hair."

He realized she had no idea. The communication through the prison was spotty at best and empty of anything with humanity. "Emma didn't. She lost her Beach Betty badge the first round. It never came back." He knew the two women had occasionally been friends and beach buddies. Surfing was something Jolie had only tried but ended back on the beach with Emma, watching the guys ride the water. It was nothing like riding horses. By their thirties, none of them were up for water time unless it involved a boat.

He softened the news. "She finally let go on Good Friday. We scattered her ashes at the five-mile line. She wanted to be at Trestles or Rincon but couldn't make up her mind. So now she's at both."

He looked up. She could see the wet eyes. His head cocked gently as he continued to study her.

"It looks like you cooked off some of that whiskey fat and built more muscle."

She snorted and was back on safe ground. "The food sucked. If it were a restaurant out here, it would receive an F and be shut down overnight. Most of what they slop out is carbs. They hope you'll just get fat and slow, but the weights in the yard could make for a good burn."

"What about the gangs we hear so much about?"

She thought about the breakdown of whom was in which area of the yard. "Arrangements can always be made." After she had helped her cellmate fend off an attack, the Aryan Nation didn't want to have anything to do with Jolie, and the blacks had disowned her cellmate long ago. The two had found common ground with speaking Spanish and their heritage of being from southern California.

He leaned back toward the desk—opening a folder. "Speaking of arrangements… we've deposited enough in this checking account to pay bills and live on for a few months until you get your feet under you." He flipped a checkbook toward her from the folder.

"The day-to-day is your responsibility. The rest of the holdings and land tax, we will continue. The dogs are long gone, as are all the livestock. The early belief was you would end up serving the full twenty, or even worse, get in trouble and go for more."

"Even three-to-five is too long for livestock. You did the right thing."

He nodded at her acknowledgment. He shifted as he felt more comfortable with getting the basics out of the way. "I didn't know what you would want to do, but just in case, I sent an inspector up to the cabin. We've had a crew resetting all the plumbing that had gone to hell. The electrical is fine, but they advised pulling in a better powerline or installing a large enough solar array to be off-grid or sell the extra back to Pacific Gas & Electric. With the solar, we can get an engineer to size the array and match it up for either being off the grid or to grid tie and sell the extra power. It's the feeling of the concern to look at going commercial and getting credits to pay for all the grid tie and produce an income."

He shuffled through a few more reports. "The propane is all checked out up to the cabin. But the appliances are shot. So you'll have to go shopping for hot water, stove, and if you want to do a propane fridge, then a fridge as well." He looked up. "Personally, I'd hold off and get the power squared away and install efficient appliances throughout. We can make some recommendations, or we can take it over and just get it done for you. You don't have to decide now… Let me know in a few days or so, and we'll go from there."

"What about the well?"

"It got its annual check about six months ago, and they replaced the sand screen almost all the way down. You have more than enough water for livestock and a large garden. But if you plan to build a water park larger than a slip and slide… we'll need to talk."

"Anything else?"

"Nope. I think everything is covered. When are you planning to go up?"

"I need to find a truck. So probably in a few days."

"What kind of truck?"

"Beat to crap, ugly as pig shit, but with both doors, glass, and runs dependably."

The man scratched at his face and then used both hands to rub his face. "What was it you used to call them… a double-doable or something?"

"Double R. Rodeo-ready. Beat to shit and run all day, with dogs in the back you can leave it overnight at the rodeo and nobody will touch it."

The man snorted a soft chuckle. "Right. Where are you going to look?"

"I figured I'd risk a few bumper stickers about grapes or rapes and go troll the underbelly of Ojai or Santa Paula. If I get desperate, I'll head out toward Point Mugu and bribe a few pickers for their short truck." She stood with her palm out at the man with his hands on the arms of his chair. "Don't get up. It ruins the fantasy of you still being tall and handsome. I'll call before I head up the hill."

"What are you doing for a phone?"

She scratched behind her ear. "I suppose the phone line is still good up to the cabin… Why?"

The man leaned over, and his hand hovered over his large console desk phone. "It's probably long gone dead or turned to crap. It's worth checking, but I was thinking more of a twenty-first century kind of phone." Pushing a couple of buttons, the speakerphone was ringing. He sat back.

"Logistics. Manual here."

"Manual, it's Mike. Do we have any spare phones in stock?"

They could hear the man lean away from the phone and rustle something in a shop. "I've got a couple of survey phones. Here, let me try one."

The small cell phone on Mike's desk vibrated. He leaned over and looked. "Works perfect. Can you bring it and a matched charger up here please?"

"On my way, boss. Anything else while I'm fetching?"

"What do you have for hunting and homestead defense?"

"If you don't mind an eighty-year-old lever-action, we have a 30-30 nobody uses. I might even have a box of shells."

Mike looked at Jolie. She thought and nodded.

"That'll work… Thanks."

Jolie half-sat on the back of the chair. "If I get caught with it… I go back. No questions asked." Her face was stone.

The man rocked back in his chair. "I figure you being back will stir up something sure as hell. When they found your knife, they never thought about looking for anybody else. Whoever used it will come looking for you. If I had a knife, I would have offered it too. But I know your daddy had it custom-made. I've been hankerin' for one just like it. If you know where it was made, I think I might take up pig hunting."

"Tim Jostell, down in the Burbank or Glendale area. I'd have to go down and see if I can find him."

The man took in a deep sigh as there was a light tap on the

door. "Let me know if you find him. I've got an itch for fresh wild pork chops. How are you getting around now?"

"I borrowed a car from a friend of a friend on the inside, so I could take the driving test and get around. But he'll probably need it back soon—therefore, finding a truck."

The door swung open, and a stocky young Latino with tattoos crawling up his neck sauntered in. The rifle he carried like he was born with it. In his hands were a box of shells and two other boxes.

He placed the boxes on the desk, and without preamble, tried to explain. "This is the state-of-the-art satellite phone. Normally, you use it just like this. The shell is completely waterproof, just don't take it surfing without a tether. With it like this, it looks like a regular phone and will still slip in your back pocket. But, if you don't have a cell tower, flip this up, and it activates the satellite receiver… Just make sure you're on Earth. They found out these don't work good on the moon. It was the same with the restaurant they built at Tranquility Base—relaxing view, but the atmosphere sucked. Charge it and standby will take you for a few days. If you need a solar charger, just let me know. I can get one to you in a few days. I'm the speed dial marked Q… just like James Bond." He looked up. "Any questions?"

Jolie smiled at the mix of business and smartass. "If I need anything, I'll call. Thanks, Manual."

He started to turn and then pointed at the rifle. "The barrel and pin have been dragged. So it doesn't exist. Please don't do anything to make me have to destroy it. The iron sights are set for about fifty yards. But if you put the base of the sight on the target, you're good for the full field goal."

Mike cleared his throat. "Do we have any survey vehicles we can spare for a few weeks?"

"I can find something. Auto or stick?"

"I don't care. Just so it runs all day."

"Easy-peasy. Check with me tomorrow, and I'll short a crew."

"Thanks."

"De nada, Chica." He two-finger-saluted Mike and was gone.

She looked at the man behind the desk. He shrugged his face. "If you need to call him—I don't want to know. But you probably met a few of his connections in the last seven years. We like him, and we don't want him to be transferred back."

3

FIRE

*Nobody rides rodeo because it's a cool sexy job. Most are seriously injured
before they're thirty. It's more than a calling… It's the fire in the gut. Riding
is the only way to get it out.*

Few vehicles moved in the heat of the afternoon. Main Street could have been used as a target range. The sole pedestrian was slow enough, crossing the hot asphalt to almost qualify as a stationary target. The lone dog chasing something was only given away by the slow twitch of its left front paw. The mouth was split, and the tongue lay on the shaded sidewalk.

Siesta is a necessary convention. When the heat drugs the entire town, convention is thrown under the bed to be revived at four in the afternoon. Even the birds refused to do anything but hunker down in the shade on cooler grass.

Her time-battered boots ground on the small grains of sand in front of the door. She turned to examine the town she had grown up in—but then betrayed by.

The bar was as if time had stood still. Somewhere in the

previous sixty years, the beer, whiskey, sweat, bar-fight blood, and the combined smell of a thousand hot, horny, and drunk youth in a cow and horse town, had reached a retch-inducing stench—and then froze. The smell had never gotten worse or less. The bodies changed, but the rest was always the same.

She watched the broad shoulders spreading out to fill and stretch the T-shirt. With each twist of the hands, the muscles in the back rippled like fish in a full creel. The belt rode a little higher than it had the last time she watched it, but the jeans had the same sag from the flat butt they always had. She rose slightly to look at his boots. The back of the boots pushed hard into the rubber duckboard pad. The slanted back cut on the heels was half buried but still there. Once a roper—always a roper.

Her voice was a low snarl but ricocheted off the walls as if it were a fire shot from a large pistol. "Hey, goat roper, give me some rocket fuel."

The man's shoulders flinched, and then the body froze. He pivoted on his heels as he slowly ground his way around. His face drained of color, and his eyes were wide with fear.

His voice was little more than a breath. "Rocket."

He looked around, even though he knew they were alone. Three nervous steps and his hands, still wadded in the towel around a glass, rested on the edge of the bar. He leaned forward slightly, still whispering.

"What are you doing here... I mean, you can't be here. Things—"

Her boots slammed down at the sides of the stool as she burst forward. Her hands wound into his shirt. Stretching the fabric as she pulled him half over the bar. Both of their eyes crossed as their noses came within an inch of the other.

Her growl was more air than noise. "Who did you fuck in the back of your uncle's Bronco when she was fifteen?"

He swallowed. His mouth made the word but no noise. "You..."

"Who taught you how to fuck on the back of a horse at full gallop?"

"You."

"Who did you go to the prom with?"

"Celeste."

"Who did you fuck in the coach's office during the prom?"

"You."

"Who did you fuck the night before you married Celeste."

"You."

"Who have you fucked other than your wife since you got married?"

He was silent as his eyes bounced from her left eye to her right and back.

"Don't make me get my knife out, asshole."

He squeaked and then cleared his throat. "Nobody."

She backed him up two inches until their eyes straightened. Her eyes never twitched.

"Nobody. I swear, Rocket. You and she are the only ones... ever."

Jolie pulled him back in an inch. Her growl was hot on his open mouth. "When do you want me to tell her about us?"

He swallowed hard. "Why...why would you do that?"

"When are you planning to cross me?"

"Never. Never, Rocket... I would rather cut my own balls off before I'd—"

"Save it, Randy. You already did. You married Celeste. She was taking balls off the professional bull riders before you ever shook your willie at her." She gently pushed him back. "Now get my bottle down."

He glanced up at the back bar. "Rocket... You know how you get when you—"

"Get. It."

His eyes rolled as he turned. The rodeo had never broken the ranch body. If anything, it had layered on more solid muscle.

Jolie assessed the middle. There might have been only an added layer of ten married pounds. He pulled out the step stool to get the bottle from the top shelf. Everyone knew the handblown bottle. The dark red glass made flames reaching up into the orange and yellow. The bone-white skull and crossed bones covered most of one side. A 1950s cartoonish rocket ship took off on the other side. Nobody opened or drank from Rocket's private stock—but a few could testify to the 160-proof mix of whiskey, rum, and moonshine. A couple could even certify to how fast it could strip the paint off the hood of a truck. The flames were only for show.

He reached for a bucket of small rocks glasses. She shook her head. "Pour it out."

He hesitated.

"Randy… I said, pour it out."

He turned to the sink and pulled the glass stopper. The familiar smell hit her like a remembered punch. She had forgotten how much she liked the blend. But the blend had also gotten her in trouble.

He turned as he slowly inserted the stopper. He placed it on the bar in front of her. She reached her hand out, stopped, and then touched it. The cool glass… She didn't have to look… Her fingers knew the way, every bump or fold or dip. It had been her birthday present when she turned twenty-one. Randy's father was behind the bar back then. It had started innocent enough. He had filled it with Jack. Then came the rum, and a few years later, the raw moonshine. She had told herself it was either drink or become addicted to hardcore pain pills from too many falls, too many bad horses, or too many of the wrong things. She told herself she could quit any time, and in prison, she figured out she could have… but she had no place else to go in those days. She worked hard, she rode hard, she drank hard. Everyone in the valley knew she was just drunk-working until it was bar time.

She sighed and looked up at one of her oldest friends.

He shrugged. "What happens now?"

Her large toothy smile pulled back tight as a jerk-line on her right side. Her large teeth could look friendly or downright scary. Randy weighed in on the latter instead of the former.

She leaned her head as she slid her hat off and gently rested it on the seat next to her. "I go back to being the town drunk... and maybe the town slut as well." She pushed at the underside of her breasts. "I still got great tits..."

Randy nodded toward the bottle. He had experienced this treacherous side of the Rocket before. He picked up the bottle and hefted it to show it was empty. His face was a hardhanded question.

"Got any tea?"

He nodded.

"Now here is the real question. What booze gives a person the worst bar breath? And how little can I get away with and still smell drunk?"

He thought a moment. Reaching out, he grabbed a shot glass. Three splashes later he placed half an ounce in front of her. "Mix a half cup of this in the bottle full of tea, and nobody will want to kiss you until they are horny enough to fuck the Sheriff's drug dog."

She took a sip and screwed up her face. Her body shook, and her head cocked to the side as she adjusted her face. Three more shudders and she drew a deep breath through her nose. "Perfect." Her vocal cords were rusted and frozen. They both laughed.

Half an hour later, Randy poured her a drink over ice in a large rocks glass. The kind of glass the hard-drinking town drunk had used before. She held the glass up to the light and then sipped.

Putting it down, she shuddered. "Good god, that shit is nasty."

He chuckled. "But it looks right. Take a big swig and swish it around in your mouth so I can smell your breath."

He leaned forward as she swallowed. She smiled and gave him a breathy line. "Kiss me, sailor."

His face folded in on itself as he backed up. "Oh, fuck no. Jeez… You're never getting laid again."

She held up and turned the glass as she contemplated the ichor. "It actually tastes worse."

"And you think the killer is someone you know, and they come in here?"

She jerked a twisted head. "It's all I've been trying to figure out for seven years. Someone set me up. They knew me well enough to know when I was here or on the road or off hunting. Any time I spent on the road with rodeos, I was around people all the time. Most of the time, I bunked with others. So I would always have had an alibi. If I was just pig hunting, the most I was gone was a day. Most of the time, I was home by late night. Only a big pig I had to pack out with the burro would take me longer."

"What about the dogs? I mean, fuck. I wouldn't have gone up to your place with all those killer dogs hanging out. I mean, what did they do for food?"

"If they weren't with me, they ate from the auto feeder. The water also refilled automatically. They had a month's worth of food between the three feeders, and the water was never off. Anybody up there snooping around who shouldn't be—they were just extra protein."

He leaned against the back bar and crossed his long legs at the boots. He stared at the duckboards as he slowly drew the bar towel through his left hand. "So why did you threaten to tell Celeste about us?"

"I didn't… I only asked. I wanted to know if I could still trust you with all my secrets and my life. You're the only person I have left. I went to prison for someone else's lie. I got in fights, but I never killed anyone—not even in self-defense. I've lived longer than maybe I should have, but I tried to do the right thing when I could. Down deep, I think I'm a good person, but society now looks at me the way you did when I sat down. Killer first. Trail beaten stock hand second. Or maybe ex-convict second then cowpuncher. But honest woman isn't even on the list. Those glory days where people chanted my name when I was roping"—she fluttered her fingers through the air—"gone."

She looked up. Her eyes had no tears, simply hard, stone-cold piercing blue. "I need to get my house in order. If you're junk, you will go in the heap. I'm packing light for the long ride."

"What about Celeste?"

"What about her?"

"She was your best friend."

"I fucked you on the eve of your wedding. I would have fucked you at the reception, but there was nowhere to get private enough."

"But you still let me marry her. Or her me."

She shot him with her left finger and thumb as she sipped more of the drink. Her face wadded up and turned dark. Her tongue oozed out of her tortured lips. "Shit. Pure shit. This is going to take some time to get used to."

Randy cocked his jaw toward his right shoulder. "It's why I'm here at ten in the morning… just in case a town drunk stumbles in. Don't forget to leave a good tip."

"Can I just fuck you instead?"

He gave her a hard stare of silence. Their eyes never twitched.

His voice sounded like a breeze coming down a long dry canyon. "Do you think it was easy for us these last seven years?"

She snorted dryly. "Who was the one locked up?"

An angry growl edged his voice. "All three of us."

4

DIRT

* * *

There is no soft, cushy grass in a rodeo arena. If you wanted to work where it's clean, you would have stayed at the Boot Barn riding the shoe-dog's pony, helping city folk try on gaudy boots that almost look like real shit-kickers.

"Give me a break, Norm. I was the best horse breaker in California before, and I'm the same person now. For seven years, I ate, slept, dreamed, and thought about nothing but horses. I can tell you the quirk of every horse I saddle broke for you or anyone else."

The man gripped the top of his ballcap and wiped it from the top of his bald head. The wispy cloud of gray stubble stood out on his walnut-colored head. "Rocket, you know I want to help, but I've got a stable to run, and there are folks who come here now…" He looked up for her blessing to not say what he meant.

"What? Because they drive fancy cars and pay you fancy money to shack out their precious pony so miss Suzie Too Good can come act like she knows horses. Prancing around your lily-white painted riding arena and thinking they are riding? Norm, I thought I knew you. Your father busted his balls from Del Mar to Bay Meadows just to buy this land and put you through school. Those hard years broke him. In those days, as a black man, he knew he was never going to rise above a groom. But he worked hard at being the best groom on the west coast. He could have gone back to the Bluegrass, but his heart and you were here. He destroyed his health so one day you could be on top of the horse, not standing in the shit. And now… I see he and I were wrong. You're not only standing in the shit, but you are standing with your hands cupped under the ass—ready to catch those rich folk's shit and still ask for more."

He jammed the pitchfork into the pile of manure—burying it past the tines. He spun on her. His anger was a great thunderstorm on his face, and his eyes had gone from a shadow of brown to coal pits of hell.

His nose stopped inches from her face. "You don't know shit. The times have changed, and you weren't here to know it."

Her hand reached out and rested on his chest as she eased him back upright. She stepped in and kept their closeness. Her voice was low and quiet but not soft. The hard steel edge was still there. "No, no, I didn't. I have driven around. I've seen the change. The city came to the valley, and the stench is worse than an open sewer. But you've changed. You got a taste of the Cadillac life and then dove right in. You can dress it up any way you like, Norm. But the bottom line here is you sold out. I bet you don't have a single green in that fancy barn. Hell, you probably don't have any stock with a wild twitch left. You're not rodeo anymore. You're just a pussy ride in them fancy pants."

She leaned over and spit. "Hell, I was going to break your first two for free. But now… shit. I can see I came to the wrong farm." She turned and headed for her truck. "Sorry I dirtied up your fetchin' farm. Send me the cleaning bill."

The man stood and grabbed at the pitchfork. "Fuck. You lost

your balls, Rocket. Your father must be rolling over in his grave right now."

She stopped mid-step and slowly turned around. Her face was in the deep shadow under the wide brim storm hat she had always favored.

"The old Rocket I used to know would have already found out about the second farm out near the grape yards."

The large smile took time to stretch. It wasn't much more than a slash mark across her face. "You have what looks like seven Montana or Wyoming mustangs. Down on the back pasture with the cattle. You have John's old paint calming some new wild monkeys. They're twitchy as hell, and you won't have a rope on them before next fall. In the far field in among the oaks, you have old stock mixed with some chestnuts that look like they would make some good rodeo ponies, but there's also a stallion. My guess is you're holding out hope he's going to be a good bareback or saddle bronc. Move the peach and the sand mustangs into the small pasture on the north side of the barn. Let them get used to the fence and ground. They'll need hay. I'll come see them in about a week."

He flipped his hat back on his head. "You still a drunk?"

She walked back to within arm's reach. "And a slut if anyone will touch a forty-six-year-old ex-con." She pushed her hat back enough to lighten her face. "But I'll make you a promise."

She waited for his nod. The facts and cards were on the manure pile.

"Any day I come out to work on your stock, I'll let you smell my breath." She gently moved the brim lower. "I never did, nor will I ever, drink before the day's work is done and done right."

5

LONGE

A longe line (pronounced lunge), is a thirty-foot rope used to exercise a horse in circles. The time is spent teaching the horse to respond to voice commands and get the horse used to its new reality.

Jolie slit open another envelope and pulled out the bill. The charge was only a maintenance fee, but it was still there… just another bur under the saddle blanket. She set the envelope on the pile and slid the bill and return envelope into the spiral slinky-dog mail holder. This was the part of life she had never liked. She could always pay the bills; it was just the doing she hated.

The holding company had taken over the day-to-day when she went away. But, with her back, they returned the pedestrian day-to-day of the cabin and homestead to her. The real holdings were beyond her reach, and they had other shareholders to answer to, as well.

Her head rocked over as she looked out the dirty window. *I need to clean.*

The window reminded her of the large window across the open atrium from her cell. In prison, the window was a torturous taunt—freedom, and everything good was on the other side of the dirty glass. The scary world was on the inside. Here, the rolls were mockingly reversed. It was the open freedom that was the scary unknown. Hiding in the cabin was where safety was— behind the door her grandfather had built.

Buried somewhere in the thick wood of the door was a thumb-sized ball of lead. Her grandfather had fired it from a Sharp's seventy caliber rifle. To make sure, the man had also shot two clips of fully jacketed rounds from his M-1 rifle. Nothing even dimpled the paper on the inside.

What the man hadn't known was his trusting young wife had sat feet from the door. She held the smaller iron skillet in front of her face and cradled the large cast-iron soup pot on her lap— protecting their soon-to-be son. Thankfully, the pot never had to protect her heart. Decades later, when she shared the story with a young Jolie, the girl had placed her hand between the pot and the pan. As her open palm came to rest over the woman's heart, she asked, 'What about protection for your heart?' The woman nodded as she turned white from the realization. 'Honey, I suppose that was in the hands of your granddaddy and the good man upstairs.'"

The noise of boiling water drew Jolie's attention. She swept her legs and boots off the time-scarred table. She stepped to the stove and turned off the flame on the only working fire ring. Wrapping the towel around the handle of the pot, she carried it out the back door.

What the child Jolie had called the submarine, stood about thirty feet from the house. The patches of yellow paint and outlines of the windows and door were only a shadow of the submarine she had tried to match as a freshman in high school. Most of the propane tank remained the age-dulled snow-white.

She threw the scalding water on the upper side of the tank. It ran down the side, but just below the halfway mark, the water turned funky and tried to freeze—showing the level propane left in the tank. She grumbled. "A couple of months or more." She also remembered the propane was cheaper when all it was used for was cooking or heating water. In the fall, the price would go up. Her lips tightened as she gently patted the heel of her hand on the tank—her mind picturing another envelope in the slinky-dog.

The pan hung from her hand as she turned. *Another errand to run when in town.* The movement caught her eye. She could count on her one hand the number of cars she had ever seen make the drive up her half a mile of bad road. In truth, it was only the first hundred yards they didn't maintain. Her father used to say it was to keep the city folk from looking for a picnic area.

The blue jeep slowed around the large tree. The sign her father had placed on the tree was still there. Few took the warning to heart. Most laughed at the 'You are now in rifle range' sign. Her father had only shot out the windshield of one vehicle—his own brother's. Years later, as his brother lay dying in the hospital from cancer, he had scooted him over and climbed in the bed. The two brothers laughed and told stories about growing up on the homestead until morning. By late in the evening, there was only one brother left.

The jeep rolled to a stop. The woman took off her dark glasses and folded them on the narrow metal dashboard. She sat eyeing Jolie and the large pan. "If I get out... are you going to brain me with the stupid pan?"

Jolie took a deep breath. Even as best of friends, some of their meetings were contentious or at least got off on the wrong foot.

She turned and headed back into the cabin. "If you had any balls, you'd come in and find out, ya chicken shit. The beer is warm, but it's only seven years old." She stepped over the threshold but left the door open. The low groaning of the jeep's door was shortly followed by the soft sound of tennis shoes on the porch boards.

As the brunette stepped into the dim interior, a dusty throw pillow hit her face. The giggles started a half-second later.

"You're an asshole. You've been in town for four weeks and haven't come over. You fucking stopped to see Randy, but your best friend—the one who taught you how to masturbate, the one who taught you how to give a great blowjob, and the one who let you fuck her boyfriend the night before we got married… no. Not even a fucking phone call."

Jolie sallied out of the dim living room. "Fuck you. Seven years and you never visited. You knew where I was. You knew the day I got home. You could have come up here any day or night. But now you're married and getting fat, so it takes you a month." She leaned over to one side. "What's behind your back?"

The brunette smirked as she swung out the six-pack. "I figured you forgot how to turn on the refrigerator and would need a cold beer by now."

The two hugged as Jolie snuck two beers out of the carrier. "Refrigerator is as dead as the freezer. I'm just hoping the bottle opener hasn't rusted away." Jolie turned to the opener bolted to the end of the counter, just above the trash can.

Two caps in the trash and they clinked bottles.

They sat in the shade of the west porch. Tennis shoes and boots braced on the railing. The view was the same as when they were in high school—many years before. The hanging tree was fatter. The old truck, parked before the Korean War, was still home to the occasional squirrel, raccoon, or lizard. The small patch of sun-washed grass still invited through the trees. Only the corrals changed.

The horses used to be around for a season, and then there were new ones to break or train. Now, the gate yawned open… not even a dog lay in the beaten dust. The manure had all been raked out long ago—or baked into more dust. The lack of animals hung in the small leaves of the scrub oaks and on the parched wood of the homestead. It sucked the life out of the air. Even the soft gurgle of the beers and the wiping of a mouth on a sleeve whisked away as if no life sounds existed.

Jolie couldn't figure out if the homestead was dead or just holding its breath. Without her mother to help, she wasn't sure if she was up to the job of breathing life back into it or whether it was just a Sisyphean job. She rolled her head to the sound. "Hmm?"

"I said, do you remember Cletus Dragomir—the kid with the huge ears?"

Jolie snorted at the almost forty-year-old memory. "Stuck straight out. Kid couldn't run for shit. As soon as he got up to speed, his ears would slow him down. PE teacher put a ball cap over his ears so he could run with the other kids." By this time, they were both laughing too much to do anything but huff out a couple of words.

"Kinder than the rubber band."

Jolie slapped her hand and bottle into Celeste's chest. "Oh, god. Sue… Sue something…"

"Suzanne Dimwit."

"No… Dimsworth. Suzanne Dimsworth." The peals of laughter echoed through the spar woods. "I can see doing the rubber band to flatten her ears at night—maybe. But why for god's little green apples would a mother send her child to school like that? I mean… kids are cruel. Why give them ammunition?"

"Because her mother wasn't much smarter than Suzanne…" The two age-drawn hands clinked bottles and took another sip in unison—old habits. If one looked left—the other also did. They never called each other before school—they just showed up dressed alike. Some teachers insisted they take tests in separate rooms. It didn't matter. It neither helped nor hurt their matching scores. Even the Kolinsky identical twins weren't as connected.

Jolie rubbed her right heel on the top of her left boot. She needed to remember to rub some mink oil into the leather and soften the arch. Her feet had gotten larger in prison.

"What made you bring up Cletus? You having an affair?" Jolie snickered in the top of her bottle before taking another sip.

"Ass." Celeste sipped. "He's up in San Quentin for murder."

Jolie's beer stopped halfway to her lips. Her eyes were focused on the hanging tree, but her mind was working overtime on the sliver of information. She hadn't thought about the boy for over thirty years, and yet… her friend brings him up in a conversation leading to the mention of his imprisonment.

Jolie held out her beer. "Here, take this."

"What? Why?"

Jolie stood and walked to the end of the porch. Looking out into the forest, her voice was flat but on the edge of rage. "Go get your other sympathy beers and get off my land." She stepped off the last step and kicked at the dirt as she walked away.

"Rocket. Wait. What the fuck did I say?" The brunette stood with her arms out as though crucified. "Rocket. Jolie. Where are you going? Come on back."

The blonde turned and snapped her hand at the brim of her hat. "Fuck you. If you're going to be the kind of person who points out every other person in prison, I don't even want to know you. That was the snake in the lake lowest thing you could have ever done. And you did it to me. Fuck you." She turned and kicked at the hanging tree as she walked past.

A few minutes later, she could hear the jeep start and leave. She was pissed at the sleazy move, she was pissed it had been her friend who pulled it, and she was even more pissed she had been such an ass about it. But prison was behind her. Even her parole officer only wanted a phone call instead of a visit.

She turned right at the branch of the old riding path. The homestead was a perfect square—two miles by two miles.

In the 1800s, the government had granted the railroads a hopscotch of one-mile-square homesteads along their proposed track. The companies sold the land to develop the railroads. Where logical, they granted them a two-square-mile township. When the rail ended going up the other side of the county, the homesteads became cheap, and the township even cheaper. Her great-great-grandfather was friends with the railroad master. The man had an ugly daughter who, at almost twenty, he desperately wanted to get married off. The four miles of scrub oaks, deer, wild boar, nuts, berries, and three streams to water cattle on, made a worthwhile bride price. The woman became Jolie's great-grandmother.

Over the decades, Jolie had hiked, ridden, and drove every game trail and road. The large rock cropping on the thumb of land where the northern stream curled was as familiar to her as the single brown freckle on the side of her left knee. The over-hang of the stream had been her father's favorite place to lie with his arm in the water. Before long, he would roll back with a large fat trout in his hand. Along with hunting the large pigs with only dogs and a knife, he had taught her to tickle fish. None of the streams widened enough to use a pole, much less fly fish. Any fishing involving a pole, she headed for the ocean.

The scream of an eagle overhead brought her back from childhood. She tipped her head, the broad brim of the hat shading the sun, and she watched the graceful soaring of the giant bird.

She expected to watch slow movement as the bird rode the thermals over the southwestern acreage. But this bird was angry. The stop and start of wing beating for reposition and height meant it was not riding thermals in the afternoon—something or someone was disturbing its nest or nesting area.

Jolie changed course.

The three men moved through the scrub forest. They liber-ally applied cans of blue and orange spray paint to many trees. The GPS in one man's hand—with the maps they all had—

suggested they knew where they were, as did Jolie. They were over a half a mile onto her land.

Her first inclination was to walk down and find out who they were and run them off. But prison had taught her patience and observation had far more reaching rewards.

By late afternoon, she had tracked them and their marking of trees over an expanse covering half a mile or more. Trees to remove—red marks; trees to reserve—blue dots. The marks created a pattern in her mind. The pattern had only small clear cuts connected by lines. She thought about the trees they were marking. There was no single species. The types of trees were oaks, eucalyptus, and soft jack pine alike. From what little she knew about timber cutting for lumber, this randomness made no sense. They were also marking fat trees as often as skinny pecker trees.

Nothing made sense until they returned to their two trucks. The clearing they were parked in was too far for Jolie to read the signs on the doors, but one of the logos was obvious and the other she had seen all her life. It was a family business, and it had nothing to do with respecting property rights of other families.

The enormity of the men and what they were up to knocked her back. Her squat became sitting on the dirt in the high summer tanned grass. The shade of the trees hid her as she watched the trucks turn and leave. The pattern they had marked on her trees was not distinct and blatant, but it did explain the sticks with orange ribbons she had noticed but not paid attention to—it was time to clean her house.

6

STARTS

*Instead of breaking a horse, the much-preferred method of horsemanship is
'gentling' or 'starting' a colt. Mustangs are wild horses and
are best 'started' than 'broken.'*

Jolie had worked with a young girl's pinto pony the
day before. The hours she spent on the lunge line
had taken their toll on her back and arms. The small
horse hadn't been physical but the seven years of not holding the
loops of line in one hand and lunge whip in the other had taken
their toll. By the end of the afternoon, Jolie had hugged the neck
and stroked the head of the pinto without it shying or startling. A
couple of more weeks would retrain Jolie's muscles and have the
pony ready for the girl to ride again. The check would match up
with a couple of the bills in her rack.

Today was an all-day affair. She had raked the grass in
several parts of the small pasture. Not to rake anything, but just
be in the enclosure ignoring the two horses. Four large carrots
jammed her back pockets. Their greens hung like tails. Jolie knew

the smell of the carrots, and the greens overpowered the smell of the sunbaked grass of the corral. Every time she stopped and bent over, she would sidestep so the wave of green swished like the tails of the two wary horses.

She had worked her way around to all four corners. With each move, the two mustangs had migrated to another corner. She never chased them or moved directly at them. The middle rail in the south fence, she feigned to adjust from its position where it was nailed solid to the post. She had similarly stroked her gloved hands over the rail in the north corner—a little fake work here and a little fake work there. The hours dragged by.

She pulled the two skinnier carrots from her left hip pocket. She placed each on top of a post with the fall of greens facing in toward the center. She leaned the rake against the fence on the inside where the mustangs could smell the tool when she was gone. Her gloves she sluffed off and laid on top of yet another post.

Norm walked down from the stable as he watched the woman sitting in the middle of the corral. He paused at the fence and then leaned over and slid between the rails. He watched the mustangs. The sunshine dappled on them as it broke through the leaves on the large oak.

Jolie looked out of the side of her eye at the tan Ostrich skin boots. She never moved. The boots and starched chino slacks were never something the man she had known before would ever wear. A lot had changed in seven years. Maybe longer… if she had stayed sober in those days and paid attention.

His voice was soft but smooth as slow molasses. "What are you doing?"

Out of her left eye, she watched as the tan horse nibbled gently at the greens of the first carrot. All the other days, she had left before they had gone near the carrots.

Her hand eased out and patted the dead grass next to where she was sitting. "Just working hard for every penny you're paying me, Norm." She patted again. "Go ahead, 'Norm. Take a load off. You look plumb tuckered out from all your watching me from the room you have over the stable. What is it? A dirty-leg room? The place you take your better female clients for a little rest and exercise with the big black stallion?"

The big man surprised her as he grabbed the front of his chinos, crossed his boots, and scissored down to the grass. "You know… you always had a nasty mouth on you."

She pulled a long stem of the grass and stuck it in the side of her mouth. The second mustang was sniffing at the other carrot.

"Nastier mind too. You do know them grass stains are almost impossible to get out of those fancy chinos. People will think you've been rolling around in the pasture with the horse whisperer."

He frowned at her with pursed lips. He wasn't sure he liked what had come back from the prison system. She had a harder edge to her—less easygoing knock-about rodeo.

"Why does everything out of your mouth have to be nasty, mean, or just dirty?"

She watched the two horses as they worked on the two carrots. The taste was good, but they were still sideways to her— watching. Wary. Wanting to relax and trust, but not sure how.

"Why do you wear city boots and dandy pants? Did you jump the fence while I was away?"

"What kind of question is that?"

She sucked hard on the grass as she slowly pulled it out of her mouth. "Well, I don't see any woman in evidence. If you plan to drop a colt or six… time is ticking."

"Now you're just disgusting." He gave her a hard look. Her face was still a question. He jumped. "No."

She put the grass straw back in her mouth and went back to watching the horses. "Hmm… touchy."

"What do you want from me?" Of all the people in the valley and surrounding, she was the only one who never asked him for anything but work. No favors. No extras. No freebies. Just honest work, and he always got more than he paid for. "And… why are we just sitting on this grass?"

She leaned forward with the flexibility of a ten-year-old. Her chest was flat against her thighs. Her heels dragged back as the knees bent and she was still lying against her thighs and now watching the horses again. The move was more like watching a snake than a limber human.

She started to talk about prison—but stopped. "When you only have a knife, and five hundred pounds of boar breaks the brush, you can take the kill to it or let it come to your knife. If you take the blade to it, you better have more push than you weigh to drive all fourteen inches through the armor and into the heart. Once it's there, you still need the blade as leverage, so it slices the heart in half." She half turned her head and looked at him. "Do you have that much weight, drive, and strength? Because I don't." Her chin returned to between her knees. "But if you wait those few heartbeats, the pig will reach thirty miles an hour by its third step. The speed turns the quarter-ton of weight into a full ton of kinetic push, driving the shoulder over the blade being held stationary. As the hunter is pushed up and over the pig, they push down on the handle. The fulcrum, from the inch of armor, levers the tip of the blade up through the heart, cutting it in two. The hunter waits, and the pig kills itself."

The black man's voice was husky with concern. "Are you planning to kill a person or a pig? Because all I see here are two mustangs I paid good money for."

Jolie turned her head and laid her cheek on her knee. "Norm, the day I click a rope on those mustangs, I'll be sitting right here. They will come to me. They will let me pet their faces, scratch their chins, and then stand there as I lay a rope over their necks, and lock the clasp. If they don't bolt, they will get two carrots each. The lead will be only four feet hanging down. Each day, I will come out here, rake a little, pet a little, sit a little, and be with them. By Halloween, I will have a blanket on them. Next spring, we'll ride them down to the big bend in the river and let them taste wild water."

He watched her watching the horses. The Rocket he remembered wasn't patient. She took the fight to wherever she thought it needed to be. She would ride hell-bent at rodeos and even harder during roundups. He heard many times about the sheriff being called out to bar fights, only to find Rocket leaning against the bar throwing back a drink from her bottle.

"Where did you learn patience?"

She locked her chin back between her knees. "The second day in prison, a fight broke out. Three bigger prisoners jumped an older woman. She was my cellmate. My cellmate Mary had warned me not to be in the yard near her. I didn't listen." Jolie pulled the grass out of her mouth. "By the time I jumped on the back of the biggest one, Mary had taken the shiv from the tall one and buried it in the big one's chest. The sharpened spoon only had to enter most of the way of the handle and then break off. She kicked it the rest of the way into the heart with the toe of her shoe. The tall one was slow in the head… and Mary just broke the tall one's nose with her elbow."

"What about the little one? What happened to her?"

"I never saw the pencil in Mary's hand. They took an x-ray and found it jammed up through the nose and straight into her brain. It dropped her like a bad habit."

"What happened?"

"I got twenty-days in the box, and she went to the hospital for two weeks with a shiv halfway to her liver. Everyone had seen them attack her. But I jumped in. The big gal had dropped under me the second Mary kicked the shiv deeper into her chest. By then, the siren was wailing, and at least six or eight shotguns had gone off. I got hit with four or five beanbags, and because I was too stupid just to lie there, they shot me with a taser."

"What was the beef about?"

"Who knows. When we were back together in the cell, I had bigger questions. Mary was working on the seventeenth year of forty for five counts of aggravated homicide. She had cleaned a bar. Her husband and his mistress were two of them. The other three had tried to help her husband and the shit he was screwing. When the police showed up, she was behind the bar and wiping it down like she worked there. She told the police, 'There's the trash. Haul it out.' It took them four days to figure out she didn't work there. It was almost a month and the Mexican border when they figured out her part in the slaughter. In another ten minutes, she, her ex-husband's truck, and eighteen-thousand bucks would have been starting a new life."

"So you figure it works the same with breaking horses?"

"And people."

He frowned. "How do you figure people?"

Her mouth spread softly into a wide smile. Her lips were like the lazy bend in a river—gentle and wide. "I wanted to have a talk with you. But if I went to your office, I'd have to make an appointment." She sat up and yawned and scratched at the hollowing of her cheek. "If I tried to talk to you anywhere else on the property, it would be in the storm of a million interruptions. But here you are. Just me and you for over twenty minutes." She glanced back toward the riding arena. "And nobody coming this way. Just us."

His chagrin pulled back on the one side of his face. His head swung softly. "Okay, I'm here. Do I get a carrot?"

She pulled the two large carrots out of her back pocket. "As long as you leave at least half for them."

Chuckling, they each took a bite and chewed. The horses watched them.

"What do you know about Castle Construction?"

He blinked as his chewing slowed. "Big company. Powerful too. Big Red is your girlfriend's uncle or something. They're out of Santa Barbara or Montecito area. I had them put in the long barns and the arena about five years ago. They run some big crews and are always working on a pipeline of new projects. Rumor has it he built Jackson's ranch. Why?"

"Have you heard any talk of a large development up my way?"

"These days? There's always something. Why, what have you heard?"

She put her one leg under herself and leveraged up to standing. She left the carrot where she had been sitting. "I've just seen some survey stakes where they shouldn't be. If you hear anything, let me know. But, Norm, don't go nosing around. Don't even mention this conversation or anything to anyone. It might just be nothing, and then, the rustle in the chaparral could just be a gray squirrel… but it also might be an angry, protective sow with suckling piglets."

She reached over to give the man a hand. As he stood, her face was inches from his. "I'm serious. Don't say a word to anyone."

He watched her usually crystal blue eyes, drain away to ice white. He nodded.

7

WORN SADDLE

Any working tack used daily becomes worn. Small tack, like lines, get replaced. Saddles, on the other hand, just become more comfortable with time.

The bar still reeked. The sweat level was just higher on a Friday night. The crowd was settling into ignoring the same old drunk at the end of the bar.

What had been more of a younger crowd back in the day had aged. What had mostly been ranch and rodeo now moved on to success with a college degree holding on desperately to the old fantasy of the dinner plate belt buckle, a tight ass tucked into Wranglers, and a squirmy rodeo bunny. Some of the bunnies had replaced their squirm with the worm of books and had high-pay jobs of their own. What used to be a lot full of trucks, dogs, bales of hay for the morning feed, and a few horses tied to the rail, was now an empty rail with beamers and Porches nosed up. But the tsunami of testosterone and hormones still filled the bar.

Through her drooping eyes, she watched the ebb and flow of the hormone dance. Most in the joint she recognized. She knew they all remembered her… but nobody approached her. She understood. Some stench you couldn't wash off. She thought about a rider named Biscuits.

The rider had been a switcher. He rode bareback or saddle. In his younger days, he rode team roping with his brother. He had been known to shoot a clean horn almost every time. His left-handed brother had a good record for catching both hind legs, and their stretches were usually well under the average eight. They were competitive, and with his up-and-coming bronc riding, they were making enough to ring the pro circuit—until the night he was drunk and shot the intruder coming through their trailer door. Even his mother never spoke to him again.

With his brother gone, he rode broncs for another two years while everyone watched the spiral. But nobody would step over the line and put out a hand. It was on him.

Nobody ever knew what happened to him. Biscuits had ridden to money in Tulsa and had preregistered for Amarillo. But he never showed up. Someone ran his truck's plates… but they never turned up in either state.

For now, Jolie liked the reek. In fact, she needed the stench. Nobody would sit within arm's length of the stink of a woman who had driven her pig knife through the chest of her mother while she slept—unless they were desperate.

Randy set a beer down in front of her. They stared at each other. Only one person was stupid enough to buy her a beer— the one person who could never drink hard liquor.

Jolie's hands never moved. Her eyes drained from blue to white. The slight shaking of his hand didn't escape her notice. "Where's she at?"

"Safe." Their eyes were locked. "Chicken… she called ahead from the parking lot. She's waiting."

"If I'm going to drink with her, I need a knife."

"If you're going to drink with my wife while you have a knife… I'm sitting between you two."

Jolie snorted with a softening smirk. "Pervert. You always did dream of a threesome with us. And I can tell you right now and forever… that ain't our kind of gymkhana." The touch of blue had slid back into her right eye. He knew it was the best he could hope for. Celeste told him about the blow up at the cabin.

He drew his cell phone from his pocket as he walked away.

Jolie felt the weight land on the stool next to her. She didn't have to look. Her left hand slid the beer over in front of Celeste. The only thanks was Celeste's knee knocking against hers. They sat silent for half an hour.

"You've really turned into a cunt."

Jolie took another sip and tried not to grimace. "I was on the way when we turned thirty."

Celeste harrumphed. "Fuck no. You were on the way when you got kicked by the palomino you were breaking."

"Well, tough cupcakes, little girl. Don't pull shit, and you won't get called on it."

The brunette muttered lowly. "Shit. You went away for seven years, and I don't know how to be around you."

Jolie pushed herself around and faced her best friend since second grade. "How about trying just to be you. The same smartass who stole a burro and parked it in the girl's gym… on a Friday night."

The woman's eyes flew open as large as her mouth. "Oh, crap…"

"Yeah, it was everywhere. The poor thing would have died if there hadn't been all those towels to tear apart and eat."

Celeste collapsed against Jolie's shoulder. "Oh, geez… I'd forgotten about the donkey. Best stunt ever."

"No… the best stunt ever was you telling Mrs. Tight Panties I had helped you."

Celeste held up her index finger and twisted as she pointed it at Jolie's face. "You have to admit, the week in Encinitas was the best. Even if you lost the truck for a month."

Jolie squinted down at Randy who was busy at the other end of the bar. As she turned back to Celeste, she cocked her head so her hat shielded her face and mouth. "Whatever happened between you and that fishing boat guy? He was hot."

The woman's eyes went wide as she groaned into a moan and shrunk into herself. "Oh, my gawd. I had forgotten about him. In the short word—nothing. In the long… well, those tight pants didn't lie. His problem was he should have cut the kissing and fumbling around to a short time and focused on getting out of those tight jeans."

Jolie's shoulders started jumping as she laughed. Same old Celeste and Jolie. "You're saying he had his shortcomings?"

Celeste grabbed the edge of Jolie's hat and pulled in. With their noses an inch apart, and both cross-eyed, she snorted. "The second I touched him." They both exploded. Randy looked back down the bar. All he could see was the top of the wide-brimmed black hat and two sets of shoulders. But the laughter was the same as it had been in high school and the many years after.

Celeste finally leaned back for air and another chug on her beer. To keep a straight face, she focused on her husband as he worked. "You ever see a video where a whale blows water out of his blowhole?"

Randy glanced back. The hat was lower toward the bar, but the noise of their laughter was louder. He knew only one was getting drunk. The bar was loud and noisy, but the two at the end, his ear was tuned to. The Friday night could have been any one of the ones from ten years before. Maybe life could get back to the good times again.

8

WHOA

Wild hooey of Americas. If I need to explain the word 'whoa'... there's a problem between the book and the reader's seat.

The night had lasted longer than Jolie planned. It felt good to goof around with Celeste again. There was a reason they had been best friends since they sat next to each other in Miss Stracken's second-grade class. The sitting together had bled over into the cafeteria, the playground, and the bus. Celeste rode home with Jolie, and then after chores, cookies, and homework, Jolie's mom would drive her home, or Celeste's father would pick her up after dinner when he got off at the prison. Either way, the two single children had found their sisters.

Their pranks and hijinks continued through high school. By then, they were referred to as simply *the twins*—even though one was blonde and the other brunette. One rode horses at a semi-pro level, and the other rode the grandstands. Jolie was booted, and Celeste was tennis shoed. The commotion Celeste could create around her garnered her the nicknames of tornado, hurricane, and dumpster—as in a dumpster fire. Her names were as transitional as her mood swings, but no matter who was talking, everyone knew who they were talking about.

Jolie turned out onto the highway. Her elbow sticking out of the window created a playful breeze through her hair. She thought about her friend. The one name most descriptive of her life from high school, her father's death, and until turning thirty, would have been 'slow moving train wreck.' Only her finally dating Randy settled down her wild side, and she started to pull her life together.

She looked up as the interior of the truck turned blue and red.

"Fuck."

She pulled the truck over. She knew there hadn't been enough alcohol in the single glass of her drink. More with, it had been so nasty tasting, she had left half of it. She left her hands draped over the steering wheel. In the side mirror, she saw the dark form of the sheriff get out of the car and walk forward. She rested her head back and waited.

She startled as the passenger door opened. The man slid in and closed the door. They silently studied each other.

The officer snorted a single laugh through his nose. "I don't know why I thought you would recognize me."

Her eyes leveled. A part of her wished she had buttoned the top two buttons on her shirt. "Should I?"

The man barreled his lips in a grimace. "It depends. When you were roping... I mean serious roping, did you pay attention to anyone but your horse?"

"My horse? Which one?"

"A big black one... I think its name was Lightning?" He took off his Smokey Bear hat and played with it in his hands. "I think it was a gelding."

"Thunder, he was dark brown but almost black, and I always rode stallions."

"Well, the clown you ran over thought it felt like getting hit by lighting." He smiled weakly. "Well… except for the stars and stuff."

Jolie turned sideways in the seat. Her right knee cocked up onto the bench seat. Her right index finger rose as her arm elbowed along the seat back. "You used to have a blue nose and a red star on your… well, one of your cheeks."

"Red nose and red heart. It was the left cheek. The same place my mother always kissed me when I would leave the house."

Jolie smiled. Rodeo—win, bust, break, or fall, it was always warm memories. Even before prison. "And now you're a sheriff."

"Deputy. I was before." He shied his face. "Mostly because I loved being in the middle of it all, but occasionally as undercover for ATF or DEA. But mostly because, from the first day I was a clown in the kid's rodeo with sheep dodging and goat roping, I was in love."

Jolie smirked. "The dust in your nose, and the ache of the bruises, but the smell… bulls, horses, cows, people, and crackerjack popcorn."

"Especially the popcorn."

"Down San Diego way the Churros were good and greasy."

"They didn't beat the machaca burritos out in Indio."

She watched the man. He was her age, maybe a little older, but he was acting like a nervous kid. He pulled over the known town drunk but still hadn't asked for her license and registration. "Are you going to arrest me or ask me out to the next rodeo?"

He looked up, only partially startled. "Have you been drinking tonight?"

"Do you want me to blow your machine?" She knew it did— and she meant it to—sound dirty.

He sighed and softly shook his head. He quietly looked out the front window. His sigh was heavy but quiet. "I was the one who found her. Your mother."

His words froze her but hit her as unexpectedly as if he had slapped her. She had never thought about who had found her or the effect it would have on those people.

"I'm sorry…"

"It wasn't your fault. It was my job. Evidently, she was supposed to go to an important meeting in Santa Barbara—but never showed."

"It was the stakeholders meeting. She was the chairperson. It was a big deal."

"I guess so." The hat stopped turning in his hands. "They called the office and asked for a deputy to check on the cabin. I was patrolling the area and swung up. I knew something was wrong the minute I pulled up. Your truck was gone, and the dogs were acting spooked. Her car was still in the lean-to. I radioed for back-up but went in anyway. Only the kitchen screen door was closed but not locked."

Her hand reached out. "You don't have to…"

He put up one hand. "It's okay. I've had time… I need to… you need to hear this." His eyes were wet. "For me."

She nodded and dropped her hand.

He sniffed and sat up straighter. "Even when I saw just the handle, I knew it was your knife… but it was wrong. The finger grids were to the left. It was a left-handed person who shoved it in. You threw a right rope. Just then, I knew it wasn't you. I tried to tell the lieutenant and the sheriff, but it was like it was just easier for them to find and hang you."

"They never brought it out in court."

His one eyebrow jumped as he looked sideways at her. "I'll tell you something else they never looked into. Even though I made a note of it in my report." His hand-carved a curve in the air. "The rifle rack over the front door was empty."

"I took the 30-06 with me to Idaho. It was my lucky elk hunting rifle."

"You never got an elk."

"My friend never showed up in Moscow. He supposedly had the tags."

"They hung you on that. No proof you were in Idaho, no tags, no friend, and no evidence you had ever been there."

"CHP found me at the truck stop in Atascadero. I was on my way back."

"You were set up."

Jolie thought about how friendships were made in prison. It was always a give and take. There was always a price for friendships. Nothing was offered freely. "Can you prove it?"

The hat sunk in his fingers, almost hitting his boots. "No."

"Then why tell me all this? Why pull me over in the middle of the night in the middle of blackout territory?"

"Because... I thought you should know... there are many of us who know you didn't do it. And I thought you needed to know some people have your back."

Her eyes were closer to white than blue. Her heart vibrated. "I don't even know your name."

He rose on his left cheek and fished his wallet out. He held his card out. "My clown name was Punchy, and the number on my back was always 111. Put me in your phone. If you ever need me, I'm just a barrel away." He got out.

Jolie just sat there watching the side mirror until the cruiser lights turned off, he made a U-turn, and the taillights disappeared. The tears rolled down her face without her crying.

9

STEEL

Working tack is made from steel. It is strong and durable. A cowhand who shows these same qualities, as well as courage, is said to have 'steel.' Male or female, it has nothing to do with genitals.

The neighborhood had always been sketchy, but the small strip mall was where life, the economy, and karma came to take an explosive, reeking, massive dump. Jolie eyed the ridgeline of the signs. She had seen zigzag fences more lined up. Luckily, she had eaten before she crossed the San Fernando Valley. The health department stopped coding the restaurants three miles and sixty years before. The sign for Tres Jerks showed only a chicken, pig, and a bull. As she slid out of the truck, she thought how the truth should have been a rat, small dog, and a cockroach. The neighborhood to the north was south Glendale where blue-collar workers met the middle class. This wasteland, even the poor from Glassell Park didn't venture into. Stuck between the hills leading up and over into the rougher sections of Hollywood and the railroad yard workers of Glassell

Park lay a no man's land stretched between pin and ink prison tattoos and a joint rolled with anything mixed with any drug. To call it a rough neighborhood would have been kind.

She stood at the door, eyeing the handle. It was a pull she didn't want to touch. The one day she decided to wear a tank top.

The door swung open as a couple emerged. Jolie eyed the two who didn't fit. The suit was more Glendale than upper Burbank on the edge of the barrio of Sun Valley and Pacoima. The giggly young woman fit the stereotype in Jolie's mind of the young thing out front who was there because she shared the boss's bed for the long nooner.

Jolie left her boot in the doorway as she watched the two climb into the man's Lexus. She didn't think the baby seat in the back had anything to do with the blonde in the short summer dress. But the twin hunks of silicone looked like it could take care of a whole nursery. She finished kicking the door wide and stepped into the dark interior.

The décor was stark but inviting. Those who ignored the outside were rewarded for entering. Her mouth watered from the smells of the barbecue done more Yucatan than Jamaican, but the dry rubbed jerk was true through all the Caribbean.

The bartender flipped the ubiquitous white towel over his shoulder. A ripped tank top stretched tight over bulging ebony muscles. Jolie wasn't sure the large mane of dreadlocks washing over his shoulders and down his back was kosher or even approved by the health department, but she wasn't making any phone calls to complain.

"What kin I get ya?" The accent was something but probably more Hollywood than Montego Bay. But at least the voice was soft and musical.

"I'm looking for the lowlife Tiny Dick Timmy Jostell. The sleazy bastard stole my girlfriend."

The mouth started to open as the eyes spread wide. The man

looked her up and down, sizing up the fight in the woman. "You comed to da wrong place. You have to leave now." The accent might be real. It hadn't changed.

She shook her head. "No matter to me. I either beat the snot out of him here… or gut him at home."

She watched as the man's eyes got larger, but the mouth vibrated in rigger as he fought for what to say.

The voice behind her rumbled. "I'd pay good money to watch either one."

Jolie spoke to the bartender. "Does she have a gun, or can I turn around."

His chuckle sounded like twelve-pound mill balls pounding dead stone. "Oh miss, I ain't sayin'. Dis be yo mess to clean up."

She laughed with a broad smile as she turned around into a large breasted hug. The woman enveloped the rail-thin cowgirl. "Oh, child. This has been far too long."

Jolie hung into the warm comfort of the woman's embrace. Her voice was wet and husky. "Oh Pansy, I have missed this hug. I don't want to leave until morning."

The woman began to shake. And then they were both shaking. "Child, don't start."

Jolie pushed back. She wiped at the tears and snot as she sniffed loudly. "We need to talk, but I didn't get much breakfast on the way down here."

The woman turned and flapped her hand at the tall bartender. "Princess, we need two plates of whatever Cookie thinks is good enough to serve rodeo royalty." The man leveled his eyes at her. "Go on." She dismissed him with her hand and wobbling underarm. "Don't be lollygagging now. We have royalty here, and she be hangry. And the good Lord knows, you do not want to see her just pure angry… like I'm a getting' rat now."

Rolling his eyes, the man put the glass down and turned toward the back.

Jolie draped her arm along the large woman's shoulders. The two of them watched the man walk away down the long bar. Jolie pressed the side of her head next to Pansy's.

"Um a yum a yum…"

As the man turned through the door into the back, Pansy snorted deep in her chest. "I'm sure you be thinkin' the same think his boyfriend thinks every night when he comes home." She looked up with a smile at the horror-struck face. "Um huh, you heard me right. Breaks women's hearts all day and warms his man's heart all-night."

"Well, shit on the barn door. It's still good to look at."

The woman was chuffed. "Why do you think I hired him? Business is almost double since he came. I don't know who's coming for him or who's coming for the results. But I can tell you… I don't care. I jus' like the deposit slips from the bank."

Jolie smiled. Some things hardly change. They took seats in the large booth. From the placement, Jolie could tell it was the throne the woman conducted business from. She reached in her shirt pocket and drew out a business card.

Pushing the card across to the woman, she explained. "This man wants a knife just like my pig knife."

The woman stared at the card. Soon the wet eyes leaked streaks of crystal down her cheeks. She looked up. "Sweetness, Princess wasn't telling you to leave. He was telling you my Timmy was down in Forest Lawn. He be gone almost three years now."

Jolie's face was stone. She waited.

"He ran down to the market. I had forgotten rolls for Sunday dinner. Four little shits looking to cut a name for themselves. They jumped him coming out with the rolls. There was even a birthday cake for his daughter's twenty-fifth hiding at the bottom of the sack."

"Just four?"

"The first two started with knives. But one of the others…

when they seen he be better with the knife than all four of them… he pulled out a pistol and loaded eight shots in Timmy's body, and then one last one through his head as he laid there— bleeding in the parking lot."

Jolie reached across and took the woman's hand. "I'm so sorry. He was a good man."

The woman rolled her eyes and wiped tears. "Oh, fuck that good man shit. He was the best. That little shit be always thinking about others. But he still left his mama and daughter alone and missing him."

Jolie didn't know how to take the backhanded love. "How are you two holding up?" She gently squeezed the woman's hands.

"Honey, some days, I don't know if it be Tuesday or Sunday. The days just gray and all look alike. We jus' push dat rock back up the hill like the Greek dude. Day in and day out… jus' pushin' a rock, pushin' a rock."

The bartender placed two serving platters of barbecue in front of them. "Cookie says no matter how hard it is, you gots to eat. So, you hide it all, no matter how bad it tastes. There be layers of death by chocolate cake fo' dessert."

Jolie sat wide-eyed at the food. Pansy reached out to the man's hand. "Sweetie… call down to Dotty and ask her to come up. Tell her Rocket is here. She'll know what to bring."

The food was almost all gone when the muscular young woman strolled through the front door and into the bar. The torn tank top could have been a match for the bartender's… The arm and shoulder muscles were thicker and more massive. This kind of mass didn't come with a gym membership attached. Jolie smiled and stood. The face was close to what Jolie remembered of her father. She reached out her hand to shake.

The woman snorted and slapped the hand out of her way. Her hug was just short of crushing. "This is from my father. I don't hug until the third date."

Jolie choked slightly at the deflecting humor. "I like a woman who plays hard to get."

"I didn't say I be hard to get… I just don't give away hugs." She pushed her open palm out at the booth. "Sit."

As Jolie sat and scooted in, the woman reached behind her and drew out a large knife. It was an exact match to the pig knife. The woman quietly laid it in front of her.

Jolie's hands were an inch away from each end. There was a slight vibration. She wanted to touch it, but a part of her told her if she did, it would disappear.

"When Daddy heard you was sent to prison, he said you would need a new knife. Those assholes never give anything back. He figured some cop probably one night would sneak it out of evidence and hide it at their home as a souvenir. So he made you another one… just in case you needed to go pig hunting again."

Jolie's chin rose as her lips barreled. She watched the light bounce off the polished blade. Her eyes were slits as she watched over the curve of her cheeks. She sighed as her eyes slid shut. Her right hand found the handle. It closed around the wrapped leather but never moved the steel. She could feel the power flowing through the weight.

In a second, dozens of pigs broke through the brush, fought with the dogs, and then… there was the frozen moment. Time and motion stopped. In the hundredths of a second, the pig and Jolie's eyes locked. It was the moment the pig realized—the fight was never about the dogs. Five-hundredths of a second—the first front hoof reaches out. When it reaches forward again, six hundred pounds of pig is moving at forty-miles-an-hour. As the right front hoof moves back, the knife in the air becomes the knife in the pig. Piercing the shoulder where the neck enters. The one place the armor of the skin changes from rock-hard four inches to a softer inch. As the small Californios pommel hits the armor, she starts the down pressure to rotate the tip of the blade up into the pounding heart. The hand lets go and is replaced by the moccasin. She steps on the handle, using it as a springboard throwing her over the pig and out of harm's way. The tusks dive useless into the ground.

The ache would always come. More than a days' worth of adrenaline pumped into the muscles and burned to ash in a moment. If she stopped moving, she would stiffen up and be worthless. The meat had to come out, be sheared from the bone and laid on the taller bushes of chaparral—away from scroungers. Cutting up the belly and inside of the leg's skin—strips to make a pack for the first hundred or more pounds of meat. The bulk, if there was more than another load, she would bring back the burro and pack out the hide as well.

Her eyes opened. The other two were sitting back —watching.

The young woman leaned in. "You be there… with the pigs." Jolie nodded softly. "I could tell. Your arm never moved, but your skin crawled and jumped from the muscles. Daddy would have loved to see it."

"You took over the forge."

The woman blinked slowly as she curled her lips in a closed smile. Her chest and chin bounced once. "He put me on the bellows when I was five. When I was ten, I was holding the tongs while he pounded with both hands. For my twelfth birthday, I had made my first knife by myself."

Pansy rolled her eyes into a smile. "Little Dot here has won more knife show awards than her father ever dreamed of. Her work has been in several movies."

The young woman blushed and rocked forward with her elbows on her knees. "Don't listen to her stuff. Gun shows and movies are nothing but puff pastry. Real steelworks." She pointed at the knife.

The ropey tanned hand placed it back on the table. "Let's hope this one will never have to."

The right side of the young woman flashed in surprise. "You're not going to hunt pigs anymore?"

"European boars? No. It takes a pack of well-trained dogs. My father spent decades breeding and crossbreeding to get the dogs we had. There is no such breed as a pig dog—you have to breed them up. You need mass from a mastiff, toughness from bulldogs or pit bulls, speed from dogs like Rhodesian ridgebacks, and brains from Australian shepherds. And even then, it's just a simple sampling of what went into our dogs. No… this knife… this knife is for a different kind of pig."

"So, you're talking about human. Self-defense."

Jolie's face was a sad stone. "Sadly, yes. Someone killed my mother. And they did it with my knife…" She didn't have to finish. The other two women understood.

Dotty leaned over and looked under the table. "Do you always tuck your jeans into your boots?"

"Pretty much. I don't ride in the chaparral anymore, and if I did, I'd wear slick-side chaps. Why?"

She nodded her head for Jolie to watch. Her hand lowered to the draw loop on the side of her tall boot. The loop moved up. In a flash, she had a slender knife in her hand. Jolie knew from prison a small sharp anything is just as deadly as a pig knife.

She held her boots out. Dotty ran her index finger and thumb around inside the rim and nodded.

It was going to be a late night or early morning getting home. But there were no dogs to feed.

STAKES

Prize money or the prize of doing something. Also, stakes can mark territory or mark a challenge when placed in someone else's territory.

The duff of the forest floor Jolie had always considered her perfume of choice. The acorns, combined with the prickly leaves of the scrub oak no larger than a thumbprint, rotted into a musty scent of a peanut butter sandwich at a sausage barbecue. As a little girl, she was given the peanut butter on coarse ground wheat bread, while the adults ate the sausages made from wild boar and usually venison. Because neither meat had enough fat, lard was added and ground into the rest. Jolie would steal slices of the rich smoky meat from her parent's plates.

Most of the scrub oak was easy enough to walk under. The small coastal deer raked antlers against the hanging limbs to remove the felt in the spring. The young bucks practiced antler fighting techniques. Jolie was entertained for years, watching them raise on their hind legs and bounding forward to lock their horns in mortal combat with a limber spring limb. Some, feeling their macho testosterone, would attack more substantial limbs—only to be knocked senseless. Her favorite being the three-pointer who took almost twenty minutes to regain consciousness, rise, and stumble off the thirty-foot cliff. He had resulted in some great steaks and a perfect balance for the two suckling pigs she killed the day before.

As Jolie grew into high school, her father's statement of 'our land' took on a different meaning. He had always told her about how the land was theirs, but it wasn't. The animals, trees, birds, and bugs owned the land for millions of years. Jolie's family only held a deed to protect it for all living on the part called a township. The four markers were all two miles apart. The government had intended the four-square-miles to have a town built on it—except the railroad was placed across the valley, running on the western edge. With the change, new homesteads and two new township plots were plated—driving the value of the old plots to useless.

Jolie's great-grandfather saw value in a large parcel ranging over the hills. It couldn't be farmed, and there were too many trees to clear for cattle. But there was a peacefulness in the forest land. So the young lawyer brought his young wife and three children to grow among the trees, deer, pigs, bears, coyotes, raccoons, weasels, and bugs. The setting was more of a testament to his wife than to his pioneer spirit in leaving the sleepy town of Santa Barbara. He had pointed, and it was she who took a stick and drew a large square in the dirt, saying: 'I want a large porch for my babies. I want the south porch for cooking in the summer and the west for greeting visitors.' Every other detail was up to her husband. They camped in the large tent for two years while the dream took shape.

During the years of the tent, she was known for shooting game from her outdoor kitchen under a lean-to. It never dawned on her husband when he would return after a week or two's work down in the city as to where the meat in the stew had come from. It only became obvious the night he returned at dusk and the large bear carcass was still hanging from the tree. The small woman was all but lost in the mass, cutting the meat from the bone. She stopped long enough to kiss her husband hello, hand him a wad of jerky for dinner, and return to her work. He had his job, and she had hers.

The heat of the day was a few hours off. Jolie let her nose guide her to where the pigs had rooted the duff, looking for mushy half fermented acorns from last fall. The pungent odor would swell in this hollow or wisp away on a rise. As she walked, her calves became more accustom to the new knives in her boot. The hunting scabbard for the big pig knife, Dot had finished the day before. Jolie had told her when she called she wanted to take care of something on the south side of her land and would then drive down in the afternoon before the traffic built. She imagined what the harness would feel like under her shirt. It was going to take some getting used to.

Jolie dropped the large gunnysack under the cliffside of the blue oak's deep shade. The tree was one of her favorites. When she was nine, her father brought her to the hill. He showed her the magic of the gap between the tops of the scrub oaks and chaparral growing in the wash below. The hanging edge of the dense canopy of the blue oak hanging over the cliff was only a few feet away. His grandfather's collapsible telescope allowed them to look out across much of the Santa Ynez Valley.

As she grew, she watched the valley grow. At first, there were the large green properties of land with a dot of a house or barn here and there. Then came the larger homes on smaller vestiges of green land—some with barns, most without. The next round of expensive cars brought even larger houses of ridiculous scale on sections of land lawyers had to ask for variances. The few acres of grapes rotting on the untended vines were to justify paying only for agricultural property taxes instead of honest sharing. When Jolie got a strong whiff of the stench growing in the lower reaches of what used to be honest ranchers, she had stopped going to local events.

She sat on the large sack of lath stakes with orange plastic ribbons. The first one she had pulled out of the ground shortly after the sun pinked the tips of the coastal hills. Once she understood the flow of the roads the markers were intended for, the bag filled quickly.

As she stood, she looked down. There was just a dot of red in among the dead brown of the duff. The hard, red ball had belonged to the only mastiff her father had owned.

Hondo leaned against most men's upper thigh or hips. The dog was massive in height, head, jaws, and chest. But the heart of the beast was even larger.

When hunting, Hondo was the one to tear into a pig head-on. Each dog had their specialty to torture or torment. Some went for feet, others for the tail—endlessly forcing the pig to circle and circle. Hondo would charge and dive straight for the snout. Square between the large curled tusks, he would sink his canines deep into the tender flesh and lock his jaw. The larger pigs, twice or triple his size and weight, would thrash and wave the goliath of a dog in the air like a towel. The smaller pigs would back into the other dogs as they tried to tear loose from the savage pain in their snout.

Her father would tell Jolie stories with his hands waving wildly in the air and at his face. The big black dog, now lying on the grass covered with adoring puppies, locked on the snout of the pig in mortal combat. The razorback tearing at the left ear while the Australian shepherd pulled and ripped at the other. The blue heeler would bite and slam into the rear haunch while the blue tick dog would badger the tail. Or, in the case of a larger boar, would bite lower at the hanging balls.

Whenever the giant Hondo was awake, the red ball was in his mouth. Her father thought it might be to keep his teeth from clacking, which was uncomfortable. The young girl thought it was because it was his and his alone. Even when they were hunting, the ball was in the mouth. Her father said if Hondo dropped his ball, it was only because there was a pig in the brush. It only took seconds to prove him right.

Her father, the dog, and Jolie liked this blue oak overlooking the valley. This was where they had found the old dog's body. Her father must not have noticed the ball.

With a wistful smile, she bent to pick up the ball.

The weight of the bullet hitting her shoulder was like being kicked by a horse. The left shoulder, with its nine screws, metal rod, and plate, took the full energy of the blow and dragged her over the cliff.

11

BREATH

*More important than how your fist is set on the rope and jammed
into your crotch, more important than if your lasso is hanging
three feet or four feet, more important than if your
horse is young or worn—above all else… breathe.*

Distracted, Mike reached over and without looking, picked up the phone. Few people would think to call him on a Sunday. "Mike."

"Hey, Mike, it's Dot. Dotty Jostell."

He looked up and out the window. He knew he should know who the voice belonged to. "Yes?"

The snort on the other end of the line was dismissive as well as humored. The woman's husky voice could also have been a man, but he was stuck on the name.

"I'm sorry, I forgot you be a lawyer type. I'll make dis simple fo' you. I gots a big-assed pigsticker Jolie supposed to come down and get on Friday night. You name and card be taped to it… but I guess you got scared by the size to clean your fingernails. I just throw it in the recycle and maybe one o' them little gang bangers here hurts himself on it."

"Jolie?"

"Oh, shit. Did I miss dial? I be trying to reach Mike Williams of Union Capital."

He frowned and checked his cell phone. It was Sunday. "Um… I'm sorry. Dot was it?"

"Yeah. Like on the dot, only I hit harder."

He sat up. "Excuse me for just… one…" His fingers flew over the keyboard. The image was a dark-skinned woman with bulging muscles standing over an equally muscled woman. The one's right fist was pummeling the other's nose and face. Even from the grainy image, it was still clear the blonde was not awake by the fifth blow. The mixed martial arts fight had been for the title but finished with one holding the belt as she rode in the ambulance with her friend. She had even refused to allow the announcer to touch her hand.

"You have a large belt. It took you three rounds and nineteen stitches, Ms. Jostell."

The silence on the phone was only punctuated by the slow deep breath. "Not my finest hour. She was a close friend."

"The article here says you have dinner with her parents every month. I would say you are still friends."

"Do it say I lay a yellow rose on her grave every month?"

Mike looked out the window at the waves curling toward the beach. So many parts to a person's story. "I think to have printed such would have been an invasion of yours and her privacy. It was only a story about friendships among competitors."

The voice was soft and quiet. "I don't compete no more."

He bit on his lower lip. "No… but you make knives."

"My father taught me. When my father was killed, I took it out on everyone in the ring. Now I pick up a three-pound hammer and beat on red-hot steel."

"But you called…" He scratched at the back of his neck. "Jolie was going to pick up the knife when?"

"Friday night. She call in da morning. Said she going to walk around southside and pull some stakes den head down. We hold dinner fo' her… she never show—and she not called. Nana says it not like her."

Mike picked up his cell phone with his right hand and thumbed to the number. It only rang. "She's not picking up her cell."

"Maybe she's out of range. She say she live where there be no cell reception."

His cell phone only issued the same ringing from the second number. "She doesn't answer the cabin number either. Give me your number. I'll go up and see what's what." He punched the number into his cell. "It's going to take me an hour to get up there. As soon as I know anything, I'll let you know."

TWO DAYS BEFORE

Jolie could feel the blanket of the dirt covering her body. The dirt and leaves had followed her down the cliff. With a shallow breath, she felt like she had hit every rock, branch, or bump down every foot of the forty feet. The pain in her right side reminded her of a quarter horse who caught her by surprise in a barn. The massive horse had pushed her against the wall hard enough to crack three of her ribs. When she dropped to her knees from the pain, the horse had kicked her into the next week. When she came to in the hospital, her left shoulder was braced and bound. The humorous had cracked below the ball joint. Seven screws and a rod still held it all together. But now, it hurt like hell.

The weight of dirt and leaves covered most of her body. She

wanted to move but also wanted just to sleep. Her hearing came and went with the dull ringing in her head or ears. She flexed her toes in her boots. She was sure she could feel them. At least she could feel the sore area where the knives rubbed against her calves. She curled or counted with each finger in turn. Ten.

"She went over the cliff."

"I don't see her."

"There. There's a piece of her shirt."

"Don't. Stop. If you shoot her again, it will look like murder. But with the one shot, it could have been a hunter."

"I need to make certain."

"There will be time enough later. We need to get out of here. Someone had to have heard the shot."

Something was extremely wrong. The voices sounded muffled with dirt and distance, but somehow familiar. Motors. Jolie could hear motorcycles. She guessed at quad-runners and then passed out.

<hr>

THE COLD HELPED WITH THE PAIN. THE DARK DIDN'T BOTHER her. She knew every foot of every acre of the four-square-mile area. She also knew it was over a mile of deep chaparral back to the cabin. If she surprised a sow with piglets in the dense brush, she knew she was dead. Only the long way around would be safe. But it doubled the distance.

She carefully moved her legs first. The blanket of dirt rustled with a mixture of the small dried leaves. The sound triggered a memory, which, for forty years, had all but been a throwaway. She held onto the memory and let it play out and then over and over. The pain then was less than her body was screaming about now.

The horse had been named Rabbit. The hand they had working the upper pastures nicknamed it Bunny Hop. Even at only nine-hands, the pony's habit of occasionally bunching up and hopping about stiff-legged had caused home after home to pass the pony along at lower and cheaper prices. If there had been a glue factory close, Bunny Hop would have landed there. Instead, the pony landed in their corral. It was eight-year-old Jolie's to train, and if possible, ride.

She had broken the hopping habit in the hot walker and then progressed with a hundred-pound weight tied to the saddle. The pony was right back at its old trick. Every eight turns around the corral and out came a series of pogo legs. The weight didn't move, but it wore the pony down. Lead in one hand, long whip in the other. Hour after hour, she trained her first pony.

One day, she stopped the morning's exercise and tied the pony to the corral fence. She left it there while she went into the barn and ate lunch. When she came out, she had a carrot in her back pocket and an apple in her hand. As she untied the rope, she fed the apple to the pony. She led the pony around the corral, slowly letting out more lead. Once she was standing in the center, and the pony had made twenty-four rounds one-way, she reeled it in and started it in the other direction. Not a single hop.

She tied the pony back to the fence, fed it the carrot, and removed the saddle. Once again, they made twenty-four rounds in one direction and another in the other direction. Not a single hop.

Feeling good about the day, she unsnapped the long lead and grabbed ahold of just the hackamore and a fist full of mane. The two made five passes around the corral. Smooth as a baby.

Jolie could see out the side of her eye, her father and the hand standing in the shadow of the large barn door.

She rode the pony over to the gate leading out to the larger pasture. Lifting the wire, the gate swung open. Eight steps into the pasture and Jolie looked back with a smile at her father.

And then found her mouth full of dirt and grass.

She could hear her father and the hand running. The hand

loved his Texas-style spurs and the ringing the rowels made when he walked or ran.

The boots stopped six feet away. Her father's voice was always soft, melodic, but with an unforgiving edge. He demanded excellence of himself and nothing less from others.

"You stopped paying attention."

"She tricked me."

"You stopped being in command. If you aren't going to control her, she gets her own way."

She lay there—crying softly.

"Okay, you've had enough time to see if anything is broken. Time to go get your pony and start over."

"But I hurt."

"Get up."

"But I hurt."

"Get up."

She knew the words would never change. She had seen the scars covering his body from the war, pigs, and horses. It would be years before he also told her about the fights as a young boy. It was only a few more years and her first real horse when the words changed to the standard, *Cowboy up*.

She had stumbled a hundred yards down the wash. She gently lowered down onto a large oak log. She grabbed her elbow and forced her right arm and hand back over her shoulder to find the bullet hole. Her hand came away with dirt, leaves, and blood. If it had been mostly blood, she would know she was actively bleeding. Now she knew the dirt and duff were helping stanch the flow. But she also knew she was not out of the woods yet. About a mile away, there was a small rotting well pump house in the upper side of the wash. If she could make it there by sun-up, she could hide there until it was dark again. She hoped the one wall still leaked from a small spring.

Only a sliver of moon rose above the trees behind her. In many ways, she would have preferred it to be a clouded or moonless night. She listened in the still air. There were animal sounds, but no engines. She knew it didn't mean whoever shot her wasn't hunting her on foot. She pushed down on the log with her hands. The pain in her left shoulder told her at least one bone was broken.

Cowboy up.

12

LEAD

A lead can be as simple as a short rope connected to a harness or as long as a thirty-foot longe line. Either can lead a horse to where they need to go.

The cabin was empty. Mike walked around, trying to figure it all out. There was an ice chest on the kitchen table. The small amount of food had long gone bad. The refrigerator stood warm. He looked for the plug and cord and found mice had eaten through to the copper wire years before. He wasn't sure if it was safe to try the propane stove, but the frying pan was freshly cleaned so he figured it might work—or Jolie didn't know any better.

The roll of toilet paper was half used, and there was a brush on the sink counter. The towel and washcloth in the shower looked used, so he figured the plumbing at least flushed and drained. The bedding stopped with a flat sheet and a trail blanket. He figured it was much the same in prison. The wad at the head of the bed might have been a feather pillow twenty years before. Nothing in the cabin gave a hint of Jolie living there for the last month. The house felt more haunted instead.

He softly closed the solid front door behind him as he stepped out onto the deep overhung porch. For all the times he had been to the ranch, he still felt more an intruder than the manager of the land. He could feel the rough wonkiness of the hand-hewn deck boards through the thin soles of his running shoes. The entire house was built for stouter boots, firmer clothes, and people of the land. The black Lexus was out of place next to the beaten rust and green truck. He flipped the electronic key-fob in his hand. He didn't even know where to start looking on the property, but he was almost certain if the truck was here, Jolie was somewhere on the land.

He pulled his phone from his pocket. A single small bar showed. Without moving the phone, he thumbed to the number. He waited as the connection did or didn't break.

His head snapped up as he heard a muffled ring—the truck.

Looking under the driver's side of the broken-down bench seat, he saw a rifle and a small bag. The phone was still ringing. Beside the small bag was an old brass hoof pick with a shackle and screw pin holding two keys. Drawing the rifle and keys out, he half levered the bolt to expose the shell. He knew enough about Jolie and her family. If there was a bullet in the barrel, there wasn't any room left in the slide. The model 1894 Winchester had been the repeating rifle of choice for over a hundred years. He remembered Manual giving her a rifle. He checked the side. There were no serial numbers. The rifle was as clean as he had told her.

The small jean bag held the rest of a box full of shells and the satellite phone. He checked the charge. Half. Sliding it over, he slid in and started the truck. He recognized the other silver key. It had nothing to do with the truck, the cabin, or anything on the ranch. It was the key to the bottom drawer of his desk.

He nosed the old Dodge around the barn and headed south.

The property was one of the rarest he visited. When he was young, it was one of his favorites. The owner was a soft-spoken man who looked like the gnarled limb of a weather-twisted oak. His life was horses, but the juice in his soul was a blend of the dozen dogs and his putting meat on the table.

In 1942, his mother had lied for him and convinced the recruiter he was seventeen and a high school drop-out. The recruiter did little more than stick a mirror under his nose to fog up. The Japanese had bombed Pearl Harbor the month before. The fifteen-year-old had returned to school after Christmas only to finish the fight a gang had started on him in a stairwell with three boys and a knife. All three headed for the hospital as he sat in the principal's office for being tardy to his sixth-period English class. The two knives in January had ended in their owner's legs. The principal had phoned his mother. She left her work and silently retrieved him. She took him back to the factory, found him a broom and dustpan, and wordlessly pointed at the factory floor littered with metal threads, dust, and scrap. The rest of the day, he cleaned around the forty-seven machinists. When the whistle blew at the end of the workday; he was hungry, tired, and knew he never wanted to do meaningless work ever again.

Four days later, he raised his hand and became a marine.

His ranch was clean, straightened away, and no-nonsense. He approached life and the horses the same. He allowed each of his burros, over the years, to throw a fit or balk—just once. He would calmly pet and soothe the animal. Stroking the neck and scratch under the chin, he would work the beast to a standstill.

And then he would grab the closest ear and bite it as hard as he could. A couple carried the curved mark out of their ear forever.

The beast knew why he bit them. They had gone against his will, and he was now going to eat them. All they could see was his chest. All they could smell was his anger. All they could feel was his teeth. After, he would strip the burrow of its pack or hackamore and then turn them loose into the field. If they came back the next morning, he knew they would never be a problem again.

One burro had been legendary. He had hauled it to Montana to hunt elk. The lesson happened at the end of six days of walking and not an elk in sight. When turned loose, the man had hoisted the tack onto his own back and walked the two days back to the ranch of his best friend. Resolved, two days later, he had packed up and returned to California with an empty horse trailer.

The next week, his friend called to come get his injured burro. He told the man just to shoot him and bury him—the animal had taken too long to decide. The man laughed and told him the mountain lion it killed might have had something to do with the delay. The claw marks on its haunches had eventually healed and faded, but the fealty to its owner never wavered.

When the young Mike had asked how he knew to bite the ears, the ropy thin rancher told him about the war in the Pacific. He explained how the sergeants would tell the grunts about being captured by the Japanese. If rations got lean, they would take the difficult prisoner and butcher them. There were no verified stories of cannibalism among the Japanese. But most, if not all, the Americans fighting them knew nothing true about them either. Americans ate potatoes and corn with their beef and pigs. The Japanese, beyond looking different, ate rice with their fish. Fear of the unknown, or perceived horror, is a strong force that can drive a person or beast to act against their nature or in their own interest.

He had gone on to use the Bataan Death March as an example. In the beginning, there were eighty-thousand Philippine and American soldiers taken prisoner. After being crammed into overheated railcars, killing many, the survivors were forced to march over sixty-five miles in the high humidity and heat. The sparse Japanese forces were brutal and swift to kill any failing prisoners. If the prisoners had turned on their captors during the march, they would have overwhelmed them. But, for the fear, over one-third of the prisoners never made it safely out of Camp McDonald. The rest were never the same anyway. They were part of the masses of bodies who came home—but not the men.

Mike parked the truck in the shade of a large standing oak. He could see a mound of cloth lying in the dark shadow under the blue oak near the cliff. He waited as he scanned the surrounding rise. The elevation provided too little groundwater for any substantial grasses or undergrowth. The scrub trees were thin and few, so they offered little cover.

Mike had learned long before how to let the eyes become unfocused and relax, only watching for movement. The tree with the deep shade had been his teacher's favorite place to watch the world. Mike knew he had often brought his daughter and a few dogs up; just to watch the valley.

Mike's eyes snapped into focus on the small bird flying up from one of the trees down in the wash or barranca below. A moment later, a similar bird also rose into the air. Mike relaxed. They were only getting exercise from sitting on eggs or tending chicks. Neither bird seemed startled nor agitated.

Mike pushed open the truck door with his left hand, his cane, and foot. His right hand wrapped around the center of the lever-action rifle. He didn't feel a need for it, but it was a light load to carry. Even a lighter burden if he needed it. Pausing as he continued to look around the area to see if his movement had caused a reaction, he slid open the box of shells. Cupping his hand over a mass of the bottoms, he pulled them and slid them into his front pocket. Not to create a large bulge, he slid some more into his left back pocket.

He stepped back and eased the door almost closed. He waited and watched. The cloth mound in the shade didn't move.

Unnerved by the quiet, Mike cautiously approached the mound of dark cloth at the base of the tree. From a distance, it could be a person or something else. The phone call from Glendale was at the forefront of his mind.

He circled to the north until he could tell it wasn't a person. Specifically, it wasn't Jolie.

Sheltered by the mass of the oak tree, he reached forward with the end of his cane. Prying open the mouth of the large bag, he saw nothing but a pile of sticks. The orange plastic streamer confirmed what Dot had said. Jolie had pulled these stakes Friday morning.

There was a flattening, as if a weight had been applied, in the middle of the bag. He thought about the pushed down indent on the bag. The weight would have been well over a hundred pounds but form following. He thought about the woman and how following her form could be. She had sat on the bag. He looked out across the valley, the view she would have come for and seen.

His eyes caught on the forest duff. The leaves were wrong. They were disturbed near the edge of the cliff. A foot on either side and the leaves were all flat and layered. The curving track from a foot from the bag to the edge suggested confused footing, or a violent stumble, such as a fight… or worse.

On hands and knees, he approached the path. Six inches from the edge was a cluster of dark reddish-brown drops—dried blood.

He stayed low as he looked over the edge. There were several large scuff marks on the side of the cliff as if someone or something had hit several times on the way down—breaking the fall. A heaped jumble of leaves and dirt lay disturbed and with drag marks to the north. She was at least alive when she hit.

He scanned the trees and brush as he rushed back to the truck.

He left the rifle on the seat as he started the truck in gear. The beaten Dodge, true to its nature, lurched and rolled forward. He swung the nose around and headed for the trail he knew would lead down into the wash running along the western side of the homestead.

He stopped where the trail turned right and led down into the barranca or dry wash. He set the break and got out. The trail told two stories.

There were tracks from two quad-runners. He recognized the funny rhomboid block tire track—he used the same tread on his.

The other set of tracks were the most informative. The dog or coyote tracks overlaid the tire tracks. The people on the two motorcycles had been through the day before. The coyote had hunted by the moon last night.

He stopped at the bottom of the cliff. There were knots of blood, dirt, and leaves. No pools where a body had bled out as he had seen in Vietnam. Whoever had been shot above took a tough tumble but still had been able to make their way north. If it was Jolie, she would be trying to make it to the cabin. It was the only safety within three or four miles—as well as safety, phone, and help.

<hr>

JOLIE LAY ON THE OLD HAY-FILLED MATTRESS. THE BARN WAS A product of her great-grandfather being a frugal man. To keep his workers busy, they hewed trees, brought from the northwest, into squared timbers. As they quickly learned, it was easier and faster to work the logs while they were still wet and green. As the Douglas Fir logs dried, they became harder to cut, and workers spent precious time sharpening tools to finer and sharper edges. When the many logs had become timbers of the correct sizes, he hired a horde of Mennonite barn raisers.

Jolie had met many of the hardworking and deeply religious adherents at rodeos in the Montana region. Going to town, sitting in the bleachers, and cheering for some local cowboy was sure to put a smile on their faces.

Sometimes, a simple amusement or pleasure, such as building a secret space in a barn, could bring a smile to their hearts. As a child, the secret area the size of a small car became her palace. It had also been one of the only places she never shared with even her closest friend. It was the only place she felt entirely safe.

She knew she needed help, but moving was becoming problematic. When she tried to make a run for the house, she heard trucks or motorcycles. In her fever, cowboys came and rode off. Old conversations animated her mind in the dark.

She pulled on the wood handle and twisted. The handle turned, and the four arms retracted on the back of the small board. With the board removed, the small knothole in the siding was exposed, the entire barnyard and front of the cabin viewable.

She had heard cars and trucks earlier... or was that yesterday?

Her truck was gone. The black car was not one she recognized. It was too much city and not enough country. Stranger. But where was her truck? She searched the farm from the hole but still worried someone might be hiding—watching the cabin. She fought against the paranoia, but each time she moved her shoulder, the pain justified the fear. Someone wanted her dead.

She studied the yard and down to the bend in the driveway. She knew the only place she could get help was in the house. To get there, she had only two choices. Run the risk of the yard and someone with a rifle... or her worst fear of her childhood—the tunnel from the barn to the basement of the house.

The tunnel she knew was filled with rats, spiders, and things that only her father could face.

1 3

SHYING

When a horse is spooked, they usually have a scared or violent reaction. When a horse is uncomfortable or doesn't want to be near something, they will avoid or shy away from whatever it is.

Jolie's hand floated over the tack hook. She knew if she pulled down on it, nothing would happen. But if she twisted it, it would release the locks on the door, and a portion of the tack room wall would swing into the space behind. The old fears rose in her stomach. The acid scorched at her throat. Being caught underground had scared her as a child. The fear of a furtive rat was reinforced by a small rodent spooking her first full-sized horse in the corral. The drop of a small girl from fifteen-hands in the air is not a little bump.

She had never entered the tunnel from the barn end. Her only experience was looking down the roughhewn walls from the doorway in the basement. The strung line of lights flickered their pasty dim yellow light. As far as she could see, there were only the occasional bulbs still in any working condition.

Old, half-eaten timbers braced the walls with cracking boards as thick as her wrist. The small girl knew enough to be certain of death if one of the boards was to give way. The dimly lit passageway constricted to darkness as her eyes and mind created rats scurrying along the edge and spiders hanging from webs strung thick enough to capture small children—the plethora of roots hanging from the ceiling invited thoughts of bats and other spooky apparitions of nightmares.

The small girl quietly eased the door shut on the sounds of metal tools working on rock and wood. Her eyes closed, hoping her father and the men would be safe and emerge for the evening meal—bringing no ghosts, rats, or other unwanted creatures with them.

Cowboy up.

Jolie jumped. She could hear her father's voice as if he was standing behind her in the tack room.

Her hand fell back to the hook and turned. Pushing, the wall softly woofed as the stagnate air broke out of the space. She was certain the doors hadn't been opened since her father passed. Or, at least, since her mother was killed seven years before.

The door's swinging triggered the lights.

Jolie stood looking at a room, finished with sheetrock or plaster, painted a bright white. The light was a modern can light nestled in the ceiling—softly lighting the small room and the top of the descending stairs. Three more lights descended the wide stairwell leading down under the barn. The stair treads were roughhewn oak glowing from wax or some other durable finish.

Seven years or more from the last use. No cobwebs. No rats. No mice. No hobgoblins. Nothing from her childhood nightmares. Just a clean white hallway.

She started down the long stairwell. The lights didn't flicker or fade. The walls stayed white and smooth.

Her right foot found the bottom. She eased to the corner and peeked around. The wide, well-lit tunnel continued toward what she felt was the house. She looked back at the steps. There wasn't enough dust to leave boot prints.

It wasn't a hall in an office building. It wasn't a hall in prison. But it was a hall, and it held her mind and fear prisoner.

She pushed herself along the long hall. Her shoulder and back dragged over it, leaving behind a crusty broken streak of blood. Her boots crossed each other with confusion. Her mind mixed with fear, the need to get to the house. To the phone. To help.

Near the end of the long hall, with its metal-faced door, there was a doorway to the right.

Jolie slowed her drag along the opposite wall. The large room was lined with shelves. They moved or shimmered. She worried it was her sight going, but then, she saw the handle floating in the middle of the glass door.

She reached out and placed her hand on the thick glass. It was cold, or at least cool. The cans and boxes on the shelves were the giveaways. It was a modern root cellar. She opened the door. Scanning the contents of the shelves, her examination stopping on the canning jars of yellow peaches. She wondered if they would still be good after seven or ten years. As hungry as she was, she wasn't sure enough to take the chance. She returned to the hall. After a moment of confusion, she turned to the large metal door.

MIKE'S POCKET BUZZED. HE STOPPED THE TRUCK AND TEASED the phone out of his hip pocket. The caller ID said simply *CABIN*.

He thumbed the screen and answered. "Four-seven-one-five."

The voice was husky but still female. "You ordered a knife. It's here." The line went dead.

He put the truck in gear and stomped on the gas. The truck

fishtailed but sped down the wash. As it spread out on the flats, he watched for the turn between the two scrub oaks. The alignment made it impossible to see the dirt track before you passed it. You would have to know the two trees. The only two overhanging the wash as it fanned out.

Almost too late, he pulled the steering wheel and cut right between the two trees. They had grown fatter over the years, and he scratched the truck on both sides. The limbs weren't soft, and he could feel the sun torched paint rake off in large scales. If she wanted, he'd buy her a new paint job or even a new truck.

As he slid to a stop in front of the cabin, he looked in the rearview mirror. The sheriff's cruiser was just rounding the last turn of the driveway and coming fast. Mike rolled out of the truck with his cane but resisted the urge to pull the rifle out with him.

The head rose slightly higher than the barrel of the pistol. The deputy was covered by the door and car. "Put your hands up where I can see them."

Mike raised his one hand. The other was on the cane that provided him an upright position.

"Walk toward the front of my car." As the man got close… "Spread your feet and bend forward with your hands on the hood. Throw the cane to one side."

He came around and felt Mike's pockets and frisked for any weapons. "What are you doing with Rocket's truck?"

"Picking her up for a date."

The deputy kicked out Mike's right foot, and he took the weight on his hands and left foot. "Don't be a smartass when there's a gun pointed at your head. You walk, talk, look, and smell like the city. Very slowly take your wallet out and put it on the hood of the car."

The two men heard the soft click of the heavy wood door behind them. Both heads turned.

Jolie sagged against the wall. "Punchy, can you arrest him after he takes me to a hospital?"

"Oh, sweet baby Jesus on a pony." He pointed at Mike. "You get her inside. I'll get the first aid kit."

JOLIE SAT HUNCHED TOWARD THE TABLE. THE FIRST AID KIT LAY eviscerated on the table. Punchy pulled the last strip of tape over the pillow of gauze pads. His voice was soft and almost to himself. "Muther humdinger, that has got to hurt like a son of a bitch. The bullet must have shattered your shoulder." He held up a screw. "You must be a rodeo clown—because you have a screw loose."

Jolie groaned at the bad pun. "When I woke up at the bottom of the cliff, I knew the shoulder was history. Did the bullet come out, or is it still in there?"

"I only got the one screw out, but I could tell there were a couple more the bullet mangled and pushed out of place." He pushed the bloodied wadding into a pile and snapped off his gloves. "It must have been a low-velocity rifle like a 30-30. If it had been an AR or AK, you wouldn't have a shoulder, and we wouldn't be having this conversation. Those damn bullets are so fast and fracture so easy, you hit a deer in the neck, and it will turn the head to mush. There is no justification for those damn weapons—other than on a field of war... I'll just stop here. I don't have anything for the pain, and I wouldn't advise aspirin because somebody is going to do some major surgery on you. But it's gotta hurt."

Jolie ground her head around and looked at him. She thought of all the rodeos the two had seen and lived. "I guess no more than coming out of the barrel at the wrong moment."

The man smiled and chuckled as he poked the side of his

head with his two fingers. "It only hurts bad the second time. The first one you don't remember. But the first one is when they put the plate in. All the following times, it doesn't knock you out, you just hurt."

Mike snapped the antenna on his phone back down. "We're going to L.A." He looked warily at the deputy.

Jolie rolled her eyes. "Oh, crap, Mike, this is Punchy. He and I go way back. You can trust him."

The deputy stuck his hand out with a deadpan face. "Francis Drips the third. You can call me deputy, Frank, or Punchy. Anything else could get me detention, or you shot."

Mike hesitated.

Jolie gave him a hard look. "Punchy was the person who found Mom. Now shake his fucking hand before I have to go find a knife."

Mike glared at Jolie as he reached out. "Dot has your knife ready. You didn't show up, so she called me." He turned to the deputy and examined the few scars on his face and reaching up into his hairline. "Punchy as in the rodeo clown Punchy? I think I knew your father."

"Maybe. He was Deadwood Drips. When he was in school, he was six-four and played noseguard. He always hated being called junior. In football, he played so hard he only left dead wood on the field."

Mike snorted. "He played for Cal." The deputy nodded. Mike rolled his head in a swinging motion of memory as his smirk grew. "I played for SC. You might call me Woody." He turned to Jolie. If you can hold it together long enough, I have plenty of Dilaudid at the office. I think David has some Oxy, so you have your choice of what works."

"Check the bottom drawer next to the refrigerator. Under the tea towels. Mom used to keep a half-pint of whiskey in there."

He came back out, holding up the bottle. It was almost full.

She grabbed the bottle between her legs and unscrewed the cap. Three long pulls on the bottle, and she capped it.

She smiled weakly. "Saddle up. We're good to go."

As Punchy helped her out, she asked softly, "Why did you come up?"

"I was having lunch. I hide just off the highway, but I can see the wash. Someone was driving your truck, and it wasn't you."

"You watch the place?"

He blushed.

Good to know.

She turned back as Mike closed the door. "Don't forget to lock it."

He stared at the door. The handle and latch had no lock. There wasn't even a keyhole.

Jolie stopped Punchy and stepped back to Mike. Her hand was out. "Keys, please."

He frowned as he handed her the two keys and the hoof hook on the carabiner. Jolie just smiled.

"There was a reason grandpa made this door so damned thick. It hides a homemade locking system in a hidden metal door." She inserted the hoof hook into one of the nicks and splits in the door. The hole was just above dead center. She turned the hook a few times and then withdrew it. "Inside the wood is an iron door. Fourteen deadbolt rods—four on each side, and three top and bottom. The gears are all made of bronze cast out there in the barn. The system is as strong as the door."

Punchy snorted. "Everyone thinks of the door and lock, but it's the doorjamb that breaks in a raid."

Jolie slung her arm over his shoulder. They walked down the steps from the porch. "If you're going to break in, you better bring a D-8 Cat. There are some major amounts of steel hiding under all the wood."

She took another large pull on the bottle and let Punchy ease her into the passenger seat of Mike's car. She laid the seat back as flat as it would go.

Punchy turned to Mike. "I'll get you down to Ventura, but we need to keep it under eighty through Santa B. Just keep up."

Mike smiled as he slid down into the large car.

14

CUT

Cut means to turn or separate one cow or steer from the herd. It is how cowboys sort out the cattle they want or need to brand, sell, or castrate.

Jolie was still groggy, but the orange sherbet felt good on her throat. Her eyes half drooped as she tried to give the man a hard look. Having never been a mother or a disapproving aunt, she had no practice, and it wasn't working—it just made her drool more orange out of the left of her mouth.

Mike drew the wooden spoon up the track on her chin. "Lord… we dress you up in the finest hospital gown and still can't take you anywhere for fine dining." He caught the small dribble on the right side too. "This is exactly why we can't have nice things."

"They cup kulling may Yuck Blimmy."

He snorted. "Yabba dabba doo?"

Her eyes got big as she started inhaling a snort. The soft bloody hack-boogers in her left nose hit the back of her throat with the whistle of a wounded bagpipe. She ripped into a coughing fit and turned purple in the face.

Mike waved her down and waited for her to stop rattling around. "No, I got it. Yes, they keep calling you Mister Finley. It's your name, Chuck. Get over it. The sex change was a success, and you will walk out of here a new woman. No more pecker, just boobs."

Her eyes didn't balloon the same. The right got larger, but the left was more pinned in dilation. The look was wonky and funny, except the doctor had told Mike they needed to keep her in the ICU until the eyes settled down, and her vision cleared.

Mike snorted to himself as he pushed another tiny spoonful of sherbet into the rubbery mouth. The closest to a rodeo the doctor had ever worked on was a polo player or someone falling off the ten-cent horse in front of the drugstore. As he caught another drool, he wondered if there were any more of the mechanical horses or even drugstores for that matter. He thought how his life, and society in general, had changed over his seventy-one years. He still felt like a sixteen-year-old hauling the four-teen-foot longboard down to the beach. He knew if he let his mind wander, it would write checks his body could no longer cash. But it didn't stop him from sitting on the point, eating creamsicle bars, and watching the surfers catch the waves on their shortboards.

When Jolie had gone to prison, he stopped going to the rodeos. When his wife passed away, he had stopped eating hot dogs. Stopped eating popcorn. As he levered in another small scoop of sherbet, he thought about how his life had spiraled down to his desk, car, and flying more than he liked. His butt hadn't felt any leather harder than the seat of his chair, car, or the occasional Lear. He needed a change.

"We need to get you patched up and moving, but we have to keep you safe too. You sort of dodged a bullet on this one…

"Not exactly." The short, balding surgeon in scrubs entered

with a computer pad under his arm. "Good morning, Mr. Finley." He nodded at Mike. "Uncle Peckerwood." The two laughed at his old nickname from surfing with a balsa board with more cracks and holes than a rotting tree.

The surgeon sat leaning on the edge of the bed. "I'm the man who spent way too much time in your shoulder and arm last night and this morning. My name is Jewels Nerkelzelinsky." He watched her mouth twist. "Yeah, nobody can pronounce it. Even my family never pronounces it the same way twice." He nodded his head at Mike. "Even the peckerhead here couldn't pronounce it, so he started calling my father jerk. You might say, I'm Jerk junior... but now that Dad has passed away, I'm the head jerk."

He lifted the pad so Jolie could see the screen. "The bullet was a soft slug. Probably a thirty-caliber. So, my guess is, up in your neck of the woods, a 30-30 or a 30-06. Usually, the aught-six ammo is copper clad and is a bunch faster. So, if this is to go anywhere near a forensics lab, I'm sure it will come back as a 30-30 slug." He pointed at the x-ray on the screen. "It entered here at an oblique angle, so it didn't shatter the scapula until here. It had enough kick left when it hit this plate to tear out all the fine work the surgeon did twenty-some years ago. Unfortunately, the work was so good, the rod inside the humerus, with the nine screws attached to the plate, took the last of the bullet's energy and removed anything we could work with."

She looked down at the large padding that ended at two small fingernails. She looked up.

He smiled. "You may have been a rocket before, but now you're more of a Jamie Sommers. We had the skills. We had the technology. We had your drunken X on the form... So, we rebuilt your shoulder and arm." He swiped the screen to disclose the next x-ray.

She stared at the mass of metal and where it went.

His finger started at the top. "Normally, the socket is here on the scapula. But, because of the damage, we needed to rebuild to here, so we did what is called a reverse replacement. We ran anchor screws further into the bone and rebuilt this shaded area here with composite. The Glenoid sphere is on the shoulder side, instead of the humerus. This allows us to use a flatter socket on the humerus, which has a freer motion around the sphere. It's usually a weaker setup, but it will give you almost all of your range of motion back. And with your muscle development, you will do just fine."

She pointed at the long white bar on the x-ray.

He nodded. "Yes, this is why our date last night took so long. Normally, there is just a long spike we insert down into the humerus. It would come to about here. But you still had fracturing at that point, with stress crazing lower. So, we took all the measurements, and our friends at UCLA printed a new humerus adaptation and brought it over. You probably don't remember, but in a way, you had two surgeries. We kept you in calming sedation between, but the 3-D printing of metal parts takes time."

She tapped the screen near her elbow. "Ow mush?"

"You have about three centimeters of just *you* left of the humerus. So don't try to be a stand-up comic." He held his thumb and finger about four inches apart and then pointed back at the screen. "This is where the bionic woman starts. This is the most aggressive we could do and still leave you your arm. With time, you will be able to do most of what you did before, as long as you are gentle with it. It's going to take a long time to get back, and the nerves suffered heavy damage... but you have both hands."

He took the fingertips in his hands. "Do you feel this?"

She swayed her head with half closed eyes. He could tell she was tired. "Good. We gave you a solid nerve block. When it starts to hurt—call out. It will get worse. What you need now is sleep. I'll check back in with you before I leave this afternoon."

The surgeon stood and looked at Mike, his head barely

twitched. "I need to talk to the peckerhead a minute. I'll be just outside. Why don't you see if you can grab a couple of winks?" Mike stood and placed his hand on Jolie's knee.

The two stopped in the hall, but out of earshot. The larger older man took a deep breath. "What didn't you tell her?"

The surgeon rolled his lips. "I didn't hold anything back… but if those muscles are any indication, she's very athletic. She's not going to take kindly to the time she needs to heal. I'm serious when I say she's looking at a year or two to get back to anything she was before. Whoever does her physical therapy and occupational therapy, they will have their hands full to keep her from pushing hard."

Mike watched the man's eyes. He had first met him before he was a full day old. "What else?"

The surgeon ran his index finger along the back of his ear. He looked sideways up at his non-blood uncle, and the only uncle he had ever known. "It's a gunshot wound…" His blinking left the question, but still wanted answers. "As you know, I'm on the county coroner's team. That makes me part of the chain of custody. I followed all the legal protocols and secured the slug. I have it locked in my safe to preserve the chain. If we need to, we can fill in the correct blanks and have the slug analyzed when the time is right."

Mike's lips rolled and unrolled as he thought. Trusting the surgeon wasn't the problem. His concern was how far to drag his friend into something none of them were sure off. His shoulder softly bounced and then settled against the wall as he wedged the single cane against his hip.

"Someone shot her on her property Friday morning. We don't know who, but there are a few circumstances… It's just safer this way. I understand putting her up in this ward with all the secrecy…"

The doctor waved his hand in the air. "This is nothing. Right now, there are three nobodies in the hospital. All of them would create a media circus if word got out. One entered Cedars of Sinai a couple of weeks ago. I think the paparazzi are still camping out down there. This is why we are the hospital we are. Millions of dollars get donated every year by those who supposedly spend time somewhere else."

Mike chewed on his lower lip. "Well, it's just good to have someone on the inside."

"Good to see you too. Are you coming down for Thanksgiving this year? The twins would really like to see their favorite great-uncle."

He looked back at the door to the room. "Let's see how things go for now. I think I might have to babysit."

"Well, keep me posted. We'd love to have you for as long as you can come. The guesthouse is always ready for you."

They shook, fist pounded, and then hugged. It hadn't changed in forty years.

15

TAKING STOCK

Any animals on a farm or ranch are the same as cans of
beans on the shelf at the market: they are stock. The counting your cans of
beans, or counting all your animals, the feed you have on hand,
and other supplies, is called 'taking stock.'

The afternoon light filtering through the pull-down shade turned everything to honey. The crescent moon of pink floated in a tableau of black. The short hair was such a deep blue-black the light was sucked in and not let out. The soft rhythmic breathing was loose and relaxed. The tip of the pink tongue never moved from the edge of the lips.

The whisper at the door was a hushed hoarseness but demanding. "Pink!"

The dog's head rapidly whipping from Jolie to her master to Jolie caused the ear leathers to sound like a worn pair of chaps landing over a barn rack or stall rail.

"Pink! Leave her alone. Come. She needs to sleep."

Jolie couldn't move her arm to lift the blankets. The sling, bound to her body, would be there for a few more weeks. The tiny timer clicked on the ice machine, and the chilled liquid started pumping through the sleeve and shoulder pad. She knew with the icing of the cold wrap she would drift back to sleep. The warmth of the large dog would help.

She raised the edge of the blankets with her left leg. The slit of a hole was an inviting cave smelling of the woman who hadn't had a sponge-bath in four days—the primal beast—drawn to the primordial scent.

All hundred and forty pounds of black muscle slid into the cave and nuzzled her way up to the tips of exposed fingers. The blocky head of the Cane Corso came to rest with one ear buried in the tips of the fingers. The twitch of the single finger was enough. The sleek black body flexed in the blanket cave until it spooned into Jolie's body.

"Oh, now you've done it. She's your problem now."

Jolie didn't bother to clear the moist gravel from her throat. "Go away, Jinx. She needs her sleep."

She listened to the soft barefoot retreat on the hardwood floor. The ticking of the twenty-four large and tiny paws kept ubiquitous pace behind. The aunt of the litter sighed deeply—relieved of duty.

The two drifted into the land of blankets and bonding.

JOLIE PUSHED HER BARE FEET FORWARD INTO THE HEAT OF THE large dog. With a contented groan, Pink melted further around the feet.

"She's never thrown a litter?"

Jinx rested the spatula on the edge of the cast-iron pan. The eggs cackled happily in the bacon fat. He leaned back against the counter. "She's never had a heat. At least, not one I could sense." He nodded his chin toward the mass of black fur covering the large braided rug in front of the fireplace. "Stormy never gave a hint she was anything but a neuter. Sometimes it's the way of nature. There are studs who have no clue and bitches who have no heat. But she seems to like being an aunt."

Jolie looked under the table at the large dog. The dog sensed the movement and groaned warmly. "She sure took to me. I guess I'm welcome anytime… according to her."

The old man turned back to the eggs with a smile. "You have the key. As long as the dogs like ya, it's your home too." He moved his head in circles. Jolie could hear the fine gravel of arthritis in his neck. The same was starting in hers. The shoulder would probably worsen the condition.

Jolie laughed. Her father first brought her up to the lodge when she was six and could stay out of trouble.

Jinx and he had served in the Marine Corp together. They had paired up as a two-man reconnaissance team. Jinx spoke the Japanese he had learned while growing up with the Japanese farmers in Watsonville, California. The two men would sneak close enough to Japanese camps to eavesdrop on the officers discussing plans of attack. With the foreknowledge, the American forces could jinx their attacks or the passage of Japanese fleets maneuvering between the islands.

The nickname took hold the day they discovered a Japanese lookout overlooking the straights between some islands. It was the lookout's job to let the Japanese ships know when it was safe to run the transition without fear of the American dive bombers. Jinx had listened to the lookout's voice, and when he felt he could mimic the lookout, they killed the lookout and took over the radio. The Japanese lost most of their fleet the next run through the straights.

To get her father to drive up to Montana, Jinx only had to call and start talking about all the elk or deer he had been seeing. The two always bought tags, but those weren't always the criteria for a good hunt. Even if they sat on a hill and glassed a small valley or an opposing hill for game, the time shared, and conversations or silence was enough to justify the arduous drive. As Jolie got older, she was sure the hunting was about recapturing the time they spent in the South Pacific hunting other than elk or deer.

The front door, back door, or large door on the barn—none had a lock. The car had a key, the truck had a house light switch and a little silver button for the starter, the jeep had the original silver switch and a stomp starter. Jinx and her father had commandeered the vehicle upon finally arriving back from an extended year in Japan. Jinx as an interpreter and Jolie's father as his armed guard and drinking buddy. Jolie had learned, at the age of seven, the complete traditional tea ceremony from Jinx's wife. She was half Korean and half Japanese; a result of a captured comfort girl for the Korean army. Jinx had saved her life by taking her home as a concubine. When she turned eighteen, he married her.

When Jolie was fifteen, she started helping with the driving. Her father would have started her the year before, but he wasn't comfortable with the appearance of nobody at the wheel. Around the homestead, looking between the top of the dashboard and under the curve of the steering wheel was fine. The open road was another story... even though they only traveled what her father called the Blue Highways—the back roads on a map with only a blue line. Some were a lighter shade of blue than a real highway.

The plate of eggs, bacon, and biscuits, waving in front of her nose, brought her around. She followed it as Jinx brought it back around to the table. The spare boney hands never changed. The tan was a light walnut, and the thin gold ring hung loosely between the two knuckles. The man was a widower but would always be married. She wondered if his swollen knuckles ached. She never heard him complain.

He pulled the blue checked dish towel straight and flipped it over his shoulder as he returned to the sideboard for his plate. "I don't know where you drifted off too, but one minute you were here, and then bam. You were gone."

Jolie took a sip of the warm coffee that denied the time it had been sitting. "I was here. Just thinking about how much of my growing up was here with you, Dad, and Tok."

The man's work-faded jeans shushed quietly across the wood as he sat. "Twice a year like clockwork. Elk, deer, or just horseshit." He poked his eggs to break the yokes. His knife and fork sliced them up with the bacon. He slid some onto the drop biscuits he had made in the early dawn. He looked over at Jolie, working with just a fork. "You want me to chop up your food for you?"

She shot him a single hard eye. He snorted, and they ate in silence.

The muscles screamed louder than Jolie wanted to scream. Even with the hanging movement exercises to keep the shoulder loose and from freezing up, the two horseshoes in her hand were agonizing. Even though each shoe only weighed a pound, the combined pull on her shoulder felt more like a hundred.

Jinx smiled as he watched her curling the small weight. "You make the same face your father did on Corregidor. A stray bullet grazed his butt, but the Japanese camp was only forty feet away. He wanted to jump up, dance, and scream in pain, but if we made a sound, we would have been dead or worse."

Jolie thought about her father's stoic nature. The broken wrist, the cracked ribs, the large goring he got one Thanksgiving week—looking for a small pig to roast for a few friends became a suckling pig and its four-hundred-pound angry mother. His pack-leader dog, Hondo, had been fast enough to grab the snout and have the curled tusks rip a large gash up the dog's shoulder. The two razorbacks, hitting the head, flew over the sow's back with the backlash. Her father danced in, slamming the knife as hard as he could, into the shoulder of the stopped pig. To his horror, the pig hooked into his side and threw him, the last critical inches of the knife had not buried. As the pig spun to engage the man on the ground, he kicked the handle with his moccasin. The pig dropped next to him.

Before anything, he pulled the emergency kit out of his small rucksack and stitched up the dogs and then himself. He sat with his dogs, shared his water, and ate a stick of his jerky. The hogs had taken him two hours to field dress and hang in a tree. The hike out had taken the rest of the daylight. In the dark, the friends, her father, and Jolie hiked the three miles back with the burro and brought out all but a slim shank a coyote had gotten down from the tree. Her father laughed, *if the coyote worked so hard to climb the tree, the meat is a small reward.*

Gritting your gut instead of your teeth was a genetic trait. Jolie curled the two horseshoes for the final count of twenty. Her brow soaked with running springs of sweat. She took a sip of water as she eyed the cord running through the large screw-eye in the wall. The end of the cord was tied to a narrow black band cut from an inner tube. The real work was just beginning.

The walk in the cooling Indian summer air would be her reward, as well as six more hours of ice machine. The days of pain, sweat, and the dog by her side were always the same. Only the weather was changing.

Jinx squeezed out more of the cream mixture into his palm. He had taken to making it for his own joints. He traded elk meat for the large block of bear fat. He cut it into half-cup cubes and then froze them until he needed to mix more salve. The juniper oil he squeezed from the berries off his own trees. The DMSO he bought.

Rubbing his hands together, he warmed and emulsified the grease and oils. His hands gained as much from the massages as Jolie's shoulder. He worked along the sides around the surgical scars.

"The scars are healing nicely. Another month they will just be pink. Mixing the aloe and vitamin E was a good trick." He could sense he was talking more to himself than to anyone else in the room.

Her voice was soft and almost drifting. "Do you miss Dad?"

His hands slowed slightly but never stopped. It wasn't a surprise question, but it wasn't one he had ever expected. "Not as much as I miss Tok." His hand turned as he rubbed, and the edge of the heel applied a focused movement. "There are days when I stand at the door with the binoculars. The elk are grazing only a half-mile away. They are fat and slow. The yearling spikes are playing at mock fights. The felt is dripping from the large racks on the bucks. They don't have a care in the world. My hand is halfway to the phone, and then I remember." His hands paused with a sigh. "And then I turn and look in the kitchen…"

"You can always call me."

His eyes closed as his face shrugged. "Not for the last seven years."

She reached with her right hand and placed it on his hands. They didn't need words. The years hadn't been easy on either of them.

16

SCANT

*A 'scant' is a lightweight lasso used for
small calves, goats, sheep, or children.*

The two men stood back from the sliding glass door. The movement of their right arms and coffee mugs were like they were tied to a stick. In the middle of the yard, they watched Jolie as she made rodeo show-off circles with the lariat. The eight-foot loop slowly floated a foot above the ground then rose to above her head and, soft as a feather, drifted back down to her boot height.

"How's she doing with her left?"

Jinx took a sip of coffee and thought about the best way to describe a wad of rope around her ankles. Or neck. Or Pink. Sometimes both or all three. "Needs work. But she's out there for an hour in the morning and one or two in the afternoon. Otherwise, she's on the ice machine sleeping or doing something on the computer." He looked over at the man who had shown up out of the blue, dropped off Jolie, and said he'd be back. He had left a fist full of exercise instructions and equipment Jolie would need to regain the use of her arm and shoulder. A month later, he drove up as if he had never been gone. "I'm not one of them physical therapy guys, but I'd say she's doing good."

Mike chuffed. "I talked to the surgeon. He said if she can put her arm up as high as her head, she's right on track."

Jinx nodded in understanding of city folk. "What did he say about the five chin-ups and twenty push-ups?"

Mike gave the man an assessing eye as he sipped on his mug. Drawing in his lower lip, his tongue then upper teeth cleaned the bottom lip. He looked back out at Jolie. She had switched to her left arm. The loop was wonky but floated for at least four or five heartbeats. "Let's not tell the surgeon just yet. He doesn't have much hair left as it is." He glanced over. "How much pain killer is she taking?"

Jinx thought about what to reveal, but the man did know enough about everything to have found his way out to the ranch.

"Most days she waits until after the news and then takes a Dilaudid with a couple of shots of whiskey and goes to bed. It's the weight I'm most worried about. She won't eat enough to put the meat back on them bones. The prison weathered her down to nothing, and this didn't do her any favors. I've had to help her bathe, and there are just old rodeo scars pulled over stacked ribs. Her legs are just as thin as the scant rope she's working with."

The loop of the lariat caught the large black dog and Jolie. The two hit the grass and rolled around a bit and then rested.

"What's with the dog?"

"Pink? Just friends. I don't think they're dating serious or anything, but they are both over twenty-one."

"I just wondered. All her dogs were taken when she—"

"For someone I don't know, you've been asking a lot of questions." Jinx lowered his brow as he looked sideways at the other gray-haired man in the city clothes. His tone wasn't angry or aggressive, but it was confrontational with a honed edge.

Mike smiled. He had wondered how far he could push this man. "Ask your questions… I'm kind of plumb out."

"Who exactly are you to Jolie?"

Mike rolled his lips, thinking about the complex relationship. "Have you been down to her ranch?"

"It's been years, but yeah, I know the spread. Some corrals, a barn, a few scrubby little trees, and a duck pond."

Mike smiled. "I don't know where she hid the duck pond, but you're shy by a little over twenty-five hundred acres. Between the town-stead and five other homestead properties she possibly doesn't know about, our company manages the entire fifty-eight-hundred acres. On any workday, our duties include overseeing leasing mineral rights, royalties on the oil, and the seasonal flow of cattle grazing. Her business is almost seven percent of our business. When she was arrested, we automatically took over all details of the property. Most of what I've been doing, for decades, has been in the quiet background. Paying the utility bills or doing maintenance on the property was just a tiny uptick in our management work. Our job is to make sure nothing goes wrong, and Jolie never has to worry about where her next meal is coming from."

The old rancher evaluated the stock of the man. "Does she know that?"

Mike sucked on his lips and then jangled his head. "No."

"Why?"

"I don't think her father even knew what he was worth. Every March, he was given a thick stack of paper to look over and sign. His taxes usually took our accounting people about a week to prepare. All he ever asked was: *Did I make money?*" He looked out at the woman trying to throw a lasso left-handed over the large black dog. "She never even asked. She just signed where the tabs were. In the nine years after her dad died, and before she went to prison, she never asked for a draw. I've never known her to do anything but earn her way. When she broke bones doing the rodeo and couldn't ride, she taught kids, adults, and hell, even dogs. She always paid her bills. I don't know what it would do to her if she knew what she was worth." The man wiped at his chin. The thin stubble rasped as quietly as his thoughts. "I think if her great-grandfather could see the kind of offspring he had provided for, he would just nod and go back to work. It seems to be in their DNA."

The rancher nodded only once and raised his mug for the last slurp. Mike could tell the man was thinking more about the woman's father than the roper in the yard. Fifty years is a long history. You tend to get to know a person.

"I think Big Foot had some idea what he inherited."

Jinx looked at his empty mug and remembered where it all began. "In nineteen fifty-two, I knew I'd never be able to live near the big cities anymore. I grew up in the truck farms of Watsonville, down in California."

He glanced at Mike's nod of recognition.

"When we came back, I had a job interpreting. As much as I knew it was an important job, it meant I lived in Los Angeles or San Francisco. I hated it. All day, my ears and mouth worked hard, but my hands just lay in my lap and fidgeted. There were no horses, and the longest you could see was down Pike Street to the bay and across to Tiburon. There was nothing but people the whole damn way. Even on the water, there was this boat or that boat. Big ships and little sailor boats—nothing but people." He pointed out across the plains toward a tiny home and barn a mile away. "That's my neighbor John Teasdale's place. He's like me —'sept he only has four hundred acres."

He looked at his empty mug. "Big Foot and I came up here elk hunting. It was a long trip in his old Studebaker truck. We had a couple of rucksacks, two hundred pounds of dog food, a bed full of large dogs, and our rifles. I don't think we stopped smiling for the entire month. The next spring, he done sold off a piece of land some city slicker was salivating over and bought us this spread and what he called the hunting lodge. He told me just to get my ass up here and run my ranch. He bought it lock stock and barn—then gave it to me. It wasn't right. He saved our skin in the Pacific and then saved my skin from the city. But twice a year, I could see in his eyes, it was saving his soul too."

His lips rolled in taut as he wiped at his eyes. He turned back to the kitchen and sink. Coffee and lollygagging time were over.

He rinsed the mug and hung it from the rack. "When's the flight land in Bozeman?"

Mike walked over and rinsed and added his mug. "Couple of hours. Don't tell her. I also ordered a whole dinner with plenty for leftovers. We'll pick it up at the café as we come through town." He turned and leaned back against the counter. The woman, dog, and rope were on the ground again. It was like forty years was wiped away—the little girl, dogs, and a short lariat in the barnyard.

"Thanks, Jinx. I knew about the land, but not why. Land is my job, but why people do things is not something you can see in columns of numbers." He bumped off and stood with his hand out. "It feels good to meet the other half of the family finally. You and she are all that's left."

The thin hand, spiderwebbed with brown stains of hard living, slid cool into the larger man's. "Now that I know who runs the land, we'll talk later about what happens when I'm gone." Their eyes wavered in the reality of age. "Now git. You have a heap of driving to do."

17

PUNCHING

Punching doggies means driving cattle to market to get a payday.
It's the work to harvest a reward.

The thumb dug into the shoulder. The groan was edgier than the ones when Dot worked the other shoulder and arm. "You have scar tissue trying to layer in here." She reached over and drew the flat jade stone out of the hot-water-bath. Taking it in both of her hands, she slowly ran the edge over the pink surgery scar. Underneath was a lump the size of a thumb. The lump flattened.

"Son of a bitch. What the hell, Dot?"

The black woman chuckled. "Cowboy up, bitch. Think of it as chunky peanut butter. I needs ta spread it out smooth, or you will always have the lump. The lump bind you and do nothing but grow. When you shoulder freezes totally, and dat lump is huge, and you get rich, you get some happy doctor to go in there and cut it out. But if you think this hurt, wait for Doctor Happy's grenade fest in yo' ass."

"And you know this how?"

"When I was doing mixed martial arts, I didn't like anyone touching me. The female masseuses couldn't do shit. They would use stones, sticks, and even walk on me, but it didn't fix the injuries. Finally, I went into a surgeon for my hip. I thought I had cracked the femur or pulled the hip or some shit." She dragged the scar ball slowly.

The blonde gritted her teeth and groaned. "Jeez… but it was a scar ball?"

The scarred hand eased the hand-sized jade back into the warm water and pulled out a solid rod of rattan bamboo. She passed it through the towel to dry it off.

"Three balls to be exact. The surgery be scheduled for two hours. The surgeon was in there for six." She started working the shoulder with the heavy bamboo rod. "It was the first time I had ever heard of an ice machine. I wanted to marry it. Nine days later, I walked into his office without a limp. I swung my leg up and caught it behind my shoulder and head. Scared the bejeebies out of him."

"It didn't hurt?"

The woman slowly rocked the rod along the shoulder and down the back. "Fuck. I wanted to scream. It hurt worse than the original injury, but I wasn't going to let him know. I was bullet-proof. I was Megatron and Wonder Woman rolled into one. We shook hands, he released me to physical therapy, and I left."

"Just like that?" Jolie turned her head and stretched the muscle.

"Oh, fuck no. His office was on the twenty-fourth floor. I got in the elevator and screamed all the way to the seventh. I didn't want to scare the two ladies and the little boy who got on then."

Jolie laughed in the doughnut headrest.

"I wish we had met before. I liked your daddy, but I think I would have had more fun with you."

"You did meet me. I was ten. I saw videos of you doing your

rodeo roping. I used to think Daddy was just funning me by speeding them up. But I timed it once with a stopwatch. You were like a bullet, and your horse was just a black blur. I think when Daddy introduced us, I just stood there with my mouth open."

"Thunder."

"What thunder?"

"My horse. His name was Thunder. The only thing faster was the speed of light. Our last rodeo I noticed him favoring his right front hoof. Everything looked fine, so I just thought his frog might have just been a little sore. He was about a second slow in the third round, but I chalked it up to being tired. We had been on the circuit hard for over a month—we were both exhausted."

Jolie rolled over as Dot held the sheet.

"What happened?"

"It was a green break. For the finals, he lit out of the chute full bore. It was like he had reclaimed his youth. I shot the lariat and nose looped the calf. I was over the top as Thunder hit the stops and jerked the dally. Three seconds and it was all over. I was holding my hat high to a silent crowd. As I turned, he crumpled the rest of the way. The pressure of the dead stop and my stupidity of thinking he was bulletproof had shattered both front legs. The bones were sticking out like a porcupine. The crowd knew the second before I did. They put him down where he laid. I cried for two weeks straight. I didn't get on another horse for over six months. Never rode fast again."

Dot stepped back and plopped into the chair.

"I never knew." Jolie closed her eyes as she stretched her face.

"I never talked about it... I guess... you're the first I ever told. I just climbed into a bottle and never wanted to come out. Oh, there were articles and speculation. I was tired, I was old, I had an affair, and it went bad—all the juicy but wrong reasons. The truth was—my heart died with Thunder." Dot rubbed at a keloid along her upper arm. "I think I understand.

The day I lost my friend, the light just went out. I never fought again."

Jolie looked over at the long knife lying on the desk. "You just beat on steel now."

Dot rose. "It keeps me somewhat sane." She swung her arms around her body. "Listen, I want you to go lay down with Mister Ice machine and get some rest. When I get back from my run in a couple of hours, we'll go a few rounds on the speed bag and maybe let you cozy up to mister heavy bag. Jinx and Mike hung him last night. I took him out for a little date—he's probably recovered by now."

Jolie pulled a faded UCSB sweatshirt on. It would have fit Mike, and probably was his, but the giant fit made for a great nightshirt. She slid into the sweatpants. Leggings or jeans still put too much strain on the shoulder. Kicking her feet into the fuzzy slop boots, she jerked her head at Pink. "Come on. You can chase Dot to the end of the fence so I don't have to pick up your poop."

Jolie pushed her slippers deeper into the belly of Pink. The soft grunt brought a smile to her face. The four candles on the table danced in all four sets of eyes. The dinner wasn't the promised fare, but it was the bounty of a hunt. The men had hoped for some of the last grouse on the prairie, but they settled for elk steaks from the previous month's hunt, golden sweet potatoes, and roasted brussels sprouts. Everything harvested from the ranch.

The conversation had lazily flowed from poor hunting but a great horse ride to tall tales about supposedly legendary hunts to hunting Japanese to managing property and, finally, the art of forging steel. The large knife and four boot knives lay gleaming in the candlelight.

Jinx leaned his weight back in the chair as he clutched his coffee mug to his chest. "My farrier, Fernando, will be up here Wednesday. He's got a full mobile blacksmith's setup. I'm sure he will be interested in seeing these knives and talking pounding metal with you."

"I think the kind of metalwork I do and what he does are very different."

Jinx shrugged. "Don't count him out. Every bit of wrought iron on this ranch was done by his hand and his mobile smithery. He looked up at the large metal and antler chandelier. "The twelve-point elk antler rack over the fireplace… hit it sometime. It's just painted iron—the hat rack of antlers in the front hall, same. I liked seeing what his talented hands did more than I did picking up fallen antlers in the forest. In the forest, they serve a purpose. Squirrels and skunks chew on the old antlers. Wolf cubs chew on them and fight each other for them. They eventually break down and become just more stuff on the forest floor used by smaller and smaller creatures."

"I wouldn't want to get in his way. If he's got work to do…"

Jinx snorted with a smile. "Who said anything about work. I've got four horses and a mule. He can have them all shoed between a lazy lunch and nap time in the afternoon. He comes up for Thanksgiving. So he'll be here at least a week, and if he feels like it, maybe longer. By Saturday morning, he'll have his forge going, rack of tongs set up, and his three anvils placed. By lunch, the shoeing will be done, and he'll be looking for something else to make. Don't stay in one place very long or he'll size you up for a wrought iron rocking chair."

18

GROUND-TIE

*When a horse is trained so well, it will stay where
the reins are dropped on the ground.*

Jolie backed through the back door with two large coffee mugs steaming in her hands. The second the cold air slid through the armhole of her sheepskin vest, she knew she had made a mistake. There was no going back. Mike had glanced up at the sound of the closing door. Dot had been quick with her barefoot.

Jinx straightened as he looked back at what Mike had stopped to watch. "Come out here dressed for San Diego weather is a good way to lose some fingers and toes."

Jolie growled. "I've got my boots on."

The men chuckled and took the offered coffee. "How soon?"

"Dot says about forty-five minutes. The turkey was fatter than she had planned. I'm done chopping all the chopping she wanted. From here, it's all hers."

Jolie looked along the span of the bridge. "Tell me again why you're making a bridge over a two-foot deep wash that only has water in it two or three days a year."

Jinx turned and looked along the thirty feet. The rise in the middle was only a foot or so. Three could walk abreast comfortably. "It's a dry bridge."

Jolie hmphed as she jammed her hands deeper into her pockets. "A dry bridge. Oh, well, that explained everything."

The wrinkled rancher wrinkled more. "When did you become such a smart mouth?"

"When you stopped being able to paddle my butt."

Jinx smiled at Mike. "Ready to break a cowgirl?"

"Don't get any stupid ideas." Jolie stood her ground, but her left boot turned out toward open range.

Jinx looked down at the foot and snorted. "Do you know what a gazebo is?"

"Sure. You used to have one. It's just a covered porch out in the middle of the lawn. In city parks, bands play in them. What's a gazebo have to do with this bridge?"

The man hung his head in the *I'm about to teach you*, position. "In the Victorian times… yeah, back when I was a kid, smartass. They were called follies. They didn't serve any real purpose, other than to build them and to give people a little pleasure to look at. This bridge doesn't serve any real purpose other than the path leads up to this end and away from the other end. It's useless, but people still build them. We have many dry bridges. We elect politicians to go work for us in Washington, DC. They go, but don't do anything but raise money for the next election… but we still build them or vote for them. They are useless, but we still have them. Someone says something, and you feel hurt, so you build a dry bridge to get vengeance. It's useless, but you do it anyway."

He could see her struggling with the concept. Sometimes in life, building those useless bridges that take us nowhere are built before we even see how impractical they are.

He reached over and rested his hand on her shoulder. "Why don't you go wrestle Fernando away from his hot lover. Give him some time to wash his hands and face." The farrier had shown up more than once with a black face and arms above where his gloves didn't hide his skin.

Clutching her body with her fists buried in her pockets, she stiff-legged her way around the barn to the sheltered workshop. The two men watched as she rounded the corner and then backed out. Her head snapped over to see the two men laughing.

"You knew about this." Her finger was pointing.

Jinx nodded. "It goes out in the front. You never come up enough." They slapped at each other and started strolling over to the shed.

Jolie was already running her hands over the open fretwork of the life-sized statue. Even in raw steel, the horse was brownish black with the mane flowing in the hot air. Only the two hooves hovered at the ground. The horse was more forward at a full tilt than upright—the form on the back, known as Rocket, laid out along the back of the neck. The hand had just released the thinner scant lariat now racing forward toward the unseen calf. Every piece of steel was lateral and depicted speed. Even the saddle was perfect. It was her rodeo saddle, but somehow moving —the way she tipped only the toes of her boots in the stirrups and held them swept-back. Everything was pure Rocket and Thunder.

Her face was smeared sooty from the metal and wet from the tears as she turned. The large Filipino stood smiling. "I've got about another week to finish her, but I think you can see where I'm going."

"But how did you know? You were just in diapers or something when I was roping."

Jinx cleared his throat. "How many photos do you think I have? You were the hottest roper on the circuit." He pointed at the fat folder on one of the worktables. "Did you ever slow down to read a newspaper? Just in newsprint, he had a hundred photos or more to work from."

She turned. "But you couldn't have done all this in a week. I was out here helping you with those barn hinges on Monday."

He snorted and smiled. "And Mike was out here most the day on Tuesday and yesterday while Jinx worked on the dry bridge. You and Dotty have been busy. Everybody like a little bee in spring. Buzz here and buzz there. Make a little honey and go fly in the sunshine."

Mike laughed as Jinx cocked his head. "Dot is whistling." The black streak followed by six more raced around the corner. Pink made one turn around Jolie and raced back to the heat of the house. "I think we have just been called for dinner."

THE TURKEY WAS A CARCASS OF BONES. THE BOWLS WERE ALL BUT empty, and the pie pan had nothing but crumbs of crust in the bottom.

"Jinx sent me the first set of photos about two years ago. Last year I brought up the drawings. I had already started working on the saddle and your legs. Those were the most difficult to get right. Over three-quarters of the horse is wrought iron. The general curls are wind patterns I've seen over the California coast. Each of them had to feel right. I surf and hang glide, and the wind has its own shape."

"But the horse or even the saddle and legs weren't in your truck when I helped you unload." Jolie picked at the crust on her plate.

Dot smiled. "You were sleeping the sleep of the dead with your girlfriend on Saturday. The FedEx truck be stuffed full of boxes. I don't think there be a box under fifty pounds and none over a hundred."

"Eighty. Two were eighty. But they had me limited. There

were three crates sent from Orange County to Bozeman. They broke the bands and converted to a delivery truck because we don't have a forklift here like I did in Laguna."

Jolie laughed and pointed at Dot. "That's why you snuck time with my ice machine Sunday."

They all laughed at Dot's expense.

Mike leaned forward and sobered. "Dot tells me you're going back down with us. Are you up for what might happen?"

"I can't hide up here forever. And being up here is exactly what it is—hiding. After the surgery, I couldn't defend myself. Now is a different matter." She leaned in. "I spoke to my parole officer yesterday. She's been the greatest. She understands why everything was under the fence, but she also needs to have a face-to-face at her office there in Buellton. She must have a video interview on record every quarter. I'm five months since the last one."

"How are you going to explain where you've been?"

"Tell the truth. Jinx called. I flew. The hunting was amazing until the horse spooked and threw me off. My shoulder shattered, and I've been in the hospital since. But the hunting was fucking beyond anything we could have hoped for." She faced Jinx. "I need to buy about five or six hundred pounds of elk meat."

The man nodded in understanding. "I know a few people. And if it doesn't need to be this year's, I've got about three hundred vacuum-packed at the locker in town. I was going to give it to the police and fire, but…"

Mike screwed up his face and closed one eye. "Don't give those guys second-best. We'll stand for all they need or want. Just send me the bill. I want to be on their good side if I'm coming back up to hunt and ride."

Jolie smirked. "How much frozen meat can one of those handy-dandy planes of yours carry?"

"I rent what I need. But we can also have any amount air

transported down, so we don't have to sit on cold meat for four hours. What's your thinking?"

"Word needs to get around the valley. Especially word proving I wasn't on the ranch the day someone got shot. Nobody has a mouth bigger than Celeste. She may think something is up, but when I open drawer after drawer of elk meat and tell her to take what she wants, any doubt will be gone."

"How are you going to get her to ask?"

"I'm going to start with a big-assed bag full of the gamiest steaks this side of the Tetons. I've never known her husband to turn down a steak or anything free—especially not twenty pounds of two-inch thick long-hung fillets."

Dot looked up from petting and bribing Pink. "Oh, did someone say elk steaks. I've got a big mouth."

Jolie smiled and put her hand out. "Don't worry, Mistress Torture. I think we can get you covered with better than just elk. I'm sure we can pack your parting gift with deer also. I think there can be a secret meat locker down in the city. Of course, the jerky doesn't need anything but a safe to keep the riffraff out."

Mike's face was still sober. The reality of Jolie going back to the place where she was almost killed was all too worrisome. "Okay, so you being up here all fall is one thing, but how do you draw out who did it. It's one thing to know who is encroaching on your land, but it's another to finger someone who is willing to kill for what they are trying to steal."

Jolie rolled her weight back into the chair. "Old school for drawing out a predator was to bait the trap with an injured smaller animal. Rabbits are easy to trap, and if they're injured, they put up a wild noise. Any large animal in earshot is going to look into an easy dinner."

Jinx scrunched his eyes until they were just another large wrinkle. "What if you attract more than you were fishing for? You might be thinking wolf, but enough bait and you might get a puma and bear to the party, as well."

She rolled her lips and rubbed her bottom teeth against the top lip. She was smart enough to recognize a man who had more experience with hunting men than anyone else she knew. "I think in this situation, the only animal to take the scent would be the puma and wolf partners. I heard a man and a woman talking after I went down the cliff. I had heard those voices before—I just couldn't place them. But if I hear them again, I'll know."

Mike twisted the empty mug between his hands. Jolie smiled at the small scars and scrape marks on the man who, until now, only wrangled a desk. The weeks of riding and ranch work had weathered the man down to a better fighting weight. Even the single cane was spending more time hanging in the barn then being used. His movements and walk were graced with less effort.

He looked up. "Back in the day... um, the early-sixties, Big Jim Castle was just a surfer bum wandering from Rincon Point up to the Trestles. If you needed some weed, he was your guy. If you worked a real job and needed to pull a string of doubles, Big Jim was your guy. Somewhere along the line, he changed. As I understand it, there was a run-down old house he and the surf buddies were camped in. He found out about buying property from the sheriff or banks for past-due taxes or abandon notes. He got his buddies to put in the work for their rent, and then he sold the houses. It wasn't long before Big Jim was surfing less, dealing drugs more and fixing up houses. As he got more and more houses during the early seventies, he weaned off the drugs. Except what he needed to keep his work crew happy and working. By the eighties, he was throwing up large developments and shopping malls."

He watched the mug as he slowly pushed it in a couple of full circles while he thought.

"What I'm saying is... he has a shady past. But selling drugs and stealing people's property for taxes or when people are at their lowest down-and-out, isn't in the same league as murder. I'm not sure he's up for that. He's a few years older than I am, and it just isn't a time in anyone's life to risk joining the country club you just left. How many of the inmates were in their seventies and eighties?"

Jolie's one eyebrow pushed up as she examined her own hands playing with her mug. "More than you would think. My cellmate was seventy-one. Tough as nails, but still, no spring chicken. I think if she keeps her nose clean, she'll be out in another fifty or sixty years."

"And the wounded rabbit?"

"Dot's going to mark me up a bit in the morning, and I'll put the sling back on."

Fernando cringed. "Ouch."

19

———

BANGTAIL

A horse's tail cut short in line with the hocks.
Most racehorse tails are cut thus to keep them out of the way.

She pushed her hat back on her head to expose her face. She checked it in the mirror. The bruising was still purple and pecker in the center but starting to spread yellow at the edges. The spread was puffing out her neck on the left side the way Dot said it would. The art of marking up a fellow opponent to drive up the betting was an unspoken talent not often used, and excess could cause clotting in over-abused veins. Dot and her former fighting friend had become experts at where a hematoma would create the most visual impact. But, as expert as they were placed, they still ached as Jolie nosed the ugly orange truck into the parking lot.

She warned Pink as they got out. "*Heza.*" The Japanese word for knee. The command meant for her to stay at her knees. Unlike most dog training, where the dog heels on the left side,

Pink's training was purely protection. So she was given the choice of where to be in relation to her sense of danger.

As they walked through the door, Pink body checked Jolie, squeezing her against the doorjamb as she studied the empty bar. *Damn, that's going to take some getting used to.* Three heartbeats and Pink had released her to a qualified all clear. Her jeans rubbed on black fur the entire way to the bar.

As she banged the twenty-two pounds of frozen steaks on the bar, she looked down at her guardian. "*Yoko.*" The dog looked around as she laid down.

Randy turned around and almost dropped the beer glass he was wiping. "Holy crap. Where have you been?" He put down the glass and flipped the towel over his shoulder as he walked the distance of the bar. As he neared in the dim light, he took in the massive bruising and the full restrictive sling with a body stabilizer. "Oh, crap. Oh, crap."

"Oh, Randy, you were always the sweet talker."

"Fuck, Rocket. What the hell happened to you?" His hands and eyes waved about and didn't know where to settle. "One day, you were here, and the next, you were gone."

"Uncle Jinx called and said he had an elk problem. I got the okay from my PO and jumped on a plane. Best fucking elk hunting ever." She pushed the plastic bag of steaks over.

He peeked inside and then drew one out. "Holy Rocket shit."

"Nope. Just steaks." She nodded at her bottle. It took a moment for his brain to change gears. Jolie smiled. *Just like a dog trained for a food reward.*

He reached up as he kept glancing back at her. His hand missed the bottle four times.

"If you break my bottle, your pecker will never work again."

He fluffed his lips as he drew the bottle down. "You don't look like you're in any condition to do anything to anybody."

Jolie ducked her lips and shrugged her face. "Maybe not, but my dog is another matter."

He smirked as he set down the bottle. "Yeah… dog…"

Jolie slammed her hand flat on the bar. "Pink. Gado." A hundred and forty pounds of black hellhound appeared silently on the bar. Randy's face was inches from two rows of sparkling white teeth and hot breath.

Jolie rose to look. She wondered if he could hold his water or not. His legs were shaking. She reached out and petted the neck. "Tatsi." Stop. "Yoko." She guided Pink to lay down on the bar. Her eyes were on Randy. The shaking was moving up his body. Jolie still wasn't sure about him and his water.

His mouth was forming words, but no sound. His eyes were caroming between the two females.

"Yeah, I thought you would like my new puppy. Her name means "goddess of unseen, unheard, and instant death." Kind of like Thunder was in the arena."

He took a step back. "Thunder?"

"No. That was my horse. This is Pink." She smiled as she buried her face in the side of the dog's head and neck. Pink's eyes never left the man.

He backed up another two steps and regained some reality he could grab hold of. The glass slid into his hand as he pulled the towel down to dry it. "So, you disappear for months, you get a dog, do some hunting…" He pointed at the steaks. "Are those really for me?"

"Well, you do have to take them home. So I'm assuming you'll share a side cut of them with Celeste. I mean unless she became a vegan or something."

"No. Not a vegan… but what happened to your face and shoulder?"

Jolie fluffed her lips and face as she waved at her sling. "Eh. This was a week ago. Just as I was about to take a shot at a six-point, the stupid horse spooked and threw me. I landed in the brush and rocks. Shattered my shoulder—again—and cracked my face in three places. Kind of like breaking the wire expecting a calf and you get the bull some rider just pissed off."

The two laughed at the analogy. Randy's eyes never left the shining black face with a tiny crescent of pink.

The bar door opened. Three young men tumbled in laughing and joking. The one in front took one look at the large dog on the bar. Pink snapped her attention his way and white teeth shown in the dark. Randy and Jolie never moved. Two seconds later, the door slammed shut as the front guy pushed his buddies out.

"I think your dog could be bad for business."

"She gives me peace and quiet." Her thumb continued to work on the cork in the bottle. "Crap. Help me here, Randy. Make yourself useful as a bartender."

His head rotated back and forth. His eyes never left the dog.

"Oh, shit. You are such a pussy." Her fingers snapped at the floor. "Pink. Yoko." The dog took one last look at the bartender and slid over the edge of the bar.

"Give me a bucket with a couple of shots of coke in it. I need to take these oxies, and this rocket fuel is foul."

He splashed a long shot into the rocks glass and placed it on the bar. "Where in the world did you find that beast?"

She pushed the bottle at him. "Here, splash some in. I found her in hell. It's a tiny town in Montana. It freezes over every winter—just in case you were wondering." She fished four aspirin into her hand. Holding them for a second to make sure he could see the four white pills, she threw them into her mouth and sucked on the glass.

"I hope you know taking that much oxycodone is dangerous in itself. But you're also fourteen miles from home, and with alcohol…"

She reached out and stroked her hand on the side of his face. "Awe, how cute. He cares." She stood. "Besides, I'm on my way home. After I stop for some groceries and beer for the Vicodin, I have at the cabin."

She turned and strolled toward the door. "Enjoy the steaks. And tell Celeste if you guys need meat, I have four large elk worth of meat in the locker. She and I can go play in the freezer anytime." As she glanced back, she held her closed hand with the thumb and pinkie up to her ear and mouth. The two females slid out the door.

20

ALAMAR KNOT

A badge of honor, the Alamar knot was tied when a Californios (pre-statehood) stock horse had graduated to become a bridle horse. An Alamar knot worn by a horse means it can be called on to do just about anything and do it well.

"She's about as good around horses as you are. In fact, I think I'd trust her more."

Jolie laughed. "Oh, gawd… you are getting old. These are young green mustangs, and I was close to laying a rope on their necks. But if she might spook them, I might leave her in the truck or something."

The sound on the cell phone faded and then returned. "…kind of like a mastiff. They will wait for the livestock to calm before they make their next move. Don't be surprised if she makes friends faster than you."

"I'm losing the signal, Uncle Jinx. I'll take her and let you know what happens."

"You take care of yourself."

"I'm on it like a hen on a June bug. Love ya, Jinx."

"Love you too and have a great Christmas."

She thumbed off the cell and rotated the antenna into place. Mike's one eyebrow tried to raise, but he only succeeded in cocking his head.

"He said to take her to work. Let her lead the day. He thinks the horses will find her more interesting than me and might even come over just to smell her."

He snapped his small knife closed. Leaning up and back, he slid the knife into his pocket. Sitting back, he worked his closed eye into a shrug. "What do you think?"

"I think she smells good too."

He snorted. "Jinx was right. You're a smartass."

She stood and moved toward the door. She slapped her butt. "Yeah, but it's still a tight and cute smartass."

The man just wagged his head. "Just don't get it shot off. And thanks for bringing the meat down. I guess it wouldn't have fit in my trunk." He smiled at Pink. The dog was never more than a few inches away from Jolie's leg. "Watch out for her, Pink."

The door closed quietly. He stared at it for a while, almost wanting to will the girl back. She was twenty-some years younger than Mike, but the last couple of months had been good for him. The clean Montana air, learning to ride and hunt, and the good food had all been good for him. But he knew it was the solid give and take that had brought him out of the barn and to want to trot a bit at least.

He spun around and looked at his past. He had built the building and designed his office and its window, on the singular concept. The low ocean rollers were curling and breaking off the north point. Nobody was bobbing on the water to catch the twenty-second ride. He guessed they were further south, down to Rincon or even out off Point Mugu Navy missile base. Surfers, real surfers, would ride the highway looking for the right waves.

He glanced back at the quiet buzz of the phone. Line three. Never a good day when line three lit up.

He lifted the handset and drew it to his head. "How bad is it?" His eyes drooped shut as he listened to his chief of survey.

"Have they filed anything yet?" His attention was on the voice at the other end of the phone call, but his heart was a few hundred yards off the point of land in the distance.

"As long as they haven't cut a tree or disturbed a single scoop of land, we have nowhere to file an injunction. Gather all the stuff you have and take them over to Jacob and his team. We need them up to speed and ready to throw a noose as soon as they make any overt moves." He held the handset a half-inch from his ear. "Good idea. Go shoot every mark and every stake you find. Take a couple of teams. If we end up with pictures of the same tree from four angles, I don't give a rat's ass. We can hash it out in court on their dime. James needs to learn he has fucked with the wrong anthill, and it is actually a hornet's nest. Get the photos and print them in standard... Wait... fuck the tiny shit. Print them ready for court. Thanks, Eric. Keep me up to speed." He gently laid the handset in the cradle.

The set was running three small and two large waves. The large front wave was starting to swell up. In his mind, he was making it grow. Someone was going to get drilled.

PINK STOOD AT THE GATE AS JOLIE OPENED IT. THE SLENDER GIRL with freckles and mop-head of twisties stood a body-length away from the dog. Her eyes floated huge in the soft mocha face. The face was frozen in fascination at the large dog whose black fur absorbed the light and never let it go.

Jolie looked over and smiled. She knew Pink and what effect she had on people. Some were scared shitless, and others, like the girl, were wary but fascinated. "You can pet her, you know. She likes to be scratched under the chin first and then along her neck and shoulders."

"It won't bite me?"

"It's Tonisha, right?" The girl nodded. "She. Pink is a woman like you and the singer Pink. I think if the singer was here, you might be in awe of her, but would you be worried she might bite or hit you?"

"No." The voice was soft and gentle. Jolie guessed it was why Norman hired her to tend the horses.

"Well, Pink here is a lot smaller than these horses, but from what Norm has said, you aren't afraid of them."

The girl looked at the horses and laughed. "Golly and Molly? They ain't scary. Sneakers but not scary."

"Sneakers?"

She pointed at the four carrots making Jolie's tail. "The carrots. They be like sneaking my carrots while I'm raking. They never wait until after I pet them. They jus' like to be big ol' sneaks."

Jolie turned and leaned against the post as she frowned. Her hand hung and found a black ear to rub. "You've touched them?"

The girl lolled her head into her shoulder in dismissal. "Of course. I mean the first few weeks they was jus' getting to know me. But then they started sneaking, and then I would scratch right here on their head, and sometimes they jus' stand there, and I can hug them on the neck. They just lonely and want to be loved."

Jolie harrumphed softly. "Well, let's see what they think of Pink." The two grabbed their rakes, and as they swung the gate closed, Jolie watched Pink raise her head into the slender brown head.

For such a force of nature, who scares the hell out of people, she also has a way to calm the beast. Now to see if her charm works on horses.

"Just a minute, Tonisha." The girl stopped and turned. Jolie smirked as she drew two of the carrots out of her back pockets and jammed them down into the young women's back pockets. "I want to see this sneak thing."

The girl's mouth was a set of pearls to make a queen proud. She set about raking the grass here and there. Jolie and Pink were just observers. The two horses hugged the fence rails as they watched the older, the newer, and the new.

Her wide-brimmed black hat shaded her voice as Jolie coached the girl. "Good. Stay to my right like you are now. Give Pink about a horse length between us to move in. See how she moves back and forth between us?" The girl nodded as she racked at nothing—just moving a few leaves. Gentle movement in the sunshine. "She's letting them know she's okay. They remember me, and they know you, but she's the new piece in the puzzle they are trying to figure out."

The three moved lazily toward the middle of the paddock. The horses had separated and circled from two sides.

"Here. This is where I always sit. We'll sit close and let Pink move around us." They laid down their rakes and sat. Jolie took her hat off and laid it on her rake. With her right hand, she reached up and pulled out the braid-band. With a slow roll of her head, she gently finger-raked out her mane of tan-blond hair. Pink sat on the other side of the girl.

"What happened to your arm?"

Jolie looked down at the sling and winged out her arm. "I had a bad accident, and it shattered my shoulder and arm. It's healing, but it will take time."

"It looks like it still hurts."

Jolie rolled in her lips as she closed her eyes and turned her face into the sun. "It aches. The real hurt was doing something stupid." She turned to face the girl but watched the horse cropping at the short grass a few feet from the calm black dog. "I let my guard down when I shouldn't have." She looked out at the break of trees along the edge of the paddock. "Do you know what you want to do when you grow up?"

"I know I don't want to be a groom or stable sweep." The girl smiled. "I like math in school. This last year I started calculus. I'll be a freshman this fall, and they'll let me take trig. There are a lot of jobs math does. I jus' needs ta see them all."

Jolie smiled as she felt a tug at her back pocket. She gently reached and felt a soft nose. As it snorted in her palm, she helped the carrot out of her pocket. The greens were half eaten.

"See. They likes ta sneak."

An hour later, Jolie sat on the bottom rail as she leaned into the middle rail. Her right arm was cocked along the fence, and her chin rested on her loose fist. Her focus was on Pink in the middle of the paddock. She was lying on her side as if without a care. Both horses cropped at grass within a few feet to either side. The leads hung from their necks.

"Well, the leads are on. A little later than promised—but on."

She didn't flinch at the man's voice. The electric cart had given him away. "I had a little detour delay." She rolled her head to look at the man resting his arms and chin on the top rail. "But it wasn't me. Tonisha's a natural."

He hummed as he watched the horses and dog. "Hmm, she doesn't have any fear. Her first day, we set her to cleaning stalls. I forgot to stop her before she got to the two stallions on the end. When I remembered, she'd finished the first one and had thrown a hackamore on the second and tied him off outside the stall. She thought he was nervous because he'd never seen her before. She's the only one who washes him down without tying him off. He just stands there with his lead on the concrete like he was trained to be ground tied. Damnedest thing to see. She'll brush out the others, but him—she starts with a shower, washes his mane and tail, puts that girly cream rinse stuff on him, and brushes him out until he shines. Every bit of it out on the pad with his lead never moving."

Jolie snuffled softly. "Once these two had snuck their carrots and gotten a hug each from her, she ran off and got the leads and snapped them on like she'd been doing it for years. They weren't sure of the training leads, but pretty soon, they settled down."

Norm rolled his head on its side so he could watch her. "And your new dog? Or is that just a small pony rolling around out there?"

Jolie snorted a breathy laugh. "Her name is Pink. This is the farthest she's been from me in over three months."

"Trained as a…?"

"Natural. With the livestock, she's like a Martine, the Spanish mastiff. She calms them, protects them, and if one goes astray, they go roundup the master." She sighed. "She was glued to my side by the third day up in Montana. She is good at hunting—never gets in the way, and you can trust her never to go retrieve your stupid duck."

They both laughed. Some things just aren't worth fighting through the bones and buckshot.

"A while back, you asked me about Castle Construction…"

She looked out of the side of her eye. "I did?"

He scowled at her. "You did. What I'm wondering is if it was just in passing or a serious specific question?" He rolled along the rail to face her. "You've never been a small-talk sort of person. All these years, you've been a direct straight shooter. Even when you were stinking drunk down at the Roadhouse, everyone knew your mind."

She took a last long look at the two mustangs Tonisha had named Golly and Molly. She rolled out of the railing and planted her feet spread outside the fence. She rested the heel of her right hand on her knee, letting the sling float. "So, what's your question, Norm?"

He thought about his place in the valley. There were those who wanted to be powerful. There were those who thought they were powerful. And then, there were those who were. He knew he was in none of those camps. He may have the largest stables where the powerful played, but he was still just a servant and a black man in a white-privileged valley.

He sat down on the other end of the second rail. His voice was low and soft as a summer breeze—nothing to carry farther than the next section of fence. "I've heard mumblings."

She stretched her neck back. The sand in the bones ground like a small beach. She knew she was getting old. Not rodeo-ready. "There are a lot of mumblings in a valley this size, Norm."

"They involve little stakes with orange plastic ribbons on them."

She shook her head and stood. "I see those shit stakes all over this valley." She snapped her fingers at her knee. The goofy in the dog vanished instantly. Pink's flip-over spooked the horses, but the black flash and pink tongue were at her side before the other two were halfway to the other fence—the four paws set for anything needed. "When you're ready to talk to me about whatever it is you're hiding folded up in your pocket, Norm, I'll be around." She nodded at the mustangs. "They'll be rider-ready by the Fourth of July if Tonisha doesn't beat me to it. She has more balls than someone else around here." She tipped her hat and walked off.

His voice was a low rumble, but it carried in the dead air. "You didn't used to be such an asshole."

She spun on her heel and walked back. The man was aware of the large dog at her hip.

She took his chin in her hand and drew him up. As their noses came within inches, she could tell what he had eaten for lunch. She never liked kippered anything. "The woman you like to remember was eight years ago. I was a slut, a drunk, and a broken rodeo rider. I was also innocent. Someone took advantage of that innocence and took a knife…" Her teeth bit down and strained her words. "My knife. The knife of my father. And drove it through the heart of the only woman we ever loved—my mother. The knife of the two people she loved, who loved her with everything they had—and betrayed everything good in this world."

She gently released his jaw with a small push.

"That is the day the person you remember—died. The person I am now is the product of seven years hard time. I've been gang-raped by brooms and mops. I've had shives stuck in me and stuck shives and worse in others. I've been on the wrong side and on the right side. I became a person without a friend and made a friend I would take a shiv for. You have no idea who I am anymore. You go home to your pretty mansion at night. You sleep in your fancy bed with silk sheets and dream of even finer things. I close my eyes and see only my mother and a world seven feet by ten feet, and it didn't bring her back. If you can bring my mother back, you can tell me who to be and how to act. Until then, I break your horses, and you'll pay me. If you have anything more to say, say it. I don't do pussyfooting around anymore. You either cowboy up, or I nut you for the gelding you are. Are we clear?"

The man squeaked and then cleared his throat. "Clear."

Her eyes were almost granite gray-white. The muscles along her jaw stood out as if carved of granite. She turned. "Pink. Hiza."

Norm cleared his throat. "Someone in his company has been surveying and staking your southwest quarter."

She didn't slow. "Find out who and then talk to me. Otherwise, stay clear, and we might take that Fourth of July ride together."

She climbed into the orange truck and stared at the selector on the column. "Crap." She looked at the pink tongue inches from her face. "Damn it, Pink. I hate an automatic. Especially in a truck."

Pink licked her on the nose.

SHABRACK

A thin saddlecloth, thinner than a blanket or pad.
Sometimes called a 'sham' or false covering.

The Roadhouse was moving. Not the usual Friday or Saturday night shaking, but it was a noisy solid pack for a Wednesday night. By eight o'clock, the place smelled like stale beer, last month's garbage, and fresh beer turning rancid by the minute. Four guys had already been cut off and sent home— still wearing their work ties to a honky-tonk should have barred them at the parking lot or at least been a red flag to the bartender.

The blurry-eyed tramp, slurring jumbled greetings and f-bombs, slapping any ass walking past, and drinking from her own bottle was her own brand of trouble. The Rocket was back.

The redhead in the shaggy pixie-cut shaved on one side, bent over and hefted another pony keg into the slot. Stabbing the snout and running home the knurled nut, she recharged the system while her belt slid down from her tank top far enough to disclose a few inches of her butt-crack. Standing, she hitched up her hip-huggers, scooped a pitcher up under the tip of the tap, and pulled the long arm with the bull and rider on top. The foam kicked and frothed, then kicked and finally ran beer. She poured the foam out and rinsed the pitcher.

"We have Ribbon."

Randy called back over his shoulder from the other end of the bar where he was filling an endless line of beer glasses and pitchers. "Thanks." He nodded at the cluster of dirty glasses and pitchers on the bar where the three waitresses in the Daisy Duke outfits had been stacking them. "I'm running out of room here."

The redhead rolled her eyes at the duckboards as she sighed under her breath. "Useless fuckwad." She started for the other end—ignoring the "Great ass" comment from the drunk.

Thumbing at her mildly infected nose ring, she nodded back at the drunk as she hip-pushed Randy out of her way at the sink. "What's with the drunk at the end with her own bottle?"

"Why?" He topped off the pitcher of beer and shoved it across the bar to the waiting waitress.

"I mean is she straight or lesbian… what's her story? She was scoping out my ass."

Randy glanced back down the bar at the woman under the dusty black felt cowboy hat. "Rumor has it she'd ride anything rodeo at least to the bell." He let the glass foam over—leaving a good head but not excessive.

"Rodeo? What the fuck does that even mean?"

His hand worked another glass and beer as he nodded down at her tight low-rise jeans and carved belt with a large buckle. Then leaned back slightly to take in the pair of roping boots now popular with the local gals who had no clue about what to do with a horse. The Santa Ynez Valley was full of cowgirls and boys who the closest they ever got to horses was driving a Ford truck. Some even wore the blue shield as a buckle because they thought it made them look more rodeo.

Scooping a pitcher under the tap with the bull rider on top, he pulled the long arm and leaned closer to the woman. "That is the famous Rocket. Don't touch her bottle. Don't mess with her head. And, most important—don't fuck with her. She's fresh out of seven years up in Lompoc. She busts wild horses all day, and drinks until she can try to sleep the sleep of the dead."

"Why? What did she do?"

"She rode a horse to death."

The redhead screwed up her face and scratched at her loosely covered tit. "They put you in prison for killing a horse?"

The truth and a story flashed through Randy's head. Thinking of Rocket, the legend, and the hands-off she had asked for, he leaned back near the shaved side of the head and the fifteen studs in the ear. "No. The prison she got for shoving a sixteen-inch Bowie knife through an old woman's heart while she slept."

The young woman had heard some gnarly shit before, but this made her eyes turn to hubcaps. "No fucking way."

Randy rolled his eyes into a slow blink. His left hand pushed the pitcher across the bar as his right hand crossed his heart and held up his two fingers. "Truth."

The redhead half his age grabbed his T-shirt and pulled him close. "Who was the old woman?"

He looked at her eyes—only inches away. His heart beat out the slow five-count. "Her own mother."

Her eyes hit a fuller expanse and froze.

Randy nodded sadly. "Don't fuck with her." He turned and walked down the bar, leaving the young woman to get her head around some of the strangest life can deal. He knew the glasses were in danger and waited to hear the first one break. He stopped at the end of the bar. The blurred eyes cleared. The slur was gone.

"Well?"

"Her mouth is good for at least a hundred or more tonight.

But at least five hundred by Saturday." He shook his head and eyes. His face was mush.

Ignoring the passthrough where he knew a large black dog was lying next to, he backed up to the bar and push-jumped to sit on the top. Swinging his legs over, he dropped outside the horseshoe. "I need a cigarette." He stiff-legged his way to the door and pushed out, and then took a half step back. Without turning, he softly commented. "Celeste just pulled in."

Jolie's eyes lost their clarity and returned to the glaze of drunk. The main event had just started.

"HOLY SHIT." The voice was strident and tinged with real fear.

Jolie could feel Pink stirring at her foot. The shoulder pushed into her ankle and calf. She reached down and ran her hand along the other side of the head. "Yasashī."

"What the fuck is that?" Celeste leaned sideways over the bar staring at Jolie.

Jolie lifted her glass and took a sip. "For just once… jus' one fucking time, I wish you could come in here acting like a normal human been. Jus' once." Her mouth slurred, but she kept still as if any movement would cause her to throw up."

The brunette spotted the sling. "Oh, jeez. Randy said you hurt your arm, but he didn't tell me you damn near tore it off. What the fuck, Rocket? Are you back wrestling bulls again?"

Jolie slopped her head around. Her voice was as low and slurred as her eyelids. "Jus' once." She rolled back as she leaned her sweat-stained armpit on the bar—almost splayed out. Her eyes rolled and bounced open a few times as she worked to focus. "Celeste. How the hell…" She belched good, healthy, and long. Wiping her mouth on her sleeve, she smiled—proud of herself. "Did ya lick the steaks? I mean did you like…" She rose on her one hip as if she were farting. The relief washed over her face.

"Oh, honey. You are a total mess." Her best friend reached over the bar and grabbed a wad of napkins. Blotting at Jolie's face at what she perceived as possible puke or snot or both. "Honey, you need to go home."

Jolie slurred. "Bug you jus' got here. I got lots to tell you." She pawed at the other as if missing the grab. Finally, she settled for Celeste's hand. "Did I tell you we got four elk… I got so much fucking meat at the locker I'll never eat it all. I need you to come…" She belched again. Having to work at it was starting to hurt her throat. "We can go shopping at the meat locker like old times. No little peckers, though—just big ones."

"Jolie… let me take you home. You've had a few too many."

"Nah. I'm jus' vine. Vite. Fine. Fine. It's just the shine talking." She fell into Celeste's face to give her the full effect of the drink on her breath. The raw garlic and onions she had chewed on the way over didn't hurt either. "Listen, chica, I'm serious. I've got more meat than four whorehouses could handle in a year. You need to go with me and take some." Her hand and finger squirmed in the air, pointing generically down the bar where only the redhead was staring with repulsion. "I know Dandy… I mean Randy likes meat."

"I don't know, Jolie…"

Jolie grabbed sloppily at Celeste's shirt and pulled her to within an inch of her fuming mouth. "What? You didn't become one of them pussy veggie people, did you?"

The woman leaned back as far as she could. "No. I mean… No. I just think you need to go home and get some sleep. How are you even driving with only one arm?"

Jolie slumped back against the bar. Spreading over her stool, the woman's lap, and the bar. The next move would have them all on the floor. "Sheee-et. The old truck fucking blew a gasket. I had to fly to Montana. Uncle Jinx had an orange piece of shit the highway crew sold him, but it's a pussy automatic. Nobody thinks I can"—she pulled her left knee up and shifted the air with her right hand—"drive a stick. Fuck it. I can drive it in my sleep."

The two started to slip and head for the floor. Celeste kicked at the bar and steadied them. Seating Jolie back upright, she started to get her to stand. "Come on, Rocket. Time for the barn." She looked around her friend.

"Was wrong?" Jolie stumbled.

"Nothing, honey. Just making sure your new horse was following us."

Jolie's eyes bobbed as her head rocked back. "Of course, she is. She's trained just like a mule. Choo choo."

"Just making certain, honey. Just making certain. Come on." She led the two out to the parking lot.

Celeste guided her to the beat-up faded orange truck. "Really, honey, I can drive you home." Her argument had the weight of last week's sunshine. Jolie pushed it past its limits.

"S'all right, honey. This truck knows how to get home. I just put it in gear, and I can just let Pink here do the driving." She stumbled into her friend, who straightened her and helped her into the truck.

"But drive careful. We don't want you getting pulled over or anything… now that we just got you back home."

Jolie slurred and wavered. "Yeah, girlfriend. We need to go shopping in my meat locker. Fuck, I've got more meat than the football squad we partied with in high school. Good times, Cellie." She leaned back into the seat with large eyes and took a deep breath through her nose. "That's what we need more of… good times."

Celeste patted the windowsill as she closed the door. "Well, drive carefully, and we'll see you this weekend."

Jolie started the truck. Two fingers saluted her friend from her nose and eased the truck toward the street.

As she slowed her approach to the street, she watched her friend in the side mirror. True to form, the woman was blowing a tantrum. She bounced off the two trucks as she kicked the tires and pounded the metal with the soft of her fists. The high-pitched scream accompanied Jolie's smile as she nosed the truck out onto the highway and headed for home. There were arrangements to be made.

She was still replaying the sound of Celeste's voice in her head as the cab of the truck lit up blue and red. *I just wanted to be certain…*

"Evening, Rocket."

"Evening, Punchy. Are we holding this meeting in my truck or your SUV?"

Punchy looked in at the black beast with glowing eyes and the crescent of a pink tongue. He could smell Jolie's breath.

His hand waved the fumes away. "Jesus. You got diesel fuel mixed in with that skunk juice?"

"Oh, I never thought about using the skunk too. Good call there." She held one eye closed with the other eyelid lifting. "It might taste better than all the old tea. This shit is nasty, but thank goodness I only need to swish a few sips around to knock out horses and elephants. What's the pull-over for?"

"Just checking in. I heard you got a new dog. She looks dangerous." Pink could have been out of polished onyx.

"She's good. Pink, give Punchy a wet kiss."

He put out his hand. "I'm good."

Jolie's left hand shot out of the sling and grabbed his hand. "Stupid. I want her to record your scent." She dragged his hand and arm into the truck. "Here girl. Gnaw on this for a minute." The dog sniffed and then started licking. Jolie didn't release the hand, and the man stopped struggling.

Jolie turned to the deputy. "She can keep this up until you've had the best sponge-bath of your life. If she didn't growl, or just stonewall your hand, I know you can be trusted. But then, there was never any doubt in my mind." She let go, but the hand remained in the wash.

"What kind of dog?"

"She's called a Cane Corso. They're from Italy or something, but all of her commands are in Japanese."

He leaned in so he could pet under her jaw and finally up to her floppy ears. "I like dogs with natural ears. Most people pin them so they will look meaner than they are." He withdrew his arm and backed out of Jolie's exhaust. "Japanese, huh. The K-9 units are all taught in Dutch or German. They always sound angry. I think Japanese would sound nicer."

Jolie gave Pink's head a rough rub. As she returned to looking at Punchy, her head dipped on the one side. Her look was all questions beyond questions. "Still watching my property?"

He leaned his head shyly and shrugged. "It's in my territory…" He smiled loosely. Jolie remembered the smile floating just above the rim of a barrel in the middle of the arena.

He nodded his chin toward her arm; now, out of the useless sling. "How's it doing?"

She smirked. Rodeo to rodeo. "Better each day. The top of the arm and along the back of my shoulder aches the most. But… it feels better once I start working it out."

He bobbed his head. "Liniment if you can stand it, or DMSO. It helps. I use it on my knee or WD-40 if I run out of the good stuff."

"Does it keep it lubricated."

He snorted. "Nah, it just has a lot of the DMSO in it." He fingered the sling. His face asked the question.

"Camouflage. It's the old wounded bird routine."

His face compressed in confusion and then cleared in a smile. His radio squawked in staticky garbage only he could understand. He acknowledged but stood still. Jolie didn't have to look to know that only one foot was turned toward his patrol car.

"What time you take your dinner break tomorrow, Punchy?"

"Eight… well, eight-ish."

She smiled. "I've got a bunch of prime two-inch thick elk

steaks, and I think they're delivering a barbecue in the afternoon. Right after I buy it."

He smiled. "I'll swing by early and help you get the barbecue out of the back of the truck."

She smiled. "You've got a deal, sir." She put the truck in gear. "Have a safe night, officer."

He called after the truck. "That's deputy…"

He watched the red lights until they disappeared around the curve. The smile was slow. The tip of his tongue wet his lower lip as he rolled it in over his lower teeth. He looked up at the great throw of stars. Tiny diamonds on a black velvet cloth. He felt a long way from a rodeo barrel. The smile pulled back and pooched up his cheek where the young bull had ripped his face so many long years before. It just had never felt so good before.

2 2

TIN TACK

Thin, cheap, fancy-looking, and shiny. Mostly used for parades. Also called show tack. Looks like high-quality decorative silver but fake.

Orm watched from his office. Even from a distance, he could tell the sling was dirty, needed washing, and served no medical support. It wasn't like the old Rocket to resort to anything resembling a sham, but the new woman she had become was just scary enough to have anything up her sleeve or in a useless sling.

The mustang he had resolved himself to accept as Golly was loosely trotting around the paddock. Jolie had her out on about a twenty-foot longe line. The shallow loop occasionally dragged, skipped, and popped between the horse and woman. The horse had plenty of room to circle further away from the woman with the long whip but seemed more at ease to just turn lazy circles on a loose lead.

It was their second week on the longe line. Both mustangs now came to Jolie—and the first carrot. She took to randomly slipping the hackamore on, then to touch nose to hand, and last to get the carrot. Norm had watched as the urge to get the first carrot had become a small pushing and shoving game they had probably played on the open plains of Montana or Wyoming where they were rounded up and saved by the state. They had cost him six hundred dollars total to have them brought to him. He had bought eight over the years. One was still unbreakable, would probably never be ridden, and five years later, even untouchable unless first tranquilized with a dart. But the stallion had sired three spectacular riding horses and five strong riding mules—each selling for more than the total cost of all the mustangs combined.

His eyes wandered along the string of five student riders and their teacher as they posted on the trail toward the new training field for jumping and field racers. If the sport involved riding and competing, Norm was ready to try providing the arena, trails, or grounds for the wealthy to try their hands and horses at the rungs of the ever-changing ladder of popularity and one-upmanship. If one of the trendsetting young women in L.A. tweeted, chatted, or was photographed riding their new pet camel, he would have some serious thoughts about scrounging the middle east for the best of the dromedaries—no matter how dramatic it would appear.

Jolie reeled the longe line shorter and shorter and finally stopped Golly. The horse stood blowing softly. The workout, no matter how little it affected her, was still exercise. Jolie dropped the whip and stepped the last few steps. Norm watched with a sliver of awe as the mustang never backed up. The wildness was tempered as she didn't shy but only leaned her head into the petting as Jolie started the scratching under the chin, and then up around the hackamore's wide noseband.

Norm could see, as her fingers slid under, the noseband was loose on the mustang. Nothing in what Jolie had done with the two had been demanding. Everything she left to the horses to decide and only in their time. She would show them the way, reward them when they took the direction, and encourage them with affection. Even the longe whip lagged further behind than with most exercisers and trainers. He still didn't understand how she had looked at them and made such a bold statement about what they would become. Especially the goofy-footed Molly. She was never going to get the hang of cutting cattle, much less be fast enough or solid-footed enough to perform snap turns where the rider's lower foot could drag the ground. Wyoming mustangs had no Doc Bar blood in their heritage. But he knew she would stubbornly defend her prediction.

The phone on his desk buzzed softly. His focus retreated first to Jolie and then to the glass in his window, and finally, his awareness of being at work in his office. He spun his chair as his hand floated in the air, finally settling on the phone.

"Yes?"

"Sir, it's Jeffrey at the gatehouse, sir. Sorry to interrupt you, but we have a Michael Williams here at the gate. We don't have him on any list, but he insists he be allowed in. What would you like for us to do?"

"Did he say Michael or Mike?"

"Sir, his driver's license says—"

The edge crept into Norm's voice. "Mike or Michael?"

"Neither, sir. He only said Mr. Williams to see the mustang trainer."

Shit. Norm's eyes sagged shut as his forehead found his right hand. "It's Mike. Put him on every fucking list. Write his name on the wall by your door and apologize to him for my mistake for hiring a social maladroit. She's up in the small paddock near barn three. Can you direct him, or do I need to come down to hold his hand?"

"Excuse…" Norm could hear the kid's Adam's apple hit his brainpan and then his belt buckle. "Yes, sir. Barn three, sir."

Norm blindly restored the phone to its roost. Looking up, he stared at the small black and white photo of a seven-year-old girl posting on her first pony. It was his favorite photo of his wife. Even their wedding photos hadn't come close. The girl's joy was pure. No complications. Not a single hint of anything terrible in her life. The day was bright and sunny, the pony was perfect, her riding was flawless, and she had won her first of many ribbons before she moved on to trophies which would eventually be as tall as she was. The day the photo was taken, she was all smiles, reins gathered in her control, and her pony minding every nudge of her knees. Losing her parents while she was in high school, losing all three of their tries at children, and finally losing her dance with cancer were years away and utterly unfathomable.

Now he would have to go ask her sister if she could do something about her son. Or if he could just fire him. Some days it was good to have some family left—and some days, not.

The sound of the car drew him from the single photo he had left of his wife.

Norm recognized the older man rising from the car. The man had been on the property three times. The first to assess the potential. The second he had brought the two lawyers and a notary. And now—this.

Mike walked over to the fence. Jolie was working one of two horses on a longe line. There were four pool worms laid across the lane of the circle the horse was trotting in. The plastic foam tubes were soft, yellow, and only four inches thick. The horse treated them as if they were about a foot high and jumped each time. There was no preparation, just trot, jump, trot, jump— around and around. He didn't know if the horse was more bored by the trotting in a large circle or the jumping, but it definitely didn't have a happy or nervous look on its face. It appeared as if it was just its turn to go in circles or the woman in the center would crack the whip.

Mike put his shoe up on the lower rail and leaned in. "How often do you have to crack the whip?"

Jolie smiled. "Never. They aren't brain-dead surfers off Rincon Point. They are behaved young ladies from the best parts of Wyoming."

"How many times around?"

"It depends on the day. Sometimes only twenty each way, and some days even a hundred isn't enough." She snap-glanced her head as she kept turning. "What are you doing here, Mike?"

He looked around.

She rolled her lower lip in. Mike could see what word she had said. The prison had been no school to teach manners. He wasn't a prude since he had said much the same while surfing, but for some reason, it was like getting shocked by touching something metal after walking across a carpet. It doesn't hurt… It just…

She scratched and kissed the nose of the horse and unsnapped the long rope. As she walked, she yanked up the longe line. "This is a long way to drive just to take a girl out to lunch."

"We can get some hoagies or something. We'll talk and eat at the same time."

Once out on the highway, Jolie turned. "Okay, you insisted I come with you and leave my truck. You wouldn't talk at the horse farm. So I'm guessing you have a sneaker wave crawling up my board, and you want to warn me… but why all the secrecy? You think someone is listening at the farm?"

He glanced over. His hair did the wave hop only a full head of thin white hair can do. She wondered what her hair would look like when she was seventy or so. Her mother had more pepper than salt when she was killed at sixty-eight. Her father's hair always looked like he had just drummed out of the Marine Corp and buffed it down with silver paint.

"Other than Jinx, Dot, and me, how many know you got shot?"

"No one. I fell off my horse hunting a month ago. Why?"

"You didn't tell your best friend or the bartender?"

"Celeste and Randy? No. They only got the cover story. I

might trust Randy, but I'm not sure about Celeste. So everyone got the same story about hunting."

He nosed off the highway and drove along a small road wandering along the backside of Jolie's land. His finger pointed to surveyor stakes along the narrow backroad. "Someone in the state or county thinks the traffic on this road constitutes a widening and upgrade."

Jolie watched as the stakes slowly passed. "As far as I remember, there are only a handful of ranches up this way."

He eased the car left onto a dirt road. The tracks weren't deep, so it was fairly new. "Someone is hoping to build about two hundred more small ranches. Well… something with the necessary ten acres to qualify for lower property taxes. Big homes, small ranches, small taxes. Sound familiar?"

She sulked down into the seat as she looked around. The topography was starting to look familiar. "Yeah. Big hat and no cattle. Just a fucking cattle dog with nothing to work." She sat up and whipped her head around a few times. "Where are we?"

His smirk held no mirth. "It must have been a while. I was wondering when you would start recognizing your property."

She pointed out the window. "I pulled all of these stakes…"

He stopped the car. "No, you only pulled about a hundred stakes. They put them back and added a few hundred more. I wasn't joking about them wanting to divide your land into two hundred ten-acre plots and build big million-dollar homes. Their problem is, they have to prove you have abandoned the property for the last five years. By surveying and staking it out, they can show hostile takeover at least."

Getting out, they scanned the low sloping hillside. Scattered in among the eucalyptus and oaks were little stakes with red, orange, and yellow plastic ribbons fluttering gently in the air. Jolie tipped her hat against the sunshine. The tiny dots of bright color speckled the next and the next hill. She could feel Pink pressing against her leg—calming her.

Grinding on her heel, she turned to Mike. "Tell me where I stand."

"Well…" He started to walk. "The good news is the stakes you ripped this past summer were the basis survey for all of this. With them gone, they had to resurvey the entire project to prove up the viability for them to get finances to move forward. This"—he waved his arms—"is the result of their first venture capital. The good news for you and the bad for them is this is still your land. So if you, say, got a boy scout troop to walk this square mile and gather all these stakes to have a little bonfire or weenie roast, they have no recourse."

She stopped and looked south with her hands on her hips. The view was one she had never thought about. Terraced right, every mansion would have a spectacular view of the valley to the southwest. The valley generally never changed much. Most of the large ranches changed hands to the next generation. The villages like Los Olivos were hidden in the valleys where panoramic views never saw them. She knew where they were, only because she had grown up in the valley, but to any city slickers, the view would be excellent.

"I'm hearing a but in there…"

He stepped up beside her. "More of an 'or' in there. I'd forgotten how amazing this view was. When you were small, and I was new to the firm, your father asked me if I would be interested in some acreage along this knoll. I was still surfing more mornings than not and couldn't picture living this far from the ocean. If I had been smart, I should have taken the offer."

"How much land did he offer you?"

"About one forty. This entire knoll down to the road."

"How much?"

He smiled to one side as he faced her. "That was the other part. The curb rate would have been a cool million. I think I was making about two grand a month at the time."

They both laughed softly as their gaze returned to the

southern tip of the valley.

"A million then makes this development today worth some serious money." She rolled her lower lip and chewed. She figured he had the necessary numbers but was afraid to ask. The six-hundred-dollar check from her last job felt hard and cold in her hip pocket. She was way in over her head—and had thought she was doing fine. She wasn't sure if she wanted to know the numbers.

He looked down as his shoe played with the small eucalyptus seed ball. "It also makes the people who have a lot to lose… very dangerous."

She tipped her hat sideways as her head hung so she could look at him. "Really? Dangerous, you say? Like they might turn me over their knee dangerous or maybe send the class bully to come slug me in the arm dangerous?"

He thought about her warped humor. It used to be poking fun but now had a surgical edge to it going straight for the carotid artery.

"Shoot you in the back kind of dangerous."

"Oh. Just the little things." She raised an eyebrow as she looked past him at the other hills. "So, after the boy scouts, what then? Do we even know who's behind it?"

He turned, taking in the distant dots of orange and yellow, and continued until he was looking at the rise behind them. "We've been digging into it. I hired a couple of guys from Los Angeles. I knew them when I would surf down that far. They ended in the FBI, and then retired from the California DOJ. They never hung out a shingle, but most already knew what they wanted to do in their retirement besides golf and fishing."

She frowned at him. "Nobody surfs anymore?"

He sighed as he ground his head back and forth. "The waves are polluted."

"From what I heard, they always were."

"Yeah, but back then, us kids were the pollution. Now it's

more kids but also toxins the docs can't identify. They even have names for the problems like Surfers Nose, Wave Cough, and Eye-a-Bunga. Once you get them, there is no getting rid of them even if you quit riding. It's just not worth it."

She snorted and spread her hand across the view. "Then now you're ready to buy my hill."

His response wasn't what she expected. "Well, I guess we could call it option 'C' in our arsenal."

"What are the first two options?"

He turned and gestured toward the car. "I'm hungry."

As he drove, he thought about everything he had been studying for the last five months. "If we get lucky, we find out who the actual owners are of the shell companies crossing back and forth in the Caymans, Bimini, and St. Barts. We're only four shell companies in, and we're getting stonewalled like we were asking the net worth of Switzerland. But if we fail there, your troop of boy scouts comes into play as well as filing a cease claim."

He turned right on the highway. "We also have some papers. All I can say is we must have forgotten to get your signature on them about three years ago. We will probably have you sign them anyway."

"What kind of papers?"

"The ones directing us to survey the second hill for the hog farm you plan to build there. Of course, nobody would want to be downwind of the shit ponds. And if there is a massive rain, it would probably overflow, and anyone's mansion downhill would be up a creek."

She thought about where he was going. If she had signed papers, and there was any movement such as survey or tree clearing, the abandonment claim would be null and void.

"What about the turkey ranch on the close hill?"

They were still laughing when he pulled into the winery for lunch.

CANTER

A three-beat gait of a horse between a trot and a gallop.

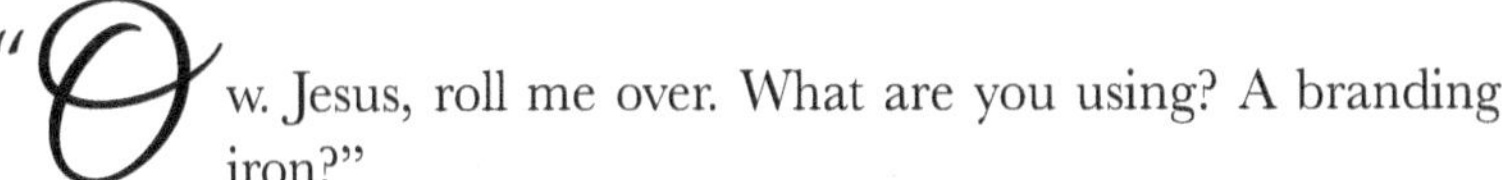

"Ow. Jesus, roll me over. What are you using? A branding iron?"

Dot kept digging with her knuckle. "Shut the fuck up, wimp. You don't come down here for a month. You wear dat silly rag like it be a disguise. You don't work out the muscles, so you get what you work for." She pulled the arm up over Jolie's head. Bringing her knee up against Jolie's shoulder, she pulled the joint to flex.

"What the fuck?" Jolie started pounding the mat of the fighting ring.

Dot chuckled. "Okay, I owe you one. Dat one was jus' me havin' fun with yo pain." She rolled over into a standing walk. Taking up the two chilled bottles of water, she offered one out to Jolie. "But seriously now. You need to work yo shoulder out or be froze—den there nothing you can do. Short of another surgery." Jolie noticed how Dot's language moved in and out of ebonics with what she was talking about. The more physical the subject, the more accentuated the annunciation.

Jolie handed the water back. "Just put it on my shoulder."

Dot shrugged and dumped part of her bottle on her bare shoulder.

Jolie jumped. "Not like that, you silly goose."

Dot put the bottles down and pulled the thinly padded gloves off the top buckle. She offered out the one pair. "You thought you just drive down and get a rub. Fuck, girl, you only started to be warmed up. If you thought getting shot was all there was, you go home and wait. But the next time, my guess, they come close to make sure. It's my job to make sure too. You be all kind of booby-trap land mine."

The owner of the gym sat in the gloom at the edge of the ring. He didn't know who the older white woman was and didn't care. If Dot said to let her in and keep everyone else out, then closed he was. He also wasn't so sure about the black shadow of a dog. Even though it seemed friendly with Dot, it kept ten feet from or close to the man watching the women fight. The tiny pink of the tongue and the piercing blue eyes were all the man could see in the ring's shadow.

The door opened. A flood of harsh white light pierced the dark around two male figures laughing and joking as they entered. The bald man barked from the corner of the ring where he sat on a worn stool. "We're closed today. Get out."

Grumbles at the door became a closed door.

Between jabs, Dot glanced over. "Maybe you should lock the door, Max." She swept the leg, and Jolie stepped over it as she deftly reached out with her left—only touching air.

"Can't. The kid is bringing us lunch, and he doesn't have a key yet."

Dot held up her hands, and Jolie stopped. "Look. Everything is three beats. One, two, three. Punch, feint, punch. It's a rhythm.

One, two, three, one, two, three, one, two, three. It's like dancing the old waltz."

"That's a four-count. A trot or canter is a three-count."

"Fuck dancing. I don't care if'n you can or can't, this here be all threes. Punch, feint, punch. Or to mix it up, you punch hard, wait a beat, then left right. *Boom. Boom.*" Her fists were blurs in the air. "Got it? Here, work in my hands."

Jolie thought about riding her favorite horse Thunder. Down a dusty road or across a field, his presence was always the same as if they were taking a victory trot around an arena. The trot always became a canter with the same *pow pa-pow, pow pa-pow.* Her fists reinforced the memories. The anger and pain of losing him through her vanity bled out with each hit. Pow pa-POW, pow pa-POW!

Dot whipped her hand out of the way. Sliding the glove between her thighs, she drew out her hands. She walked over and poured cold water on her hand. The padding hadn't helped.

"Yeah. Like dat. Wherever you went jus' now. Dat how you win." She shook her hand as the door opened. She and the man cursed at the same time as she shook her hand in the air.

The dark shadow backlit by the door held up the two bags of lunch. Max waved him in.

Pink moved slightly to track the new target. Jolie slid through the ropes and jumped down. Her hand found an ear. "Yoko." Pink waited out the ear rub and then lay down.

The older man talked around the sandwich he was chewing in the side of his mouth. "How long you here for?"

Jolie looked at her arm and the bruise surfacing from the previous day's exercising on the beach. "Until I'm bruised enough where Dot can't see me in the dark—so I can sneak off. Why?"

Dot slugged her arm a bit more than pushed. The two were becoming even more like sisters.

Max looked at Dot as he talked. He knew she would have the

final say. "I've got a couple of mixed kids who are coming up. I think you'd make them stretch, but it wouldn't seem like you were going easy on them."

Dot squinted one eye. "Mixed? Who?"

Jolie frowned at Dot and then Max. "Mixed? As in race?" She slipped Pink a bit of her sandwich.

Dot slugged her harder. "Mixed martial arts. What I used to fight. What we are doing. Did they shoot you back of the head?" She shook her head for drama and to hide her smile.

Eyeing Dot, the man tore another bite out of his sandwich and weighed what he could say. "Tawny for one. You tear her up too much. She needs some good fights, not just lessons. I think we can run her out this spring at Pasadena. Maybe even take her over Fontana way for the opens."

Dot chewed and thought about the girl in question. Nodding. "Who else?"

"You know the skinny kid who rides the bus up from Chinatown?"

"The redheaded boy with the zits? She'd kill him."

Max leaned back, laughing like he was trying not to fart. "No... oh hell no. Crap, she'd mop his body from buckle to buckle. I don't think he'll ever be ready unless one of the schoolgirls who walk past here wants to beat him up. No. The Asian kid. Mathew, Luke, John, Peter... whatever his name is."

"Jay. I think he a Jacob. Just don't call him Wing Ho like you did when he first came here."

He ignored being called out on his old school habits of nicknaming according to a person's appearance, ethnicity, or habits. It took him a year before he found out the black girl who was always on time was also really named Dorthey. She hated her name, but Dot stuck. Not many fighters were punctual. She also had a habit of dotting other fighter's eyes.

"So what do ya say? Up to mixing it up with some kids?"

Jolie looked at Dot. The woman pushed her lower lip out as

if to say 'why not.' She tapped at her head. "Full headgear and heavy gloves. I don't want you hurting the kids, Rocket."

Max snorted. "Rocket?"

Jolie leaned her head over and looked at him with one eye and nodded.

"Oh… this is going to be fucking beautiful. Rocket vs. Wing—"

"Max!"

THE WET SAND WAS COLD ON THEIR FEET, WHICH KEPT THEM jogging. The tiny lights out to sea were easily confused with stars low in the sky. The week had created some bruising, but the workouts had loosened Jolie up more than any amount of mucking stalls or working horses could have.

Their breaths were easy; the talk was short plugs in the air. Both were smiling at the exercise, the empty beach, and camaraderie.

"What now?"

Jolie thought through three sets of three footfalls. She had begun to notice she did things in three anyway. Right, left, RIGHT. Left, right, LEFT. Even her hitting had become switch-hitting. The first fight the young girl had escaped. Then, in practice, she had even taken Dot by surprise and clobbered her headgear with an unexpected left. The woman laughed from the mat how she was not going to teach Jolie how to kick. Two days later, one of the other fighters at the gym had taught her a few of the basic kicks. One more time on the mat was the last time she caught Dot by surprise. The mat had become Jolie's friend until she settled down and did the serious work.

"I go back. I break horses, get drunk, maybe get laid." They both nodded good evening to the elderly couple swinging their arms and doing the power-walk octogenarians did on the beach when nobody else was watching. The two women glanced back with smiles. Jolie nodded. "That's me in thirty years. I want an old codger who will power-walk with me on a midnight beach."

"What happens with your land?"

Jolie stopped. Her hands on her knees. She wasn't blowing hard, but it was a rest to figure out how to explain the property. Standing, she pointed toward the pier. The lights were just twinkles in the dark, and the men fishing were invisible from a distance.

"How far is the pier?"

"About a mile. Maybe less."

She turned and pointed at the next pier with fewer lights, a dark brushstroke against the twinkling lights of the city clutching at the bay behind. "And the pier there is another mile. So between these piers is two miles."

Dot nodded. "Yes 'um."

Jolie held her two hands out, slightly cupping her fingers. "Now imagine these two miles and take it back from the beach the same two miles."

"That be a whole bunch o' city. Would take you most way to eighty-fourth."

Jolie nodded. "But imagine it's just trees. Deer wander on it. Five-hundred-pound wild boar eat my acorns, my grandfather shot a bear from the front porch of the house I live in. Squirrels, raccoons, badgers, weasels, chipmunks, lizards, snakes, bees, and even frogs. We all live there."

Dot's eyes sparkled from the city lights. "It still a lot of lands to take care of."

"That's the point, Dot. I don't take care of it. Nobody does. Before the Indians, there was nobody. But all those animals and more were always there. Nobody should take it away from them —not the developers, not me, not anyone. The land around in the valley, if it's not farms or ranches, it is being paved, and houses are thrown up. Then they plant some trees and a bunch of grass. The trees aren't native and need water—lots of water. The grass needs water and fertilizer which runs off into the streams and pollutes the water, so the algae bloom and kills the fish. The cars foul the air, the people jam the roads, and they build more malls to attract more people."

Dot rested her hands on her friend's shoulders. "Chill. Breathe. I only wanted to know what you be doing about the stake things."

Jolie sighed. "Want to come run in the forest and pull stakes with me? I have a shit load of elk meat to barbecue."

"What's it taste like?"

"Better than prime rib." Her eyes popped big. "Oh, wait. I even have some elk prime rib."

"What do you eat with it?"

Jolie laughed and started slow jogging back to the pier and her truck. "Beer. The thicker, darker, meatier beer the better."

"I don't have any knives or swords I have to make for at least a month."

Their four feet kept count as they jogged, sparred, and punched their way through the night. The four paws shadowing them was enjoying the night, the sand, and the water. She kept running in and out of the rush of the foam as it chased them along the beach. This sand was nothing like the sandy soil of the ranch. She could get used to this vacation stuff.

2 4

HOBBLE

*Ropes or leather tied around the front legs to keep
a horse from moving more than grazing.*

The girls laughed to watch Pink run around the small bonfire of stakes. She would bite at one of the ends, but the heat would follow if she pulled. Jolie never had to tell her to drop the stick; nature took its course.

Gathering the stakes had become even more fun. Once Pink understood they were removing the stakes, and either putting them in their bags or throwing them into the back of the six-wheeled gator, she was off and running. She would pull out a stake and race back to the gator, drop it in the back, and race off to find another stake. Soon they figured out she was only pulling the ones with red ribbons, so they switched to only orange. After a few, Pink had caught on to the new game and only pulled the orange ones.

Jolie leaned into Dot laughing. "Okay, yellow, orange, red,

and repeat." The two had to walk farther, but again, it only took the dog a couple of series to figure the pattern.

Jolie showed her a stake with a red ribbon and pointed up the hill at a single stake with a matching red ribbon. The dog started off and then dove into a mound of scrub brush. She surfaced with a large blue-bellied lizard in her mouth. Proudly, she brought it to Jolie. Laughing, Jolie pointed at Dot. "Oh, no, honey. That lizard is Dot's. Give it to Dot."

Pink looked at her like she was crazy but finally took it over to Dot. She held it in her mouth until Dot begrudgingly put her hands out. The dog gave her the lizard, which only remained dead for a moment. The flying lizard startled the martial arts master, whose squeal made Jolie fall over laughing. Pink ran to her master to make sure she was all right, and then back to find out what had gone wrong with the gift.

The red ribbon stake was long forgotten. Stake hunting was done for the day. Steak was in order.

Jolie kicked the last of the stakes out of the back of the six-wheeled cart. "She never kills them. They are much more fun to watch my reaction when they figure out they are free to escape. One let me pet it for several minutes, though. It's the toads and bullfrogs I wish I could teach her not to touch. They're just ooky."

"Ooky? As in the Adams Family spooky and they're ooky?"

Jolie snorted. She hadn't called anything ooky in a long time and had forgotten where she first heard the word. The two danced around trying to remember the words but just settled for acting like kids and creeping around what would become another bonfire when the sun went down.

With the charcoal lit, Dot stood watching the flames as the black chunks became red. The creep of the change had always fascinated her as a young girl. It was almost as interesting as watching a caterpillar spin a cocoon, but faster.

Jolie kicked the sides of her boots against the tree turned

porch column. The dust cloud was small and almost useless. As she pulled open the screen door, she wondered why she bothered. The maid hadn't shown up in the last forty years, so she probably wasn't coming in the next week or three.

Jolie saw Pink start to rise. "Yoko. You stay with your Aunt Dot. I'm just getting our dinner." She stepped into the kitchen.

She pulled open the refrigerator. The interior was dark and empty except for the jar of pickles. The dark green was probably not pickles. She didn't know what the shelf life of a jar of pickles was, but she was sure it probably expired her first year in prison —if it made it past the rapid trial.

She turned to the large ice chest. The bag of ice was a slumped bag of mush. The four thick steaks were still individually sealed in the shrink bags. She eyed the last five beers. "Fuck."

"Jolie?" The voice didn't waver, but it stank of uncertainty.

"Yeah." She softly kicked at the ice chest. She bent to rescue the steaks.

"Better come out here. Popo just rolled up."

Jolie scrunched her face as she stood. "The what?"

"Five-Oh. The fuzz. The man. The fucking cops are here."

Jolie placed the six pounds of steak on the large platter and carried it to the porch. She put the platter on the table next to the barbecue and walked to the edge of the porch. Punchy was just climbing out of the car.

"You're fucking late. We called that fucking nine-one-one four hours ago, and finally, you come wandering up here taking your own sweet fucking time. What the hell do we even pay taxes for?"

Punchy double-hand grabbed his belt buckle and stood slowly rolling his head around on his neck and shoulders. "Because I like my fat paycheck."

"What if I were having a heart attack?"

"You'd die." He stretched backward.

"What if my horses had gotten loose?" Her fists buried on her hipbones. She peeked at Dot's unbelieving face.

"They'd come back when they got hungry." He slowly crossed the yard.

"We've got goochies in our henhouse. What you gonna do about it?"

"Shotgun. Kill the chickens."

"Well, damn, Mister Deputy. If you have all the answers, where's the beer?"

He snapped his fingers and walked back to his cruiser. He opened the truck. When he closed it, he was bent over. He stood, holding a large ice chest, almost the size of the one in the kitchen.

"You needed more ice too. When I stopped in for lunch, I ate the last two hard-boiled eggs... they were hard-boiled, right?"

Jolie shrugged. "Nope, just old and spoiled. You'll probably get some clown gut rot, and then we'll have to bury you in a barrel." She opened the ice chest while he was holding it. Her whistle was low. She let the lid fall. She passed one of the beers over her shoulder to Dot who she could feel behind her. She leaned forward and gave Punchy a short kiss. "I saw the roll of Danishes. Were you planning to stay for breakfast?"

"It was a thought." He looked at the freckled mocha face with the large wild afro. Jolie forced her lips not to smile as she watched the gears grind in the man's face. Dot wasn't moving other than to rest her chin on Jolie's shoulder. Her arms slid around Jolie's thin waist protectively.

Dot waited the three-count and then whispered, "If either one of us farts, it gonna ruin the suspense."

Two minutes later, they settled down enough to cover introductions.

THE SMALL EMBERS OF THE FORMER PILE OF SURVEY STAKES glowed orange crumbling in the dark pie of ashes. Soft pops and cracks witnessed the last dying throes of the fire. An exhausted Pink lay sleeping under Jolie's hand. The last bottles of beer stood guard next to their respective consumers. The low Adirondack chairs, in their weathered gray, shimmered ghostly in the dying firelight.

"Any of the stakes left?" Punchy's head rolled over.

Jolie's head rolled the other way. Dot shrugged. "Damned if I know. Ask Pink."

Jolie looked down at the dog between her and Punchy. She groaned as she rolled onto her side. Jolie looked up. "I guess not. We can go look in the morning."

He watched the embers. The light on his face looked more like a dark tan. The embers glowed red in his eye. "I'm supposed to be in Santa B by eight. They have an inmate going back up to Lompoc. Another deputy from Solvang is meeting me shortly after six, and we'll ride down together."

"Kind of off your usual beat, isn't it?"

He rolled his head into his shrug. "Occasionally, we rotate. I pull the short straw about two or three times a year. Most of the times, it's the westies who want more than a thirty-mile beat for a day. They see the same streets, same houses, same people day in and day out. The prison run gets them out on the freeway for the day. Dump the mate and go get some clam chowder. Grab some sunshine and be back in the hole by five. Dick duty, but it beats the same old grind."

Dot stood and stretched. "I'd rather pound some steel or my girl here." She stepped through the chairs. "Good night. Nice meeting you, Punchy. Keep the faith."

Jolie reached out and caught a couple of fingers which she let slide through her hand. "Sleep tight, Dot."

Punchy's head hung back. "Good meeting you too, Dot."

The time was soft. The stars watched from overhead. The embers were almost out. "You know her from where?"

Jolie snorted softly. "You jealous?"

"She's a good-looking woman."

"After you get past the scars and hair?"

"Scars? She has scars?"

Jolie jabbed at his shoulder, slow and gentle. "You always were a weird child. Hiding in that barrel when good-looking women are riding by."

"Only the good ones stopped." He chuckled. "Seriously."

"Her father was a knife maker. He was the one who made Dad's pig knife. Dad brought the raw belly hide from a young sow. Tim used it to wrap the handle, so the knife would recognize where it was supposed to go."

"I thought you told me you stuck it in the shoulder at the base of the neck. That's a long way from the belly."

"It was just to guide it into the pig. Where is up to the hunter."

"So, like father, like daughter?"

"In a roundabout way. She used to be a professional fighter. Mixed martial arts. She got carried away one title fight and wound up killing a good friend. The coroner said it wasn't her fault. The woman had something wrong with the vessels in her brain. Any other fight could have been the last... but it was Dot." She looked over at the former clown. He understood about matches gone wrong. "She never fought again."

He took a deep breath and sat up to the edge of the chair. "So she went home and took up the hammer and anvil."

Jolie put her hand out, and he pulled her up. "I think there was a lot of soul-searching between the two."

He looked at her face in the dark. "Sounds a lot like a certain rider I remember."

She hesitated a moment and then leaned into him. He recognized her hug was more emotional exhaustion than a hug. He was there for as long as it took.

2 5

I R O N

Working tack on horses is made from steel.
Working tack of a ranch is wrought from iron.

olie rolled over into a wet tongue. Punchy had left in the dark of the morning.

She pulled her head back as her hand cupped the head and ear. "You know, your breath doesn't smell like Punchy's." She sniffed. The smell in the air was strange. It took a moment for her to recognize it for what it was. She looked back at Pink with big eyes. "Do you smell that? That, my dear, is coffee and bacon." The blankets exploded as they jumped out of bed.

Jolie grabbed the doorjamb, gasping, and trying to decide which part of her anatomy to grab, rub, or stretch. She just breathed as she pictured her stomach as a calm pond.

It didn't work.

Cleaning the hall, and then showering, toned down her

excitement, and warmed up the muscles. It all had rudely reminded her of her age not being half of what reality was.

She stepped into the empty kitchen. The coffeepot was half-full. As she watched, the small red light winked out. It had been on for two hours. *Just strong enough.*

The soft, distant sound of metal, clanging on metal, jerked her around. There was nothing there. She looked through the window at the barn. Nothing. More soft clatter.

She grabbed her coffee and the last two pieces of cold bacon —passing one to Pink. Chewing, she pushed her way through the screen door. "Dot?"

The only reply was more metal dragging over other metal. Jolie had forgotten about the metal heap around the side of the barn. Everything broken but metal got thrown on the heap. Eventually, there would be a use for it.

There never was. But it sounded good. And every other farmer, rancher, or hoarder would tell you the same lie.

Jolie rounded the corner of the barn as a steel wheel to an old wheelbarrow flew through the air and landed to one side of her. Jolie jumped and then felt embarrassed but playful.

"You missed."

"I threw it backhanded."

"Don't make excuses for a shitty aim." She was wondering if she would ever get used to the line Dot had been grinding into her for bad hits.

The woman came around the pile with some metal stakes in her hands. "Did you know you have a complete blacksmithy here?" She held up the metal stakes. "And mo metal I can pound in a year."

Jolie frowned. "I remember Dad beating out some stuff, but usually the farrier would have their own stuff. This shit hasn't been stirred up in at least thirty years. What would you even do with this stuff? I mean…" She waved her hand at the pile as she took a sip of coffee. "It's just junk."

Dot reached over and grabbed a square rod of metal leaning against the barn. By how she held it, Jolie could tell it wasn't light. "Come here." She walked toward the front of the barn. Jolie shrugged, rolled her eyes, and followed.

Standing in front of the large doors, Dot stuck the end of the rod against the giant hinge. There were five on each door. They were as wide as two hands held together, and overall, they stretched as long as either of the women's height.

"These hinges be forged from a rod like this. This be iron or ductile steel. The hinges were forged into shape and annealed so's they never be brittle. They strength is they mass and workin' in a team. The blacksmith heated them red-hot den throwed them in a barrel of oil. The oil penetrates like liniment. It always be there, cuz it stop it fro' rustin'. You never oil this, do you?"

Jolie thought and then shook her head with her face in the mug. She swallowed. "I don't remember my dad or mother ever oiling it, either. How could you tell?"

Dot smiled and reached out. She grabbed and swung the giant door open. The team of hinges groaned, but there was no squeal of rust. "Oil catch dirt and dust. It grind in and make way to rust. This don't rust."

Jolie swung the door back closed and looked closely at the hinge. "I just always thought the black was paint someone painted on careful like, not to get it on the wood. I never thought about it."

She stepped back and looked at the two huge doors. "You know, Dot, I never thought about it, but this is the only barn I know with doors that swing out. Everyone else… they just slide to one side."

Dot snorted. "Dats because dey don't have dis." She walked over to the wall and pushed on one of the boards. When she pulled her hand back, a section of the wall followed. The door was four boards and battens wide, but the full height to the cross-banding above the large barn doors.

"What the hell?"

Dot looked at Jolie. "You dint know it was here. I find it dis mornin'."

"No. What is it?" She frowned. "I mean, I know it's a door, but why?"

"Ever have big storms here?"

"Sure."

"High winds so bad if'n you open dat big sail it get blowed to the next county?"

Jolie snorted and shook her head. "Don't open the big one, just the small one. Smart. But where are the hinges?"

Dot tapped at the edge of the one batten. "They're hidden inside." She ran her finger along the back beveled board. "I noticed this. Only one reason for dis board be like dat." She swung the door open until it stopped. It was open enough for a man to walk through, but not wide open. The five hinges wrapped around a support beam and then along the interior wall.

She beamed. "The catch and lock be some fancy smithy work. You push to release. But you have to push here." She showed Jolie where on the board. The board had some movement where it thinned to flex and trigger the latch. "Dis way, no wind open yo' door."

"But what if the wind is coming from here? It's still going to blow the door open."

Dot smiled and walked to the other side of the barn. Looking, she finally found what she was looking for. She pushed. Nothing. She pushed again. Still nothing. She looked at Jolie and held up one finger.

She disappeared in the large door.

A moment later, the side of the barn opened. Dot strolled out, smiling. "It were locked." She showed Jolie the ingenious wooden and wrought iron lock.

Jolie rolled her eyes. "I need more coffee. And some breakfast."

"You ate da last bacon. And dose eggs…? Tweren't no good no mo'. What do the fridge need fo' it ta work?"

Jolie thought. The bank account was low. She pulled the phone out of her hip pocket and looked at it.

Dot snorted. "There no cell service near the barn. I've tried. You gots ta be over to the drive." She pointed at the last turn of the long driveway as it turned into the barnyard or wagon yard if you were driving a wagon.

There was no front yard. Jolie had grown up in a world of dogs on the large porch. But when you stepped down the two stairs, you were in work territory. The barn to your left, corral straight ahead, or the road to the highway to the right. Muck stalls, work the horses, or go hunting for food.

She looked up at the grime-smeared smiling face. Jolie smirked as her thumb moved the satellite antenna into the call mode. The blank screen flashed into a small dish pointed at the sky. She found the number and tapped it with the side of her thumb.

Dot's eyes lit up. She mouthed as much as whispered, "I needs one of dem."

Jolie smiled. "Mike, good morning."

"What's wrong?"

She frowned one eye at Dot. "Why would there be anything wrong?"

"Because you're using a cell phone."

Jolie laughed. "I'm a modern woman now, Mike. In fact, I'm so modern. I need a refrigerator. This icebox thing isn't working for me… or the eggs."

The laugh rumbled through the phone. "Seven months and you give up? That's not the Rocket I knew. You just need some chickens."

"Mike, I need a real fridge."

Dot poked her arm. "And a stove if'n he buyin'" She smiled a full necklace of pearls.

Jolie chuckled. "Dot says the stove doesn't work either. And the shower this morning was cold."

"Anything else you two princesses need?"

The sound of the large black car turning into the wagon yard caught their attention. Jolie wasn't sure if the laughter was coming from the cell phone or the car. She closed the antenna and punched the off button.

Sliding the phone into her hip pocket, the two women approached the car. "Now this is what I call service, Mike. We need breakfast, and here you are."

The man looked at the bare feet, torn jeans, and dirt smudged tank top, and then looked at the dirt smears on Dot with a smile. "Oh yes, I can see now how ready you two are to be taken to breakfast."

Dot's smile closed as she pushed at her lopsided afro. "Let me run a comb through my hair and pull on a fresh shirt." She raised her arm to her nose. She flinched at her nose, and the smile returned. "Oh, yeah. Fresh cut roses."

ONLY THE MUGS OF COFFEE REMAINED OF THE LARGE BRUNCH. The thin folder lay between Mike and Jolie. Dot leaned against her shoulder and watched.

Mike tapped the drawing. "The sign should be ready in a couple of days. We'll have a crew install it."

Jolie looked up. "How big is it?"

He spun the paper around and looked for the ledger of details. He turned it around with his finger on the numbers. "Twenty-feet wide and eight high at the least."

Dot pointed at the large black European boar. "I likes the pig."

Jolie nudged back. "It's a wild European boar."

"What the dif?"

Jolie looked at Mike. The two smiled. "Taste." Jolie thought and then continued. "If both a farm pig and a wild boar weigh five hundred pounds, the fat on the farm hog will be almost three times that of the boar. The meat is so lean you need to add fat to it if you're grinding for hamburgers or sausage."

The blacksmith flinched and screwed up her face. The diet of a fighter doesn't run to eating fat. "What kind of fat?"

Jolie laughed. "Usually from a farm hog or cow. But the taste of boar meat is like a cross between a farm hog and beef but with a nutty flavor. The best to do with a boar is to make jerky and sausage. It's what you add to the sausage that influences how it tastes. Add ground nuts like walnuts or filberts, and you get more of the boar flavor. Wimp out and use peanuts or sunflower seed, you get the shit they make in L.A. and New York."

"So what kind are you going to make on your wild boar farm?"

Jolie's eyes danced. "We're not. There is no way we could ever get a health permit for all the pollution a hog farm produces. And I don't want to piss off the neighbors."

Dot pointed. "Then what is the sign for?"

Mike slow blinked as his head fell to one side. His smile was soft and malicious. "Same reason we're going to cut down about two hundred trees. She's initiating her plans to improve the land."

Jolie sipped on her mug as she eyed the man. "You're sure those loggers are willing to pay me to take all the logs and stumps and everything away?"

"If they could have just taken the logs, and left everything else in slash piles and stumps, they would have paid you more than double. But what we have contracted them for is a clean harvest. They take the logs and then come chip the limbs and trash in place. And then they throw the chip into the remaining forest, and it becomes compost. Then they bring in a big track hoe with a thumb and pluck the stumps out of the ground. There is a company up near Slow Town who water blasts them down and sells them to artists who make sculptures and furniture out of them. Everything is used. To get the trucks up the ridge to the stumps, they will run a cat up there and cut a basic road. We'll decorate the road they cut with survey markers with blue ribbons, just like the layout for the barns and cess-ponds."

"And I don't have to pay for any of this?"

Mike leaned back with his mug in his hand. The self-satisfied smirk was everything. "Nope. It's all part of us preserving the land in your best interests."

"And you talked to Big Red…"

"He's seventeen shades of pissed. There is nothing on their books about making a move on your property. Whoever it is in his company, it's not with his okay."

"And you trust him?"

He nodded. "Red and I go way back. We've locked horns enough on projects to have each other's respect. If he says it's not him—it's not him. But he is going to nose around and find out who it is." He tapped the drawing. "At least, this overt staking of a claim will put a stop to the hostile takeover."

Jolie closed the folder and rested her hand on it. Her eyes danced from her hand to the items on the table. Finally, she looked up. "It sounds good. But you could have just called. Don't you work on Wednesdays?"

"And miss a chance to get out of the city, show you these fine drawings, and come visit the ridge?"

Jolie smiled. "Is the road they are going to cut work for you as a driveway?"

He laughed. "It just might. It would need to have a foot or so of six-inch rocks mashed in, then number-two-minus, and finished with gravel, or something laid down, but it just might. Are you willing to be my landlady?"

"It depends. We have a list of appliances we need you to bend your credit card around."

Dot wiggled her eyebrows. "I need a few hundred pounds of anthracite coal, too."

"You can't cook with coal."

"No, but I can beat out a better barbecue with it."

The man stood. "Well, then. Ladies, let's go shopping."

As they walked through the door onto the street, Mike frowned at Dot. "Where do you get coal in California?"

Dot snorted. "Some ranch boy you turned out to be. At the feed store."

Jolie nudged his shoulder with hers. "The farriers buy it. Most use gas now, but there are enough left to stock coal. It burns hotter."

The two women shoulder checked each of his shoulders as they walked out of the door. If he hadn't felt put in his place by women before, the shoulder push of the large dog at his hip put him in his place.

He shook his head and smiled as he followed them to the car.

2 6

GRIP

How you hold a rope, reins, or a mane
determines how long you hold on.

The sign was new but painted to look like years of neglect and weather. The snaps and splinters of the posts looked like they were several years old. They had been confiscated from another property where the sign had supported an unsuccessful candidate for the state senate. The name had already passed into obscurity unless you were interested in a used Datsun truck or a newer Toyota Helix. Both were tough sells in cowboy country where one-tons with dual wheels and pregnant wheel-wells ruled their bloated way in the shopping malls of those who had money to blow.

The sign lay half propped with a crack splitting the black boar. A sifting of dust and dirt overall would make any logical person forgiving of a surveyor who happened to miss the sign the first nine times they had taken the turn off the highway onto the back road, and then turned on an even smaller lane. After all, it was just more garbage on the landscape.

Jolie and Dot sat in the truck admiring the skill of the team in the night. Mike hired the foursome from a special effects lab, who usually did sets and movable props for movies. They had spent over a month making the collected silt and dust cling to the broken sign, but ebb away with character tide lines to mark the years of summer bake and winter erosion. No matter how you viewed the sign, it was a masterpiece.

Jolie turned and smiled at Dot. Dot licked her thumb and reached out to clean a smudge on the woman's cheek. "Lord, we dress you up and still can't take you anywhere."

Jolie stomped her left foot on the truck floor as her right hand waved in the air. Pink's head followed the unexplained move-ment. "Fuck I hate automatics. It's just not driving." She glow-ered at Dot and bent forward to look at Pink. "You think your mommy is funny. Wait until we get back into my real truck." She got a wet tongue from chin to nose. With a right cross across the eyes. She wiped her face on her sleeve. She looked over at where the snort came from. "What?"

Dot lowered her eyes in a roll. "You don't fool nobody. You been walkin' around wid no rag on yo arm fo' five days. Who you foolin'?"

Jolie mashed on the brake and pulled the selector down. "Doctor released me from the sling."

Dot laughed and clapped and then waved her hands in the air with revival. "Hallelujah, we's got us a miracle. She done be healed. Praise o' praise…" She stopped and looked over. "You got any religion?"

Jolie nosed the truck up onto the rough plowed road. "The church of Santa Ynez, with the holy saints of pig, horse, and Holy Spirit of Winchester." She glanced over at the solemn face.

Dot sprang back into her fervor. "Bless us O' Great Pig for

we be horsed around and may be shot for our divine effort." The two laughed until they pulled up near the large track hoe.

The large arm hovered over the long dump truck. The claw opened, and the stump dropped into the bed—roots and all. The whole pivoted on the large track body. The arm lowered and reached out. The stump in the ground was only about two feet tall, but the bucket pushed on the top six inches until the roots ripped up out of the ground. The bucket reached out and encompassed the roots, and then a large thumb rotated and grasped the stump. Seconds later, the stump was also in the bed of the truck.

Jolie's eyes were large as her face tipped back into her chin and neck. "Well, he made short work of that stump."

Dot's exhale was just as impressed. "No shit." Her chest shook as a smirk cocked up the side of her face. "I think I'm in love."

Jolie, without looking, jabbed at the thick hard shoulder. "No shit. It brings a whole new meaning to a pick-up line."

"But can you drive it to a bar?"

The giggles filled the cab as Pink just sat watching the track hoe feed stumps into the back of the truck.

The large arm curled the bucket and rested it on the ground. The diesel engine shuttered to a stop. The operator stepped out onto the track. Two sets of lungs inhaled as he stretched his arms behind his head. The uncovered muscles bulged and rippled in all the right places.

Dot shuttered as the air slipped between her clenched teeth. "Oh, sweet little baby in the manger."

Jolie slumped down and watched between the top of the steering wheel and the bottom of her wide-brimmed hat. "I don't think his body has anything to do with a sweet little baby... but a wild romp through the hayloft would do."

Pink looked at one woman and then the other. She was

getting all the right signals for a bit of throwing a ball around, but nobody was moving.

The man jumped down. Nothing jiggled. His walk was slow and leisurely. His thumbs hooked in his front pockets. Jolie noticed the boots first.

"Fuck. False alarm."

Dot took a fast glance. "What? What you mean, girl?"

"His boots. Their Red Wing or Danner. He's a dirt pounder."

Dot watched, and as he got close, she too slumped. "His finger. He's sportin' a noose." The thin gold band was easy to miss.

Jolie leaned in the window. "Howdy."

"Afternoon. Can I help you ladies?"

Jolie pushed her lower lip out a bit. "We were just checking on how the work was coming. How much longer on the stumps?"

He waved his hand through the air toward the next hump of hill. "There's about a hundred or so over on the next ridge. So, I should have it done in about two more loads. I've been piling them down on the south wash so I don't have to haul them far. It easier for the carvers to get their trucks in. So we told them they could come pick them up there. Most of all, this should be gone by spring. They carve during the winter and sell all summer. The piles will sit until just after New Years and then evaporate. Most of them will come once it's too dark to carve. They work outside, and lights cost money."

Jolie rubbed her chin like she was an old hand at all this logging stuff. "What about all those holes. I have livestock I need to run in here."

The man slicked back his sweaty hair. His muscles didn't come from driving equipment, but he knew what effect they had. "My brother will be coming down from Slow Town with a power rake, and when he's finished, you'll never know there had been any trees up here."

Jolie leaned forward and started the truck. "Good job... um...?"

"Zack." He stuck his hand out. "Zack Turner."

Jolie shook and smiled. "Thanks, Zack Turner. It looks like this is going to work out great."

The man looked down but waved friendly as Jolie backed up and turned around. The two women waited for almost a quarter mile before laughing.

"That man thought he was going to get lucky and have 'piece' on earth."

Jolie held up two fingers. The two laughed even harder. Dot smoothed her hands over Pink's ears. "Don't listen, Pink. The mommas be getting nasty."

THE COALS WERE JUST ABOUT RIGHT AS JOLIE PEEKED OVER THE lip of the large half drum of a barbecue Dot had made.

"Mike, the sign really does look like it got knocked down years ago. They did a great job."

His voice wavered as she pulled the top off the steaks. "I have the check already from the loggers. It seems there is a boutique miller up in Atascadero who paid more for the clean logs of the oak and Calero walnut. The eucalyptus went for the same rate as longboard oak. So, all in all, the logging will pay for all the work. Monday, I'll have a crew go pound some stakes in to mark off the road and hog farm."

"Make sure they stake out the site for your retirement house and the Olympic swimming pool."

"I thought I was getting a wave pool."

Jolie placed the large steaks on the grill. "Sugarfoot, you can have anything you want on the damn hill. Just keep the city grubs at bay."

"I'll swing out when the survey crew is there."

"Steaks are in the freezer, and they only take ten minutes to defrost in the microwave."

"You do know how to sweet talk a man. We'll see you in a few days."

She thumbed the phone off and then held her thumb on the screen. The phone redialed the first number in the row—111.

"Steaks are ready in ten."

She slipped the phone into her back pocket. Then the large triangle adorned with wrought iron grape leaves. The tone was quieter and deeper than most, but the result of calling people to dinner was the same.

Pink raced around the corner of the barn. Dot stopped and hung her large leather apron on a hook she had made for the corner of the barn.

Jolie watched the two. It was going to be quiet without Dot in a few days. The woman needed to get back to work. Work with a payday attached to it. Which reminded Jolie of the horses she needed to work out.

"I LIKE THE MUD SCRAPER AND BOOT PULLER." PUNCHY CROSSED his legs over the new beaten metal ottomans for the Adirondack chairs. Jolie noticed he also didn't mention he lived in an apartment on the second floor and didn't wear cowboy boots anymore because of the pins and rods in his feet and ankles. His uniform lace-up boots had a zipper laced into the front, same as most other professions who need to put boots on quickly.

Dot raised her beer in the firelight. "Glad to do some good."

The fire in the middle of the barnyard had transitioned from survey stakes to oak and eucalyptus limbs from the logging. Not knowing any better, the loggers took pity on the single woman struggling on her own and not only cleaned up the limbs but cut them to size, delivered, and stacked eight cords of wood. Not once did anyone mention the lack of a chimney on the cabin. Some had used her bathroom, but none notice the lack of a fireplace. Jolie knew where the fireplace had once been, but she had never seen it. Her father removed it shortly after he returned from the war. Houses burning had left him with nightmares. He opted for the safer oil furnace.

Jolie thought about the wrought iron repairs Dot had been pounding out every day. A hinge here, a gate lock there, and the extra decorative pieces. Jolie helped where she could, but Dot was like a child in a candy store. Dot's only break was going to watch Jolie work with one of a few horses. With Golly and Dolly, she was drawn in by Tonisha and a few carrots. Jolie had never thought about someone growing up having never pet anything larger than a dog. And for Dot, even those had been few and far between.

Jolie rolled her head over and watched Pink cuddled into a ball in Dot's crossed legs. The dark head, with its tiny sliver of pink, resting on Dot's arm and armrest—pointed at Jolie. The smile pulled back on the warmer side of Jolie's face. She was sure the dog would be at full attention with any unusual noise.

"She likes you."

Dot chuffed. "I guess I'm easier than I thought."

"You know, you can always move in permanently. You've got the forge and anvils. You can bring up your shop, and we can make any shop space you want in the barn."

"I do like it here. But there be Momma…"

Jolie rolled her head back to watch the fire. "There is that. I just thought I'd offer. It's been good having you around. It gives me someone to beat up on besides Punchy." The man snorted and smiled.

"When I call Momma, she's been clingy an' such. Axe when I be comin' back 'n all."

Jolie sighed. "Yeah, Pansy struck me as being frail and defenseless. The bartender is probably taking advantage of her."

"Don't you be bad-mouthing Princess. He may be scrawny, but he be wiry. And he do keep Momma in line."

2 7

FROG

The soft area inside the hoof nail. Sometimes called the 'second heart.' As the hoof lands on the ground, the frog pumps the blood back up the legs. The frog also provided stability.

The transfer bus stopped across from the front gate. The sun was only half up over the east hills. For most, the morning had begun only an hour or two before—in the dark. For some in the bus, the day started the day before.

Jolie sat still as she watched out the dirty window. Her hand gripped in and out of Pink's short fur under the service vest Mike and Jinx had gotten her. Jolie knew the prison wouldn't let her in with just any dog, but they couldn't deny a service dog.

The paperwork had been daunting until Mike passed it onto the company's lawyers with urging it being important to him—personally. The senior partner suddenly found other business in the city and *just stopped by the prison as a courtesy call.* The two men had come to an understanding with the paperwork approved for continuing visits.

Pink was required to wear the vest, but nobody would try to create agitation about a former inmate visiting with a service dog. As Jolie saw it, they were the root of her PTSD or angst.

"Your dog must be one of them PSD dogs."

Jolie looked over Pink's head at the woman in the seat across the bus. "It's PTSD. There is a "T" in there. And yes… yes, she is. She saved my life."

The woman tugged at her thin cardigan. Jolie could see it was more of a nervous tick than about any cool weather. The fabric was worn as thin as the woman's liver spots were dark. The thin gold wedding band hung loosely between the hand and knuckle. The woman was a mother or grandmother who clung to the last vestiges of what she had loved and believed still existed somewhere in the person she was visiting.

"Well, she loves you very much. I could see by the way she climbed up as the bus turned off the highway. She knew. And you're not alone. I won't sleep good for a week. This place is as hard on us as on our loved ones."

Jolie slowly rubbed Pink's ear and head as she hugged it into her throat and chest. "Daughter?"

The woman sadly shook her head. "Lost her to the drugs a few years back. This is my granddaughter." She drew in her breath slowly. "She was following in her mother's footsteps."

The woman stood as it was her turn to get off.

Jolie grabbed her bags and slid out. "I hope she learns there are better ways."

The woman looked back. "She has fifteen to twenty years to think about it."

They stepped down. Jolie watched the guard walk with his rifle across the dry bridge over the front gate.

As they started across the street with the escorts, Jolie rested her free hand on the woman's shoulder. "Don't ever stop visiting. It's the only thing an inmate looks forward to with their heart."

The woman's eyes were wet as she looked over. "Thank you.

That means a lot to hear." Her voice caught. "You… you were in… here… weren't you?"

Jolie nodded. "I'm here to see my former cellmate. She's in for life…"

The two women understood what drove each other. The bond brought a thin smile to both.

THE BELL HORN WAS AN ANGRY TEAR IN THE EARLY MORNING. THE gate rolled back to both sides as the visitors sluggishly moved into the salle port between the gates. They had been on the first of many transfer buses to come during any day. Only the new or stupid sleep in and take a later bus. The visiting hours might go until five at night, with the last transfer bus arriving at two in the hot afternoon. Some in the last bus would never make it into the building. Or if they did, the bell would sound before they had reached the strip-search room—only to be turned around and told to come back another day. There was rarely any compassion for visitors.

Prisoners and their visitors came from all walks of life. There was no defining culture, color, or status controlling a person's life outcome. You could be a high-powered lawyer or judge, and for some twist of fate, have your name changed to a row of six numbers. Jolie had met a judge, lawyers, a doctor, and a second-grade teacher who had anger issues about her husband. All had stepped over a line and ended with a change of address and name. Some only for a year or two, and others, like Mary, for a long sentence. All of them got treated like the lowest scum of the earth—prisoners and their visitors alike. Any relative or friend who came back time after time had Jolie's respect.

Jolie lined up near the yellow line. Nobody stood within two inches of the yellow paint. To have your toe touch the yellow paint was to be screamed at by the guard with the worst case of halitosis. Jolie had watched young men wet themselves being screamed at by a larger guard. No matter how big or tall a visitor was, they could find a guard who was larger and more intimidating to scream at you for an hour. The worst thing a visitor could do was glance at the other visitors whose names were called and directed into processing. Those were replaced by those on the next bus, who were similarly replaced by the next. When the guard grew tired of screaming at the offender, they were shuffled to the back of the last busload.

"Rocket."

She looked down the hall. The two guards who had stopped her and Pink flinched and squinted down the hall. The last person they wanted to interfere with them harassing a former inmate was their boss.

The warden slowed to a halt. He looked placidly at the guards. "Are we done here?"

The two mumbled their affirmatives and moved on to the next poor soul. Their day was filled with the entertaining action of creating hell for someone.

The warden watched for a moment and then turned his attention on Jolie. "Is the dog helping?"

Jolie's eyes bobbed shut as she nodded. "They're trying to get me into therapy as well. We'll see." She held the two shopping bags out. He looked at the one that was double-bagged. His smile twitched big. "I know you haven't gone out pig hunting…"

"I was up in Montana picking up Pink here. We had time to kill, and the elk on my uncle's ranch needed some thinning."

"You know you're not allowed to use a firearm…"

She shrugged her left shoulder. "If you want to take me to the strip-search, I can show you the nine-inches of surgery scars where they put my shoulder and arm back together. I was watching them butcher. It was the men who did the hunting. I have a half ton of elk meat in my meat locker in Buellton. These steaks are just a taste and a thank you for your work on okaying Pink."

The man was in a tough spot. He didn't want to show favoritism for a former inmate, but they also had known each other for a long time. "I'll spread these around with a few of my men. About the contents of a meat locker, well, maybe some barbecue could be arranged." He nodded toward the other bag.

"The usual. I brought her a few cartons of smokes, a new toothbrush, some more writing paper, and some photos of Pink and me up in Montana. She never had anything on her wall except a photo of the seashore. I don't think she had any family… at least nobody visited her."

He took the bags and turned. "Come on."

He walked them into his outer office and placed the bags on the officer's desk. "Arturo, put these in the freezer and have this all processed for C312."

The officer stood and silently nodded as he took up the bags.

The tall warden watched the door the man had left through. He looked back at the desk and then turned toward Jolie. "You know you still have to go through the process."

Jolie nodded. "And because of Pink, it has to be a separated visit." She nodded. "I'm good with it. I've never been separated from her since we bonded. So I know I can't leave her anywhere, but at least Mary can see her."

He looked up at the clock as it ticked a few minutes past seven. "Let's see if we can get you in to see her so she doesn't miss lunch."

True to his word. Jolie sat down just before eleven.

Mary sat down on the other side of the thick Armor-plex glass. They picked up the phones together.

"Jesus peas and carrots for lunch, you are so tan."

Jolie laughed. They both knew that if there wasn't a third-party listening, their conversation would always be recorded.

They fell back to their easy talk in the safety of their closed cell. "I missed you too, sweetheart."

The slightly older woman laughed. "I thought you might bring yo—" Pink's paws, shoulders, and head appeared. "HOLY SHIT! What is that? Your horse?"

"Mary, meet my savior Pink." She grabbed at the large head and ears and leaned in for a smooch. "She's a Cane Corso. Most people pin the ears and bob the tail to make them look mean. But Pink is my lover… until I give the command. Uncle Jinx took us down to the police training grounds where he helps. Pink took down the bad guy faster than the other dogs. She was even faster than her big brother, Chewie."

"She's gorgeous. The black is kind of blue, and she looks more like a cross between a panther and a rottweiler." The woman sighed. "I wish I could pet her. She looks so soft and sleek."

Jolie watched the woman she had shared seventy-square-feet with for seven years. By the fifth year, they had regretted not trusting the other from the first day. Mary was one of the few in the prison who believed she was innocent. Jolie was sure Jeb was the other on her team.

"You might get a chance."

The woman's face locked into hard and her attention snapped over to Jolie's face. "Don't fuck with me, girl. There are shivs outside these walls."

Jolie held her hand up. She didn't know if Mary actually had any juice outside the wall or not, but it didn't matter. "Listen, girlfriend. I was watching a couple of articles about inmates raising up dogs and training them to be service dogs. Most are like Pink—PTSD dogs. But they are raising all sorts of service dogs. One made me think of you. They had a beagle trained to warn a diabetic when they needed their insulin." She shied her face and smiled with her raised eyebrows.

"A diabetic dog?" The face softened.

Jolie nodded. "The reporter was saying they were rare because the trainer needed to be a diabetic to teach the dog the triggers. Mary, you're only fifty-six. You have many dogs ahead of you. The best part is they must stay with the trainers all the time, so you'd get the bottom bunk and a warm water bottle for the winter."

The woman closed her eyes and sighed. "I'm seventy-one, but I'm not going to sleep a wink for days now. Just the thought gives me the little girls."

Jolie snickered at their term for excitement. She had forgotten how old the woman was.

Mary pointed at Jolie's shoulder. "How's the wing doing?"

"While I was recovering in Montana, we flew my friend Dot up. She used to fight in what's called mixed martial arts."

"Yeah, there are a couple in here now. One is kind of small, but the Ogre and her crew jumped her in the showers."

Jolie snorted. "I've watched some of the matches with Dot. Who walked out of the showers?"

"Nobody… but the fighter at least crawled out to the door. Ogre is up in Vacaville now, so they can accommodate her in her wheelchair and maybe teach her how to talk again. But two of the crew weren't so lucky."

"What about the fighter?"

"She had drawn three-to-five, but now it's looking like she'll be in my class when they let her out of solitary in a year. So, your arm?"

Jolie rotated her left arm. It stopped short of the usual straight up. "This is all I get over the top. There's about as much steel in me as a Colt 45. If it hadn't been for Dot and Pink here, I would have a frozen joint and almost no range of motion. As it is, I'm back to training horses, and it only aches when I do a long day, or the fog hangs in for the whole day."

"What about the person who drilled you? Oh, and I got your Christmas card. Thanks for the pictures. Your uncle looks sweet.

My dad's brothers were angry-mean stevedores who would rather beat on you."

"I think I know who one is, but I'm still looking for the other. Look, we're running out of time. I gave the warden a bag of stuff. I think you should get most of it. There're six cartons of smokes, three unfiltered and three reds to trade. I threw in a few approved toothbrushes because I know how rough you are on them. There's a six-pack of soap. Don't get all mushy on me—I get this shit at the dollar store. Busting broncs doesn't pay for shit, and I have bills to pay—but I did stick a couple of hundred on your book for anything else you might need or want from the commissary."

"Did you throw in some whiskey and condoms too?"

"Yeah, there's a couple of half-gallons of rotgut bourbon and a hundred-count roll or so of condoms. I didn't count; there were a few blackout Saturday nights between now and when I bought them."

Mary laughed. "Are you getting laid?"

Jolie rolled her head to one side and smiled softly. "Actually, I am."

"Fuck you." The woman laughed lightly and then sobered. "Seriously?"

"He's a deputy sheriff, but I knew him years ago when I was doing rodeo. He was a clown."

"You're fucking a clown? Doesn't it feel funny? I mean... those big shoes and all..."

"Not that kind of clown, you ass. But a rodeo kind of clown. They jump in and out of barrels in the arena and save cowboy's lives. He was also a roper. He did team roping. Not really pro-grade, but he had fun. At least he didn't get all fucked up from the roping."

Mary looked out the side of her one eye. "But he's broken up?"

Jolie raised the eyebrow over her closed lid. "He still passed the physical for the sheriffs."

"So something works."

The angry buzzer rang. Jolie flinched, and then half smiled at the old response. "Everything that's important works just fine."

"His heart?"

"The best part."

The two hung up as the communication was shut off. They stuck their hands flat on the glass. Pink reached out and pawed at the glass. Mary laughed, but Jolie knew her heart was aching.

NOSE HOOK

*In calf roping, when the lasso doesn't make it all the way over the head,
but only catches the nose. The usual result is flipping the calf over
backward and losing the catch.*

olie stood next to Pink. The pink tongue was busy licking a nose the size of her face. Molly stood nearby as Golly got the first nose grooming. It had become their reward for their day of training. Both had spent alternating hours on the longe line.

It had become a game with them, more than Jolie had expected. Once the usual carrots were consumed, they would hip pressure the other to be the first to get the blanket saddle. The original blankets became the game of pulling the other's blanket off while Jolie was hooking up their hackamore to the longe line. The idea being, if the blanket falls off, then the other horse gets to play at the end of the longe line. The fact of them not wearing a blanket never stopped the game, either.

When Jolie first ran the straps under their bellies and cinched the strap, there was some irritation. But the moment they realized the other couldn't pull the blanket off, they were vying for which one got the saddle blanket first.

Then there was the game of Jolie on one side putting the blanket on and the other mischievous mustang on the other side pulling the pad off before the strap was secured. They quickly learned how fast Jolie could be to throw the blanket on and then pass under the belly and pop-up on the other side in the face of a playful mustang. Soon, they became used to the activity under their bellies. It was part of getting their blanket strapped on, and defending them getting a blanket.

While it was still cool, she let them both wear the covers. It got them used to having something on them for longer and longer periods. For them, it meant playtime with Jolie and Pink. All too soon, it would mean a saddle and then a rider. She hoped they would see the progression as just another fun game.

She thought about her first rodeo horse, Launchpad. The horse would grab his tack or saddle blanket from the barn rails, and find Jolie wherever she was mucking, raking, shoveling, sweeping, or lying in fresh hay. The horse would throw the tack at her feet or lay the blanket over her. Often, she would grab his mane and tail to pull on as she jumped up to place her belly over his back. By the time she had turned herself around to sit up, the horse was out of the barn for a fast ride down the road or up into the forest. It was always his choice. He had free-range of the barn, barnyard, or even to just run away. His stall and the barn door were always open. The habit or lack of containment had started when she was in high school, and they had spent so much time together training, competing, and the horse following her around like a dog as she did her chores. The barn had become her juice, the self-indulgence of having her up before dawn. She would start with the stalls of horses awake at the sound of her rummaging the oat bag. When she had cleaned all their stalls, the sleeping horses would be awake and could be moved into the avenue and tied off to the rails or wall.

Launchpad's stall was last near the southern doors—because it could become a ride or a bath. Either one would leave Jolie hungry for breakfast and a shower before school.

"When are you planning on saddles?"

Jolie turned and looked back at the smiling face of the owner. "If you have some light ones, we can put them on now."

Norm stepped over to the electric cart and held up a beginning dressage saddle—barely thicker than a summer quilt for a bed.

Jolie chuckled and waved him in with a warning. "You have to have two, or you're showing favoritism."

He grabbed the second as the gate swung out. He placed them on the top rail and closed the gate. He kept Pink on the other side of Jolie. It wasn't a trust issue with Pink; it was because he didn't trust dogs since he was a kid. The bite mark on his left forearm was a large pink comet where the tooth had entered and then tore his arm as his father pulled the dog off.

He dropped the saddles. Jolie looked down with disdain. "Fuck you, groom. They're your horses. You put them on."

"They don't know me."

"Did you bring any carrots?"

He rolled his eyes big as he turned back to the gate. Muttering, he kicked at the dirt. "Fucking princesses."

Jolie tipped her head and watched out of the side of her eye. The man was wearing his old block-toed groomsman boots. The shadow from her hat covered her smile. She looked up as Molly shouldered out Golly and the nose licking. They really were princesses.

"What do I do? Just give it to them?" The greens of the carrots draped from his hand. They weren't the smallest carrots, but they weren't the size Jolie or Tonisha would have selected as the reward for the next step in the games.

Jolie's snort fluffed her left cheek. "They're just princesses, not pillow princesses. You need to make them work for it. Stick one in one pocket and the other on the other side. They know better than to try to hog both."

He stood beside Molly as she got her nose cleaned by Pink. The carrot was jammed down in his left front pocket. As he brushed his fingers through the mane, there was only the hint of a shy or flinch. He worked his way down to the blanket.

As he started to adjust the leading edge, Molly broke from Pink's tongue and reached around to grab at the long greens. She had already seen the saddle, and it was probably just another piece of the game. She grabbed most of the greens and pulled up. The carrot popped free of the pocket and two chews later she was eating a carrot with the greens. Only one foot had edged an inch to one side.

Norm gently slung the saddle over the mustang's back. He was hyperaware of it being the first of any real weight on the horse. The hide over the front shoulder shuddered, but the horse stayed in place. He adjusted the seat of the saddle and waited.

Jolie snorted. "If you wait too long, Golly will reach over and pull it off her. You need to be quick when tacking them up."

Norm glanced over at Jolie and then back as he felt the saddle disappear from under his hand. "Hey." The man laughed. "You little sneak." He turned. "Now what?"

Jolie pointed. "Reach underneath and pick it up."

"Under a horse?" His eyes were full of fear. He knew she was setting him up to be stomped to death.

Jolie stepped over and gave him a stone eye. "Pussy."

She bent over and stepped under the horse. Reaching, she grabbed the saddle. In one move, she stood and placed it on Molly's back. Stooping, she reached under and grabbed the girth belt. She brought it up and cinched it.

Jolie turned and gave Norm a stone look. "Now do the same with Golly."

Two minutes and both stood with saddles on. No muss, no fuss, just two carrots.

Norm stood stroking the neck of Golly as she chewed the last of the carrot. "I never would have believed it. You sure you haven't put any kind of saddle on them before?"

Jolie shrugged and rolled her lips. "Nope. And to be honest, I had no idea how they would respond. To you or the saddles."

"Shit. You set me up?"

Jolie laughed as she turned her head. "Why, Norm—you done said shit. Next thing we know, I'll be seeing real honest horseshit on them cityfied block toes."

His mouth opened, and then he just laughed softly. He'd been caught.

As they walked to Jolie's truck, their conversation was light on the horse farm. But at the truck, Norm looked around to make sure they were alone.

"How's the deputy?"

Jolie narrowed her eyes. "Why?"

He stuck his hands out flat to her. "Easy there, cowboy. I'm just asking. I've known him since he was Punchy, and I was just a groom of a groom. He's a good man. I'm glad you two found each other. If anything comes up, I'd like to think he'd have your back."

She examined his face for any duplicity. "What about you, Norm? Will you have my back?"

He frowned one cheek into his closed eye. "Where are we headed with this pack team?"

Her eyes caromed over his face as she thought about trust. Their relationship was long but not deeply involved in the trust department, even though he was the only one who was willing to even talk to her when she first got out. Her other training jobs she had only gotten because he made it known she was doing work for him, which included trusting her with the wild mustangs. As she thought about it, she realized he had shown his trust, and it was now her turn.

"There's a shit storm coming. I just want to know who's on my side of the coming divide."

He thought about little tidbits he had been hearing. "Does this have anything to do with Castle Construction?"

"Is that going to be the cut line for you?"

His eyes bounced shut as his chest chuffed softly. They opened with fire. "Castle did work for me. I paid them the heavy fee they levied because I was black and don't pray at their church. But having Big Red do the work has probably brought in most of my higher paying clientele." He kicked at the dirt as he turned to watch one of the workers drive past in a gator. He turned back and leaned in. "But any loyalty? It ended when the last check cleared. I wouldn't trust them with that fucking gator, much less with two of my mustangs. They never earned anything. They just take."

Jolie leaned her head so the sunshine flooded her face. Her features were relaxed but frozen. "Someone is trying to steal my land. Big Red says it's not him... but whoever it is, is driving a Castle truck hauling their gators. When I find out who it is, I won't stop until I find out how high it goes. If it lands at Red's doorstep, so be it."

"Just be careful."

"I already served seven. I've got a PO to talk to every week. Anytime she wants to walk into my house and make my life difficult, she can, and there's nothing I can do about it for another three years. Right now, being out is like being in, except the leash is more like a played-out longe line."

"I'm just saying..."

"And you?"

His nod was slow and measured as his lips curled in and turned hard. "Just so you know, if you draw a line in the sand of this valley between you and Castle, most of the old-timers would be standing on your side. Rodeo runs deep in this valley, but memories also run long. Your father hunted a lot, as did your grandfather. Most of the meat they never ate. It went to the homes of people who couldn't hunt or afford. My father worked in this valley long before we moved here. There was always a relationship between the Thoroughbred and quarter horse people—rodeo and ranchers. He used to tell me stories about your Grandpa Jackson and how he hunted during the great depression. He hunted for hundreds of mouths, and those families… well, I'll bet they never forgot. They don't always live in the big fancy houses, but it doesn't mean they are less powerful."

He looked up the long drive to his front gate.

"Most would probably bend over backward for you because of your family."

Jolie sighed as the useless and unused anxiety adrenaline burned off. She pawed at the truck's door and handle. Her voice was more tired than angry. "Well… twelve of them didn't."

Norm chewed on the corner of his lower lip. He reached out. His hand was light on her shoulder. "Keep looking. I think the state owes you a big apology, which reminds me. The deputy district attorney who prosecuted your case…?"

Jolie looked back with her head tilted and one eye closed. "Yeah…?"

"Rumor has it he's running for district attorney next year."

She turned and faced him, hanging her right hand from the door handle. Her eyes wandered through his belt buckle and searched the ground behind. "Ballsy move. I wonder if anyone from Castle is backing him?" The current DA wasn't old and had been reelected year after year for decades. To challenge him would take balls and a shit cart of money.

"I don't know. But now I'm curious." He smiled as she

climbed into the truck. In a show of their newfound understandings, he reached in hesitantly and scratched the side of Pink's head. "You take care of her, Pink."

Jolie rocked her head as she started the orange truck. "She's got my back."

2 9

HOOEY

*In calf roping, the three legs are brought up and hog-tied with three wraps of
the small rope the rider holds in their mouth. The small rope is called a
"piggin' string." They quickly wind two overlapping wraps, and then one
flipped over to make a half-hitch. The third wrap is called the "hooey." It is
the final wrap that ties it all together: 'two winds and a hooey.'*

Jolie sat with the couple, in the dimmer corner, away
from the sunny window. The only thing behind her
were the two dark paneled walls making the corner.
Pink was curled behind her chair with her hind foot touching
Jolie's. The list of stores she needed supplies from had been
short, but the gathering had taken time. She had spoken to more
people during the morning than in the first six months out of
prison.

The two women, who stopped her at the hardware store, had
horses they rarely rode because they didn't feel right. Jolie
suspected the riders were untrained more than the animals.

A young couple, new to the valley, had asked at the feed store for someone to teach their daughter how to care for a horse and ride. The manager had pointed to the bent over Jolie and large black dog. He told them they wouldn't find a better trainer, even if the daughter wanted to ride rodeo. Jolie wasn't sure she wanted to stand up and face the three people who had been eyeing the backside of her filthy tight jeans, or just pick up the bag of oats and walk away. The former had turned out easier than she had feared.

The couple had asked if they could buy her lunch or at least a coffee. Neither had shied away from Pink. Without thinking, the woman had leaned sideways and run her hand down Pink's head and neck as she talked. It was the most natural move Jolie had seen anyone make toward a dog the size of a small pony. As the woman continued to talk, her hand grabbed and massaged the ear until Pink leaned into her leg and the eyes rolled shut.

Jolie interrupted her with a short snort as she watched Pink's reaction. "What size dog do you have?"

The woman looked down and realized what she had been doing. "Oh." She looked up. "Um… we don't have any dogs. Meg, our daughter, is allergic to dog dander. We've been thinking about something she wouldn't react to, like a Labradoodle. I grew up with large dogs. We always had the largest something nobody else wanted from the pound. My dad was a vet and volunteered at the county shelter. As one dog would start getting older, he would bring home a pup to keep them younger longer. Our house was always full of dog hair… and love."

The woman looked down at Pink. "This one is a lover. What is he, a mastiff mix?"

"She. Her name is Pink for the tip of her tongue she never pulls in. They're an Italian breed called a Cane Corso. The Roman's bred them from dogs trained to kill rats and feral animals from the farm fields. The Corso was bred larger to be war dogs, which is where the term hellhound comes from. They pinned their ears and bobbed the tails."

The woman bent and covered both ears. "Don't listen to those horror stories, Pink. You have beautiful ears just the way you are." She bent and kissed Pink on the muzzle.

Jolie didn't know what horse they had or what their daughter was like, but she knew she would suffer hell for the woman who kissed her dog. Pink agreed with a large tongue wash across the face. The woman didn't even sputter. She was a dog person bred to the bone.

The shy husband rolled his eyes with a smile. "It looks like we need to get some dogs sooner than later. She seems to be going into withdrawals."

The woman stood. "My father's last dog passed away a few months before we moved up here."

Jolie tapped her finger on her thigh. Pink leaned back to her rightful place. "Look, let me go over my list with Herbie there, and we can walk down to the Four Bar Q and talk about your daughter and her horse."

The man started. "I'll go get the laptop out of the car, and we can show you what we've been looking at." He turned to the safety of having something to do.

The woman smiled. "Russel is the sweetest man on earth, but I've never broken him of his shyness. Companies fly him all over the world to look at their factories, and he is bold as brass when it's about his business, but after that…"

"And you moved up here… because…?"

The woman sighed. The conversation was nothing new to her. "San Diego was nice when we were kids. But it has become a nightmare to drive in. Megan, Meg, our daughter, is seventeen going on six. She has Down's Syndrome. We moved to a neighborhood with a school that would accommodate her, but after she turned twelve, she had to attend middle school. Everything changed. They tried to mainstream her with no exceptions. Her grades fell out the bottom, and she came home almost every day crying. We found a special needs school, but it was up near Pow Way and, well, it just wasn't working."

"So, you moved."

"One of her school friends… they moved up here. There is a small charter school structured toward teaching the kids their independence. Russel can work from anywhere, and my job is Meg. So, we dumped San Diego and came up. It took two days for Meg to find out about horses." She rolled her eyes.

Jolie snorted. "Slow learner. I was still in diapers when I fell in love with my first horse. It took years for me to learn it was only my father's burro."

Russel returned with a laptop briefcase hanging from his hand. "Ready?"

Jolie almost blushed. The opportunity to talk had pushed work out of the way. They stopped at the counter. "Herbie, this is my list. Can you have one of the guys throw this in the back of the orange rodeo-ready parked on the side?"

Herbie took the small list and smiled. The top item was two twenty-five-pound bags of horse carrots with their tops on. "Still working on them two mustangs I see."

"We slung saddles on them three days ago. They barely flinched. It's all about your carrots, Herbie."

"Sweet talk won't get you an extra bag, Rocket." He turned and yelled into the warehouse. "Manual. Ven aquí por favor. I need you to load out this stuff for Rocket. Don't make me send her dog."

Jolie laughed. "Still evil after all these years. Thanks. I'll come settle before I leave."

He waved his open-fingered hand. "No need. I know where it's all going. I'll just stick it on Norm's account. Don't tell him and you can pocket the tip. He doesn't pay you enough."

Jolie cocked her hat back on her head. "Herbie, he doesn't pay me at all. I just do it so I can be close to the mustangs. You know how I am around raw wild beasts."

He laughed. "Yeah, I remember that rodeo in Reno…"

As they walked out, Jolie was still laughing, and Marcie was asking about Reno.

When they had finished eating, Russel took over. Jolie could see he was used to explaining with slideshows and all the graphs and things companies like. To Jolie, it was still a dog and pony show, but this one was a young girl and several potential horses.

Jolie finally put her hand on the man's hand before he could click through to the next horse. "Let me ask you something."

The man blinked rapidly—trying to catch up to the shift.

"What do you know the most about?"

"Manufacturing flow dynamics?"

Jolie shuddered dramatically and looked at Marcie. "Let me guess. You asked him out for the first date."

Marcie laughed. "No, it was his mother and my mother. It was the spring prom."

"An arranged blind date?"

"Well, we knew each other in school, but both of us were shy." The woman poked up her lower lip and shrugged with her whole face and head. "But yeah, pretty much."

Jolie turned on the man who was now slightly flushed at the neck. "Did you know how to dance?"

He smiled. "Four years of Arthur Murray."

Marcie shook with a stifled laugh. "He walked all over my new shoes."

Jolie turned on the guy in mock horror. "You cad."

He defended himself by pointing at his wife. "She's the one who threw them into the lake."

"You threw away perfectly good shoes?"

"I was trying to hit him with them."

"Hit him?"

"Well, after he fell into the lake—"

"Where you pushed me," he muttered.

"Where I pushed him." She smiled with self-satisfaction. "He was wandering off to the other side. He wouldn't listen, so I threw my shoe at him to get his attention."

"Did it work?" Jolie was trying not to laugh.

Russel grumped in a mock huff. "No."

Jolie turned. "So you threw the other one too."

"No… I waded out and smacked him on the back of the head."

Jolie wound her face up and looked out the side of her eyes at the woman. "Did that work."

The couple laughed. "I slipped, and my foot kicked his feet out, and we both fell back into the water…"

Russel finished the story. "She fell on top of me, and then kissed me. Then she said, this better not be the way the honeymoon goes."

Jolie's face flew open as she turned on the woman. "Wow. You work fast."

The woman's cheeks and lips fluttered as she chuffed a laugh. "Hardly. The question didn't come for another seven years. We'd been living together for three years, and his watch broke. When we went in to get it fixed and were waiting to see the watch guy, we bent over and looked at rings."

Russel was feeling easier and continued. "The woman came and asked us when the wedding was to be."

Marcie snorted. "Mister Choke here told her June… which was only a month away. So, I figured if we were going to lie, I'd make it bigger. I told her I was pregnant with triplets, so we needed to get married before I showed because my family was strict Hindu."

Jolie looked at the milk-white freckled skin of the redhead. The silence was almost three seconds. "If your daughter isn't as funny as you two, she's fired."

Russel snorted. "Humor is genetic—we get it from our daughter."

Jolie saw a whole different conversation yawning open and

jumped back. "Back to your daughter. I have no idea what you said you do, but let me ask it this way. If your daughter wanted to learn to drive, would you buy her a Porsche or a Volkswagen?"

"Neither, they are stick shifts."

Jolie screwed up her face in a frown. "What does that matter? She's learning to drive. Stick or automatic… she would still have to learn."

Marcie snickered. "But he doesn't know how to drive a stick." At Jolie's look, she held up her hands. "Don't look at me. I'm automatic all the way."

The man frowned. "What does learning to drive a car have to do with buying a horse?"

"Some horses are automatics, but most are stick shift. Some have small, worn-out engines, and others have big race engines. Until you know what she can deal with, why are you looking at the shiny car in the parking lot when she doesn't even know how to drive?"

"How is she going to learn?" He cleared his throat. "I mean, is there a driving school for horses?"

Jolie smiled and turned the laptop toward her. She typed, and when the page loaded, she turned it toward Marcie. "Bring her here. Tell Norm you talked to me."

Marcie smiled at Jolie and then looked up at a few people who caught her eye. The men were a few tables away, but the sunshine was in their eyes if they looked toward the three.

Marcie's voice was low. "Russ, isn't that the guy from the development?"

Russel glanced over for a second or two. Turning back, he nodded and growled softly. "Yeah, the Castle Development asshole."

Jolie leaned her head back and looked. The face was familiar, but she couldn't place it. Suddenly, one of the waitresses dropped a plate and glass. The noise jarred everything, and she was sitting at the end of the bar on a rowdy Friday night. Celeste had been dancing with some old friends but had stopped to talk to the guy at one of the tables. The man had leaned back, and when he reached up and ran his fingers through his hair, Jolie had noticed him missing most of his left index finger. She was going to tease Celeste about dating a three-and-a-half, but Celeste had grabbed her arm and hauled her out of the Roadhouse. Jolie never asked how she knew the guy.

The man sitting in the middle of the small café reached up with his left hand and groomed it through his hair. Most of the finger was missing.

Jolie looked at Marcie. Between women, when it came to men, there was a silent language.

"His name is Tim, Tim Colt… like the gun that tamed the west. His ego is as big as the whole west. He showed us a large development he was putting together. The hills faced south and would be great for solar panels and all. The lots were ten acres and would allow for a barn and corral. Up behind, there were miles of trails for Megan to ride on or walk. We were ready to put down our half-mill, and suddenly, there was a problem. He said he was fixing it, but we haven't heard back since. He doesn't answer his phone and has been a real jerk if we ran into him. So we're looking elsewhere."

"Where was the development?"

Russel cleared his throat. "Out east and kind of south. It had an amazing view of the south end of the valley. He said there was much wildlife roaming the area."

Jolie bobbed her head with a scowl. "Oh, yeah. Much wildlife: deer, large European boars, fox, coyotes, weasels, squir-rel, snakes, raccoons, more snakes, snakes who drive trucks and gators. Yeah, I know the land he showed you. It's not his."

"It's not his?"

"The road you turned on… There was a large red barn down on the right, and just beyond was an old gray, weather-beaten barn leaning over toward the road."

Marcie put her hand on Jolie's arm. "That's right. I remember those barns…"

Jolie growled as she stood. "Come out to Norm's farm, and we'll talk. Bring the girl who isn't so serious as you two. I gotta go."

Russel roped his hanging finger. "I've got this."

"Thanks, because I'm headed out the back."

She held her signature hat low against her legs as she headed for the hall with the bathrooms. Only outside did she put it on. The nudge against her thigh never felt so reassuring. "Well, girl, I think we just found the hooey."

30

MUCK

*Horses can sometimes be 'flow-through digestive units.' 'Mucking out' or
cleaning a horse's stall can produce a heaping wheelbarrow of manure and
urine caked hay: 'muck.'*

"Tim Colt. Just like the pistol."

"Who the hell is Tim Colt?"

Jolie wanted to bang the phone about. "Yeezus, Mike, that's
why I called you. Ask your buddy, Big Dick who he is?"

Mike lifted his legs off the desk and sat up. He was about to
Google the names. "Who's Big Dick?"

"Castle. The big dickhead at Castle Construction or Development, whatever it is. Fuck… did I dial Mike Williams or the
county loony bin?"

Mike's hands froze over the keyboard. He bit his upper lip as
he thought.

"Hello?" The voice was tinny as it came out of the speaker.
"Are you there?"

His eye's shifted sideways. Not seeing the desk, but something he had known or been told years before. "Yeah." His eyes shifted. It was gone. "I'm here, Jolie. Look, let me do some asking around, and I'll call you."

"I've got to go look at some horses, but yeah. Just call me on my cell."

The clink had the metallic sound of a piece of metal being snipped.

***

MIKE REACHED OUT AND PUSHED THE BUTTON TO HANG UP before the dial tone or the obnoxious recording came on. He hated both.

He pushed another button and waited. The buzz at the other end cut short.

"Yeah, Mike?"

"Can you come over? We're moving."

The dead phone line was his answer. The dial tone returned. He thought a moment and dialed from memory.

The voice at the other end of the phone was light, full of sunshine, and professional. Mike loved hearing her voice—the professional was the only part that fit the woman who was almost as old as he was.

"Hi, sweetie, it's Uncle Mike. I need to talk to your jerk brother."

The woman chuckled. "You had better have some ass-reaming gear. He's been having too much fun today. There was a screw-up at the coroner's lab, and a guy who killed his parents, and a pregnant wife is about to get off because of the screw-up. He's in running the branding iron from ass to brainpan on three midlevel lab technicians. If any of them live, it will be a miracle. And how are you this fine morning? I hear the surf is running six-to-ten off Rincon Point."

Mike buried his face in his hand and growled. "I sold my last board and bought a saddle."

"You're so full of shit." The remnants of a young girl listening to her uncle's tall tales about surfing killer waves, wrestling great white sharks, and racing with dolphins on Hawaiian waves brought a chuckle to his heart.

"True story. I've been corrupted by Montana air, the stench of a good horse, and the perfume of mucking stalls. I'm a new man."

The professional in the woman's voice dropped past decorum and bounced in the well of a growl. "Then you better be making plans to get your sorry cowboy ass down here and regale me and my brood of grandkids…" Mike could hear voices, and he waited. "Just a moment, Mike. The paramedics are here to haul off the bodies." The phone snipped and was replaced by slow classical music.

The music ended two minutes later.

"Jerk here."

"Do you still have a hunk of lead in your safe?"

The soft sounds of an empty office carried through the phone. The soft squeak of a chair tipping back was the only distinct sound. The voice was cautious and lower. "Yes…?"

"In your humble opinion, was there enough left to identify the rifle positively?"

"Just a minute."

Mike could hear himself be put on speakerphone. The squeak of the chair was followed by some huffing of bending over and opening a cabinet and safe. His nephew had always mumbled to himself as he worked. The sound came nearer with the sound of a plastic bag.

"Mike, I'm only using my desk magnifying glass, but the lower or back half of the barrel is intact. The striations are very clear. If you have something to match them to, I'd say you would have no problem. Do you want me to call the FBI?"

The surgeon could hear the other man rubbing his face—thinking about what to do. The silence dragged on.

"Hey, Uncle?"

"I'm thinking…"

The younger man leaned back in his chair, now with the handset to his ear. "You know the old saying about knowing someone on the inside or powerful?"

"Yeah, do you know that person… because I sure the hell don't. And I don't know how to proceed with attempted murder from six months ago." His anxiety was edging his voice. "Because if I did, I would have been handling this shit six months ago."

"You did."

"Jesus, Jerk did what?"

"You handled it. You brought the woman to me."

"But you—"

"Saved her arm. Yes. But of all the people between Santa Barbara and San Diego, you brought her to me."

"I knew I could trust you to keep your mouth shut."

The surgeon blew out his lips and took a few breaths. His voice was lower. "Do you still trust me?"

"Of course."

"Then let me be that guy."

"What guy?"

"The one you wished you knew. The one on the inside. The power guy. The one who knew all the right people and procedures. The one who works cases like this every month. That guy."

The surgeon almost chuckled as he thought about the office on the other end of the phone. He could almost feel the surf he knew couldn't be heard but could be watched and felt.

"Mike… are you facing your desk or the surf?"

The voice was soft and quiet. "Desk."

The sound of the big man turning his desk chair around and leaning it back wafted through the phone. Two hundred miles and the surgeon could tell the man's blood pressure had just dropped.

"Keep watching the surf. I have some work to do, and I'll call you in about two hours. I need to drive over to downtown L.A. You gonna be good?"

The grump was soft but resolved. "Yeah. But I'll be on my cell. I think I need to go check on Chuck Finley and make sure her shoulder is doing okay."

"A couple or three hours in case they are at lunch."

The waves were just white meringue froth around the point. Nothing to watch and his eyes slid closed.

HIS BODY WAS HARD-BAKED WALNUT. HIS BAGGIES HUNG FROM the hooks of his pelvic bones, almost breaking the skin. The worn elastic top draped with a smooth gap between the cloth and his flat lower belly. The five-inch scar was almost white on the deep surfer tan. The appendix he lost just before school started when he was ten—long forgotten. Sun seared sand. Continual sets of waves. Bikinis only hidden by five-inch cut-off shorts and tops too small for even their little sister. The smell of wax never washed out of his hands. Grooves cut in his feet by the unending two-dollar huarache sandals bought on Avenida Revolución in Tijuana. Tacos, burritos, hot dogs, or anything eaten while driving and finding the best waves. As the sunshine darkened his skin, the water and sun lighten his hair and eyes. Shades were expensive except for the rich who came to the beach like weekend gulls.

And then he had buried his father. The man who worked from before sun-up and came home tearing his work shirt from his body as he walked up the front walk. He stopped to kiss his wife, grab a beer, and walk out into his heaven. On any given day, until it was too dark to see, Mike could find his father bent over in the garden. The man's tan above his belt was darker than the dining table made from the local black walnut. The doctor had looked at the skin cancer. The islands were like the map of Micronesia or the Land of a Thousand Lakes. The small freckles had long grown past the size of thumbprints when they began to thicken.

The oncologist at UCLA had told him to go home and put his affairs in order. The man put his work shirt back on, kissed his wife as she lay sleeping for three hours more, and walked out to meet the work bus to take him to the docks. The boat ride was only twenty minutes to the oil rig. The deck was always wet. The deck was always chaotic with oil, water, gear...

His personal life insurance would barely bury him and feed his family for a year. Dying on the rig was worth so much more.

The letter to Mike came the day after the men from Chevron came to the house. The letter was short and written in the cribbed letters of the sixth-grade education. Mike could hear his father's voice with each word as if he were standing over the green Formica and chrome dining table. The man had died at the age of forty-six. He now wanted his son to give up his life at eighteen. The long gun board never left the rack of the 1958 Volkswagen with the cracked side window. The sun bleached out the underside, long before he felt the law degree in his hands. The board had been his promise to himself—when he passed the next test. After the quarter finals. Maybe... next week. The weeks had turned to quarters, the quarters to years, the years to degrees. The baggies became pants. The sandals became shoes. The odd jobs became regular. The hair became trimmed, then groomed, and finally styled. Eventually, his feet of faded tan rested under a desk. A desk at the company his grandfather had married into. His father had rejected to do manual labor in the new oil fields of California.

The curl was closing with a long rip of a freight train. The hand tapped at his upper arm, the fingertips holding the pin joint. He looked over at his friend and shook his head.

He looked at his friend. When had they gone their separate ways?

THE PHONE BUZZED. HIS EYES FLUTTERED AND THEN SLID TO THE phone on the desk. He dropped his legs off the desk and reached out for the phone. Punching line four, he picked up the handset.

"Yes."

"Evidently, there is a law dating back to before California became a state. It can be applied to the eastern hills of the Santa Ynez Valley."

"Shit. And you're going to tell me it's still on the books and fucks Jolie Richards square in the back?"

"No. Because, if I had called you three hours ago and told you that, it would be like walking out into the middle of the 101 freeway on a dark rainy night."

"Ronald, I better be hearing a but in your voice."

"Yes, sir. I spent a few hours on the Internet accessing the law library in Los Angeles. I'm just letting you know I'm headed down to look at some other books my old friend is setting aside for me. These books cover case laws relevant to the restricts de Californios. More importantly, these are books I am required to wear gloves and a mask to read. They are so fragile they couldn't be scanned for the Internet, and so the lazy lawyers for Castle never learned all the laws and how they apply to the property. And, I might add, they are in Spanish. Not English or Mexican, but Castellano Española." Mike could hear the pride in the man's voice. His Latina mother would also be proud.

Mike washed his fingers through his hair. "You better be making this phone call from your car phone."

"Almost, sir. I'm just finishing the scans I need to take to my friend. I'm five minutes from being on the road."

"Give me a call on my cell if you find anything useful. Where will you be staying?"

"I'll be bunking in with my friend. I'm the godfather of his two daughters. They love their tio Ronnie."

"Keep in touch, Uncle Ronnie, and make sure your research is thorough enough to cover the weekend with the girls. If you need to take them to Universal Studios or something, make sure you use the company card and bring me the receipts."

"Yes, sir. I'm out of here, and I'll check in with you tomorrow."

"Thanks." Mike hung up the phone, but his hand remained resting on the handset. Something or someone was still hovering just outside his mind's sight.

As he walked out of the office, his arm nudged the door. Not hard, but just enough.

The thought was galvanizing. He noticed the expectant look on his secretary's face. "Shit."

Her face and eyes retreated into a flutter of shock. "Excuse me?"

He turned to his office. Realizing what he had just said and to whom, he stepped back and smiled shyly at her. "Not you, Miriam. Me. You're the best."

He strode back to his desk. Finding the number, he dialed. His finger bent slightly with each pounding poke.

The voice on the other end growled. Mike growled back equally. "Fuck you, Zipper. Meet me on the pier in twenty or get ready to hustle up forty lawyers to keep your ass out of jail."

He slammed the phone down. On the low credenza under the wall of glass sat a framed photo of a young man and his girl. The surfboard towered above them. The same aviator glasses lay folded in front of the frame. Mike stepped to retrieve them and fell flat on his face.

Rolling over and looking at his feet, he saw the two canes under the desk he hadn't used since Montana. "Fuck."

He looked up at the quiet gasp at the door. "I'm fine,

Miriam. I'm fine. I just tripped on those old canes." He first pointed and then scrambled to retrieve them.

As he stood, he leaned out of the way against the credenza. "Sometime when you have a moment, could you find out who could put these and any other of my old canes you find lying around to good use? I've decided to stop being an old man."

He snatched up the fifty-year-old dark glasses and put them on. He slicked his perfect hair back with both hands as if it was long and surfed out. He turned and grinned at the amused smile. "I might even buy a horse or two."

She laughed with him. "Surfer to cowboy. That's quite a change, boss."

He stopped at the door and gently reached over and took her chin in his forefinger and thumb. In his best imitation of John Wayne, he staked his claim. "Woman, the times are a-changing. And I'm a new man."

She snickered. "I think the voice should have been higher and whinier… you quoted Bobby Dylan. The Duke's words were more on the line of a man's gotta do what a man's gotta do."

She laughed at the raised hand as he left. She watched his legs. *Something put steel back in those legs.*

31

BANG BOARDS

Lining boards inside trailers. The boards are thin enough to flex when a horse knocks up against them without causing a bruise. Also used for tying off smaller stock like calves—or people you don't like.

The sun could go either way by one in the afternoon. It could break winter records and become a sweat burner, or it could stay distant and not warm a thing. The day felt to be landing somewhere in the middle.

The gulls on the pier chattered at the anglers. Most people thought they only squealed or screamed like a small child. Angler knew different. If the flying rats screamed at you, you might throw some jalapeño juice on some bread and throw it in the air. Gulls will dive and swallow whole anything thrown up in the air. They also have the magical ability to turn their fourteen feet of gut into a four-inch projectile bombing chute. They aren't stupid, and they do know who wronged them. Sometimes they hit their targets, and other times they don't have time to aim.

There is an old story about a fisherman who became

annoyed by no fish and many gulls. He was fishing with thirty-pound heavy-duty test fishing line—even though nobody had ever caught a shark or turtle off the pier. The story goes he tied a piece of sponge to the end of his line. Soaking it in the almost deadly Ghost pepper oil, he cast it high in the air. The first gull swallowed and shit the sponge in less than a few seconds. The second gull the same. The third and so forth on down his fishing line. He kept playing out the line until he had half a dozen gulls threaded onto his heavy-duty fishing line. And then, he started reeling them in.

Mike had never heard the end of the story because that is usually the part where the listeners start laughing so hard, they either fall off their boards, run into a wall, or fall apoplectic onto the sand begging for another hit on the joint being passed around.

The gulls weren't heavy today. But then, neither were the fishermen. It had been almost thirty years since he saw him last, but Mike could spot Big Red James Castle from half the pier away. The only way he could have improved the chances was to be wearing plaid baggies, huaraches, and a holy tie-dye T-shirt saying Cow-a-bungle.

The swayback of the man had never changed. The light chino slacks and fancy slippers screamed the man's position in life. The golf shirts were a dime-a-dozen unless it said Montecito 37. The country club charged for both courses as well as the large bar between them. Mike knew the entrance fee would pay for a modest two-bedroom condo with an ocean view. The club elites couldn't care about a condo with a view. Their yachts were parked at their other club's private marina away from any oil spills or riffraff.

Mike snorted the laugh only older men took pleasure in or understood. The man leaning his arms on the railing had a combover only half a comb could take care of.

"At least the fog cleared off." Mike waited until James looked up and realized who was talking to him. Smiling, he ran both hands of fingers through his still thick hair. The placid look on the man's face turning sour was an old fart score of two points. The only thing worth more points was catching the other guy soiling himself or evidence of wearing Depends.

The man turned and leaned on the rail. "Threatening a man of my stature is a dangerous game, Williams. I would have thought your father taught you better about knowing your place."

Mike smiled. He had long gotten past his father and where he came from by the time he graduated top of his class both times. His perfect score on the bar exam was only the better salve, and something nobody, no matter how rich or powerful, could take away. Mike continued closing the distance until he bumped chests with the older man.

"Your pathetic attempt at an insult will make this even more personally satisfying. Over the next few months, you will attempt to justify to your friends at your clubs how you were arrested for fraud, grand larceny, land swindling, and an accomplice to murder."

"What the fuck are you talking about? I've done nothing wrong. I run a clean business."

Mike smiled. "Yeah, I know. Just like the clean dope you pushed up and down the coast for twenty years. Just like the houses you sold and then burned to the ground before anyone could find out how you had stripped the copper and painted the interiors with flash paint."

The man's eyes ticked up. Mike smiled as he knew he had hit a long-buried set of bones. Mike pushed his mirrored shades in so the man could only see his own eyes. "Yeah, I know about that. I also know where you buried Shake Shack Tommy's body. Some of your old crew wasn't so tight-lipped as you thought. Not all were into your dope. Some were just common, falling down drunks who had a nasty habit of talking in their drunk sleep."

The man's face flushed with anger. "You're a fucking liar, and I'm going to sue your ass to the wall and wash it out to sea."

"Oh, yes. Tell us about that big contract of yours to clean up the oil spill in sixty-nine. You had half the stoned surfers on your payroll, but nobody was watching the money you were skimming from the Chevron rigs out in the Dos Cuadras Field. How much did you take the drill bosses for, a million? Four? Or was it seven-point-six million deposited offshore in the Cayman Islands. Hell, you'd never even been there. You had the field boss go set it up for you. Your biggest mistake? His mouth—once he started drinking rum."

Mike let the past settle in as he turned and rested his arms on the rail and looked southwest at the oil field they were talking about. The field still leaked, but everyone was told it was just natural seepage coming up through cracks caused by earthquakes.

"You know what your biggest problem is, James?"

"And this great knowledge is coming from where?"

Mike turned his head and looked at the man. "Part of your problem is you never grew up." He looked back out to sea. "The worst of it is never knowing when to shut the fuck up. So I'm going to tell you what is going to happen to you. But first, you need to shut the fuck up."

"Fuck—"

Mike's head snapped around and froze the man. He waited a few seconds and then calmly looked back out to sea.

"First, the FBI will be looking into your company claim jumping in half a billion-dollar swindle. When they are finished getting ready to start proceedings, the sheriff's department will have arrested you and maybe six others as accomplices to murder. The county will swoop in and confiscate everything you have hoarded over the last thirty years. Your home, cars, boats, bank accounts... none of it will ever be returned. It's called seizure and expropriation of private property. And this is the part you're going to love because it dates to 1862. The Union soldiers could seize and expropriate the lands and holding of southerners who were making nasty against the Union. Not only could they but were directed to do so. Just like the way the FBI is going to direct the international banking to go get your money in the Caymans, Belize, Brazil, and Switzerland. Because it is in their best interests, so you can't run. Of course, it's going to be a little tough hiring the lawyers at your country club, but, hey, you've been down before."

"Why are you telling me all this. None of it is true."

Mike's smile was slow and evil. "Let me tell you something you can go ask your lawyer. California, unlike what you believe, has no statute of limitations on murder. So, Shake Shack Tommy? Yeah, you're still good for it."

"Fuck you. That wasn't a murder. It was an accident. He died in an accident. He was told not to smoke around the meth when we were mixing it. The fire was his fault."

Mike shrugged his face. "It was your house, your meth, your crew. Dave puts you two as the only ones in the house when it went up. But, somehow, you were the only one who made it out. What are they going to find when they dig up the body? Bullet or knife, James? Did you shoot him or just shove a knife in his ribs? Was he fucking your girl? Selling on the side? Or did you find out he had turned into a snitch for the cops?"

The man leaned in. "Fuck you. He was never any good, and you can't dig up bones from the Trestles. Your little fishing expedition bagged you squat. Go run back to your little land office and leave the shark shit to us great whites. Your fishing pole is nothing but trout and perch shit."

Mike smiled and turned back toward the mainland. He waved over his head. "When they fuck you, I will spend every day in the courtroom. And if the county runs low on funds to prosecute you, I'll give them the funds they need."

"FUCK YOU, ASSHOLE."

Mike smiled as he grabbed his hair with both of his hands and pulled it to the full three-inch length. Some revenge is sweeter than others.

THE STEAKS HAD BEEN PERFECT. THE BONFIRE TWINKLED IN Mike's eyes as Punchy listened to the recording. The pad of paper was filling, and he had turned the pages several times.

Punchy stopped the phone and leaned back in his chair. "Man, remind me to never get on your bad side."

Mike leaned his head forward and looked past Punchy at Jolie. "I think we're good unless you piss her off. And then you're on your own."

The deputy tapped his pen on the pad. "Do you have any proof on any of this?"

Mike smiled. He had been waiting for the right moment. "Give me a minute."

They watched as he went to the trunk of his car and brought back a banker box. The weight was obvious when he set it on the low table. Jolie smiled at the wrought iron table when it didn't budge, sag, or groan. She had no way to know it had already passed the test of Dot and Pink sitting on it.

Punchy nudged his chin. "Going back, how far?"

"In 1967, there was a funky accident. A friend of ours had gone down to Camarillo to pick up some fresh fruit. He sold it on the beach to make dope and food money. They had a falling out, and he had moved out of the house Castle was renovating. Fred's car was old, but not that old. The brakes failed, and he ended up going head-on with a big rig. The tractor-trailer won. The cops didn't care much about another stoned surfer, so they never took a close look at the car. I bought the car out of salvage for twenty bucks. They let me use their hoist, and I looked at all twenty-six feet of the break-lines. There were two small cuts to leak fluid.

They were the only shining parts on the underside." He pointed at the box. "I borrowed a camera and took photos. They're in there with the original police report. Even after I brought them the evidence, they told me the case was closed, and they didn't care to reopen it. The district attorney told me the same."

"And you think he cut the lines?"

Mike chewed a moment on his lower lip. "He's the only one who had any motive. Anyone who lived at his houses knew the shenanigans he was up to. But nobody cared because they were poor hippies or surfers or just dopers, and whoever bought the houses were considered rich or the man. There was a strong sense of fucking the man back then."

Jolie hooked her boot on the edge of the table. "It still carries through. I still sense it when I'm getting feed or even at the Roadhouse. There doesn't seem to be any divides, but there is the city and the rodeo. Everyone looks at boots." Her right hand draped from her lap and found a black ear to fondle. "Only Pink looks into people's souls."

Punchy stared at the glowing coals, and his head only bobbed a slow twitch. "What about this Sad Shack guy?"

"He was kind of strange animal. When he was sitting out on a board, he was like a statue. He had a hundred-mile stare. Even the days when nothing was really happening, and we were just bobbing out there with the seals and talking shit, he was looking north. He was the first person I knew that I think 'being in the zone' applied. Suddenly, he would take off before any of us knew what was up, and sure enough, he had seen or sensed a rogue wave. Nothing big, but one to take him in. That was the beauty of a long gun—if you could get it going, it would slide forever."

"But the shake part?"

Mike nodded. "The shakes. It was like a palsy or something. He was good for about an hour after surfing, but then, when he got inside any building, his hands had this mild shake. Nothing huge or even noticeable, but just enough to make his signature look like a three-year-old had signed it."

Punchy waved at the still unopened box. "And all of this…?"

"Copies. All the originals are in a safe down in Los Angeles. Some are even in evidence bags, like the slug a surgeon pulled out of Jolie—which is now at the FBI lab with a report. The hard part will be finding the right 30-30 in a haystack of 30-30s."

Jolie took a slow, thoughtful pull on the beer. She crossed her boots and laid her head back. "We'll just have to make it come to us."

3 2

OATS

Semi-rolled oats treated with molasses are like candy to a horse. They can attract a horse, they can get a horse to follow you, and they can entice a horse to do what you want them to do.

Mike and Punchy sat quietly in the dark-wood-paneled office. Mike guessed walnut. Punchy smiled at the dark stain on the birch plywood. He remembered helping his uncle hang all the paneling in the new courthouse. Where the public could see, the woodwork was solid heart redwood or Calero walnut. The trim was gumwood. If the loggers had been cutting the tall eucalyptus for its straight oak-like grain, nobody would have bothered with the gumwood. Stain would blotch the same as pine. It was Punchy's job to wipe the thinned shellac on all the trim molding before staining it with a tinted marine varnish. The tinting was what he hated the most. They handmade the dark brown tint by peeling the skin off black walnuts and then cooking the stinky skins to black tar-like goo. The naphtha they thinned it with tore at his throat. After the one summer, he studied twice as hard, knowing he never wanted to be a finish carpenter.

He looked at the lower edge of the bookshelf along the north wall. He smiled. Nobody had ever cared enough to come back and retouch the bad section of stain. They had just stuffed the shelf with books no one would ever move.

The judge slowly turned the page.

His left eye appeared between the top of his horn-rimmed glasses and the foliage of his bushy eyebrow stretching across his face. The pupil pinned Punchy to the old-blood red leather club chair.

"You've read through all the documents and logged all the evidence?"

"Yes, sir." His voice lacked the usual bravado of the cowboy. He was acutely aware of which chamber they now sat. There were lesser chambers, but short of traveling to Sacramento, there was none more powerful. This wasn't hotdogging around a ranch or playing social judge for catching four underage boys with one of their father's bottles. This was what all deputies raise their hand for—but seldom saw or ever wanted to see.

The man hooked his index finger into his thick glasses and slowly moved them onto the paper in brief. His left hand moved to pinch the bridge of his nose. His eyes closed in thought. Washing his hand in a question mark over his face, he leaned back. The well-maintained chair uttered only the shift of his body on the leather.

He sighed as he looked at Mike. "The statute of limitations on much of this ran out forty-some years ago. Much of this, even then, would have been an infraction, a few fines here or there and he would just move on."

"I'm aware."

"I'd have to find someone in the building department who can even guide me through some of this." His index finger gently bounced the glasses on the file. "Pushed all into a pile, it sounds like a horror story—the kind no normal person would want to move into, much less buy." His face folded in around his eyes. "I mean, wasn't there any building inspectors back then? There had to be *some* building codes in the sixties, wasn't there?"

"There was. But the Uniform Building Code gets played fast and loose when the county and city are looking for more, bigger, and better revenue from new or enlarged houses. If a shack only a surf bum or three will live in can be cream puffed into what looks like a nice middle-class home, the guy with the family working at a company or the county is going to pay more income tax, buy more expensive food, drive a better car, buy clothes for his kids, and take his family to doctors who do the same. If the house was only a two-bedroom on a large lot but built into a four-bedroom with three bathrooms—the yard left is not as important as the new property tax base. Inspectors during a building boom looked past shoddy foundations, undersized wire, and other problems inherent with a contractor cutting corners with an untrained and stoned crew."

The man steepled his hands at his chin. "But by the seventies, he was moving into developing…"

Mike shifted and leaned in. "By the seventies, everything was rocking and rolling. The recovery from the 1968 fire was finally getting funded. They were finishing off a mansion a week up in the Montecito Heights. East Mountain Drive went from a bunch of old bohemians to respectable lawyers, doctors, and bankers overnight. Our company went from twenty properties of rugged mountain slope to developments. In six years, we added more than thirty more large tracts of land people wanted to develop as mixed use. They wanted some residential while keeping the upper wild. In seventy-six alone, we picked up almost a thousand hectares along the coastal face."

The man's face furled. "A hectare is…?"

Punchy snorted. "A citified way of saying two and a half

acres. But it's a square of one hundred meters by one hundred meters. Out in cow country, we call it a plot or a quarter square."

The man's head bobbed up. "From Rome. I knew I'd heard it somewhere."

Mike continued. "With all the building, Big Red was dropping in crews made up of a bilingual foreman and the rest of the wetbacks who never did construction before. I wasn't paying attention, but I wouldn't be surprised if he even sent trucks south to get more. Up into the eighties and the real boom, many of the crews were working with story sticks."

"Story sticks?"

"Eight-foot--long sticks with black paint on the bottom and marks like sixteen inches where plugs were to go, and eighty inches for tops of doors and windows. There were wars between developers where they would go over at night and cut an inch or two off the bottoms and repaint them. The buildings would end all wonky and have to be torn down. Except most were sold before being half finished."

The judge leaned forward and grabbed the folder with the brief. He flipped through the pages. "This Shack guy....?"

Mike sighed and thought. The twinges in his back were better but still a constant reminder. The metal hip and leg were the other two reminders, and why he hated flying with the airlines—the Trestles. One too many rides, taunting the mouth of death. One too many spins of the Surfer's Roulette. It only took that one sudden stop where resilient board, immovable train trestle piling, and squishy body meet. Mike knew all too well how the pilings could break a bulletproof body and how the violent surf could tear apart a strong surfer, much less a corpse.

"We all surfed the Trestles. Even in the good seasons, it's dangerous. If he dropped him in there during the winter, the body would have been chewed up by the time they got back to any dock. At the Trestles, the surf closes out from high and straight into the hardpan. There is nothing soft like sand. It would be like putting a grape on the table and hitting it with your shoe."

"Murder has no statute of limitations anymore. But without a body…"

Mike and Punchy both smiled. "What about attempted murder?"

One end of the brush eyebrow stood on end. "How attempted are we talking?"

Mike cleared his throat. "The FBI office down in L.A. has the slug the surgeon pulled out of the shoulder of the victim. He put back in about four pounds of composite metal to save the arm."

"Any guess on the slug?"

"30-30 and not from close range. The surgeon said the bottom half of the slug's barrel or body was in great condition. If we can find the rifle, he can make a clear match."

"Where's the surgeon?"

"Los Angeles."

"But the shooting was up here?"

Both men across from the judge rolled their lips. "Mitigating circumstances."

Punchy added. "In the interest for the safety of the victim, moving them was the prudent course of action."

The judge drew a deep breath and let it out slowly as he put his glasses back on. He looked near the back of the brief.

"It's not in there."

The man looked over his glasses at Mike. "When did this shooting happen?"

Mike cleared his throat and mumbled. "End of last summer."

The judge shifted his attention to the man in uniform.

Punchy put up both hands. "I know, I know. Highly irregular, but it wasn't like we found a body and started an investigation…"

"So, you swept it under the rug and—"

"No." Punchy realized his voice was more of a bark. "Sorry.

But, no, I started an investigation but didn't file it. We still don't know who all is in on this."

The judge thought as his finger gently slid up and down on the underside of the half-turned page. He released the paper and closed the file folder. Leaning back into his chair, he glanced at the small clock at the corner of his desk.

"I'm obviously not taking lunch today, so why don't you explain what this is really all about."

Mike leaned forward. "Let me still try to get you some kind of lunch."

The judge leaned back in his chair and waved his hand palm up at Mike.

"There is a piece of land over on the east hills of the Santa Ynez Valley. This piece is one of the old townships. That is two miles by two miles. One person owns it, but we manage the different aspects of the property, such as the free-flowing artesian well and a couple of working oil wells."

The judge turned his head and looked out of the side of his eyes. "Two miles square… so four-square miles… and owned by one person."

Mike nodded. "She owns about seven square miles total but has no idea what all she owns."

"But you manage it for her?"

Mike nodded. "About eight years ago, someone set her up for murder, and she went away to Lompoc for seven. But recently, there are some shady activities involving a hostile takeover of part or all her property… at least the township. But she got out of prison and started taking care of the property, and they shot her."

"But you don't know who did the shooting?"

"It's complicated, but all of this"—he pointed at the brief —"is related somehow."

"You think Big Red is involved?"

Mike grabbed at the edge of his chair with his leg and

shifted. "He says he's not… but at least one of the suspects is family. A grandson."

"So, you two are trying to…?"

Punchy jumped in. "Trying to find out who has the 30-30."

The judge scratched at the side of his nose. "Popular rifle."

"It is, but we think we have a way to draw it out. Otherwise, we'll need a search warrant."

"Where?"

"The Valley."

"Give me the call, and I'll have it ready."

Mike and Punchy stood. "Thanks for your time, Your Honor. It's good to know when someone has your back."

"Where is the original recording?"

"In my phone, his phone, and on micro, which is in an evidence bag with the rest of the bags."

The judge shrugged his lips and face into a smile and stood. "Err on the safe side." He stuck his hand out. "Keep me posted."

JOLIE WAS GETTING TO HATE THE NOISE AND USELESSNESS OF THE Roadhouse. In her twenties, it was louder, more cowboys, and at least one good fight a week. Now it was just noisy, more city types, dime-store cowboys and girls, and a heated argument was about all the general tempers could tolerate. The ice blue eyes under the brim of the black hat longed for a fight with at least a few bottles and a pool stick or two. The two at the other end with their thumbs all over their cell phones weren't going to provide any excitement.

She took another sip on the shit water and almost longed for real lightning.

The stool on the side away from Pink slid out. Celeste slung her leg over and sat. Her arms were bare and rested on the edge of the bar. Jolie didn't bother focusing. The out-of-focus drunk-look blurred her vision only slightly but made her look hammered. It had become a joke with Dot. When one of the kids landed a punch to her head, Jolie would stumble around with the stunned or drunk-look on her face until the kid dropped their guard—then she would step in and kick them into the corner. Dot was always there to scream and yell at them about getting suckered. The lesson never needed to be repeated, but Jolie had taken personal pleasure in learning new ways to sucker the kids. They learned never to get close to any fighter who appeared to be a standing knockout.

Jolie looked down the bar. Her head swam from wall-to-wall as if searching. She took another sip, swished it around her mouth to build up a nuclear salvo of bad alcohol breath, and swallowed. The glass hit the bar with a knock.

She swayed on her stool as she slid around and leaned her elbow out along the bar. Her fist was at her ear. "Where's your boyfriend?"

Celeste pointed down the bar. She had long stopped asking or appearing to care about Jolie's condition. She figured the alcohol mush for a brain would never know the difference.

"No…" She slurred and leaned in close. Celeste leaned away. "Not your hubbud… hu… husband. Fuck it. Randy. I mean that Smith & Wesson guy."

Celeste's head snapped around. "You mean Colt? What do you know about Colt?"

Jolie's body waved back and forth as she smiled as lecherously as she could. "He has a full load—if you know what I mean. Those pants are stuffed to the top."

Celeste rolled her eyes low. Her mind was back to high school and ready to share with her friend. "You have no idea. That's why he wears those stretch jeans. He gets more ballroom to dance in."

Jolie's eyes grew big, and she held her hands about a foot apart. Then she cackled, elbowing her old friend.

Randy looked up from mid-bar and strolled down. "Do I have to cut you two off?"

Celeste braced her sandals on the rungs of the stool and leaned over the bar to give her husband a quick peck. "I'm done. It was a long day down in Santa B. Don't wake me up when you come in." She looked back at the top of the large black hat. "But somebody could use some coffee."

She stepped off the stool and strolled out as she waved to a couple of calls from around the bar.

Jolie's eyes cleared as she leaned her back against the bar. She tried to think about Celeste's clothes. She couldn't remember her ever wearing anything considered real cowboy. The fancy jeans and boots were rhinestone. The shirts were Nudies with fancy stitching on them. Even her stonewashed in bleach jean jacket in the eighties had been punched with stitching and rhinestones by the slave-labor at the Susan and Tony Alamo cult ranch in Arizona. The official Tony Alamo of Nashville jacket was her prized possession. She had worn it everywhere, except to watch Jolie ride, for fear of some drunk cowpoke spilling beer on it. Or worse yet, spitting chew on it.

Jolie's eyes closed as she tried to remember when her best friend had stopped coming to watch her ride. The only scene she could bring up was the Santa Maria rodeo. Her father and mother were in the stands. Celeste had come. She had even been sitting with Jolie's folks during the opening parade. But there had also been a boy sitting next to her. Jolie had known by the looks they were giving each other they wouldn't be able to keep their hands off each other for more than half an hour. When the calf roping started, Jolie's folks were alone.

The voice was low. "Shot of beer for your thoughts."

Jolie's eyes opened as clear as they were at noon. "Just thinking about Celeste and when she stopped coming to the rodeos."

"Did she ever go? I mean, did she ever go to watch the rodeo… or even watch you ride?"

Jolie drew a deep breath and let it out. "I used to think so. Back before Thunder and I got serious."

Randy snorted a laugh. "That goofy horse Launchpad. I remember him. He loved pulling blankets off other horses when riders were tacking up."

Jolie laughed. Her chest was warm with him remembering her first serious horse. "You should see the two goofball mustangs I'm gentling up over at Norm's. Everything is a game with them. They take the blanket if you don't strap it fast enough. Even a western saddle is no match for them. Off it comes. If they are first to get tacked up, they are pains in the butt."

"You're shittin' me. Mustangs? And they want to get tacked?"

Jolie nodded as she turned around. "Same as you want to get your dick sucked. They know petting and carrots and attention come with the tack. So they jockey and hip check each other to be first. There's a young groom named Tonisha. She figured them out. Once we got a rope on them, it was just a progression of the game. Carrot, petting, maybe some brushing, then tack up and taking turns on the longe line. A few times I've left the saddles on them and ground tied them while I go eat lunch in the truck. They are good as gold."

"You ground-tie them, and they stay?"

Jolie laughed and then laughed at the idea of a mustang staying. "Oh, fuck no. But they're only wearing hackamores, so they start grazing what little grass they can find."

"When you gonna get on?"

"I'll probably try a fifty-pound sack next week. I want to have them close to bridle by the Fourth of July. Maybe even ride them in the parade if the crowds and noise don't spook them."

He leaned on his forearms and watched the door. "You doing okay with training jobs?"

"Why, you need help here at the bar?"

"Nah, just wondering. Your land must have one hell of a nut for taxes. I wouldn't want to see you lose it."

Jolie closed one eye and looked at him with the other. "What makes you think I'd lose it?"

His face wrinkled uneasily. He shook his head in a jiggle. "Just something Celeste said a few months ago. It never sat right with me."

"What about?"

He hunched forward, and his head ground around to look at her. "Something about losing it to taxes or having been away so long. I never thought about it, but those years… you had to be doing something."

She looked back at the door. Her hands washed and rubbed at her eyes, and she yawned. "Taxes are up-to-date in November. Next ones are due in June. I'm covered."

She stood and bent over to kiss Pink on the nose. Standing, she looked over her shoulder. "And, Randy, we never had this conversation."

He smirked his wan smile up into his right cheek. "We never do. Oh, and by the way. My bar hand is still wondering if you ride on her side of the fence or not."

Jolie chuckled lightly. Her cheeks pooched with her broad smile. "Keep her guessing, Randy. Keep her guessing."

"Good night, Rocket. Good night, Pink."

The wave was just above shoulder height. He could tell she was tired, and morning would come before dawn. With Rocket, it always did.

33

———

FARRIER

A blacksmith who shoes horses—but is also usually
the first trained eye to spot health problems.

Fernando stood in the doorway. His smile was soft and shy but eager.

"What the hell, Fernando? What are you doing down here?" Jolie leaned out and looked around the wagon yard. "Where's your big-assed truck?" A white car sat nosed to the horse rail.

The man laughed. "I was told I didn't need it." He turned and waved his hand at the broken, empty corral. "Then I get here and see why… Your corral is broken, and they all ran away. Que pasa, chica?"

Jolie rubbed the sleep from her face and eyes. "Fuck. I need coffee for this." She turned and walked toward the kitchen. Stopping at the door, she looked back. "Geez, Freddo, you're family. Get your ass in here."

She noted how shy he was as he took a tentative step into the house. He started to swing the door shut.

"No need to close the door. Pink still needs to go potty, and the flies are too afraid of the owl, so they never come in."

His arms reflectively raised as he protected his face with his hands. "Owl?"

She snorted and waved toward the one wall of the living room. The seven-foot wingspan stretched out as if the stuffed barn owl was just leaving its perch on the large branch sticking out of the wall. "If you can pound out feathers, I'd like an eagle over the barn doors."

The man stood staring at her bare feet and then down at his work boots. Jolie laughed with a snort and turned back toward the kitchen. "You figure it out. The maid hasn't been here in forty-some years. She ain't showing up tomorrow or next year. Bare feet or boots, the boards get swept out either way when I feel the need. And I don't feel the urge coming on any time soon. How do you take our eggs? Minute steak or man steak?"

The young man looked around from the doorway into the kitchen. "What is man steak?"

She turned and held up a sausage with the end bit off. She chewed as she watched the tide of red wash up from his shirt. "Okay, you get the minute steak." Turning, she pushed the eggs around the pan as she made room for three more. "So, in Montana, you weren't bashful. But come to California, and you're just a shy boy? What did Jinx tell you...? I was a wild woman and would jump your bones at the drop of a pair of jeans?"

"No." His voice was as husky with embarrassment as his neck was red.

She flipped the steak over. Taking up the one skillet, she scrapped the eggs onto one plate. Turning, she took down another plate and pushed half of the eggs onto it. With tongs, she flipped the steak and then pulled it onto one of the plates. She pulled the three sausages onto the two plates—two for her and the other one for him. "You really need to taste this sausage.

I want to order another few hundred pounds of it. Or I want the recipe."

They ate in the silence of hungry. Fernando noticed the work gloves stacked on the counter. Work starts early on a ranch, and he hadn't caught her in bed. Even a ranch with no livestock has work to do.

She gathered her knife and fork at the five on the plate and leaned back with her coffee in her hand. She watched him eat the last few bites.

His fork froze a half-inch from the last bite. He looked up and saw her watching him. He looked down at the bite, then wiped his mouth. She hadn't moved. Her blink was slow. "What?"

She took a slow sip of her coffee. The power of not moving or talking she had learned in prison. The person who moved or spoke first was insecure, and therefore, the loser. "You're the one who drove down here. You tell me."

"Up."

She thought about what the word could mean—altitude or direction. "From where?"

"Glendale."

She took a soft sigh. Her right foot was twitching, and the large black weight rolled onto it—stopping it from scratching at her side. "When am I expecting Dot?"

The man rolled his wrist over and looked at his watch. "Any minute. You do have more food, right? I mean, you wouldn't want her to get hangry or anything…"

"Shit." Pink jerked to attention. Jolie stood and opened the refrigerator. The two eggs and a dinner steak stared back at her. *Just enough.*

The sound of the laboring truck, making the turn into the wagon yard, brought her attention out of the almost empty refrigerator. Seven years of having three meals a day magically appear in front of you was a habit she was going to have to work on getting over.

She turned the stove back on to start reheating the large cast-iron skillet. Turning, she pointed at Fernando. "Coffee is in the cupboard above. Throw out the last of the old pot in our mugs and make a fresh pot. Two of the scoops so the spoon will stand up in it." She rushed out the side door through the utility porch.

She waved Dot to pull over to the barn as she swung the large doors open. The voluminous building stood as clean as any garage in the city. The new boards and repairs to all the stalls dotted the morning gloom of the interior. As the sun shifted, Jolie knew the barn became lighter until it became downright bright with the large doorway facing into the western sunset. When there were horses, the eastern doors could be opened to catch the early light. The morning side was where the washing was done on the large concrete apron. The double-ended barn with its tall doors also allowed the hay trucks to pull straight into the barn and fill the hayloft above without using the loft's end window doors. As a young girl, Jolie was sure the hay doors were only there for her to sunbathe in the nude.

As the doors swung open, Jolie grabbed her raised hand for Dot to pull the truck and trailer into the barn. "We can unload from here later, but the skillet is warming up, and the steak and eggs are probably on your order to do first."

"Fuck. You mean I needed to stop for coffee?"

"Geez, girl, where do you think you are? Some pull through in the boondocks? This is a high-class full-service joint here. We serve elk steaks, eggs, coffee, bruises, and aching torn-up muscles. Fernando is whipping up some fresh coffee as we speak." She watched as the end of the trailer cleared where the doors would close to and still leave ten feet or more. Her hand gripped in a fist. She glanced at the other end. The nose of the truck wasn't even at the halfway point. She rarely had ever thought about how large the barn was—only how happy she always was when it was full of the smell of horses and fresh hay. It would take work, but it would be there again one day.

The truck murmured to a stop. The snap of the seat belt accented the creak of the opening door. Jolie stepped into a solid wall of hug. As they hung, she sniffed at Dot's neck. "New perfume?"

Dot shook with laughter. She turned back to the cab of the truck and pulled out a large paper bag. "I stole a bunch of fresh princess rolls. They were hot when I bagged them, but a few seconds in the nuke, and we're back in heaven. It's a carb day."

A while later, Fernando peeked in the battered bag. His face was one of a child about to cry. Jolie laughed. "Afraid not, Freddo. I got the last one." She tore it in two and offered out the smaller part. Dot mock snatched at the prized morsel. Fernando jumped, and the bread disappeared.

Dot roared with laughter. "Like a bunch of hooligan guttersnipes. Ain't nobody in control."

The young Filipino-Latino looked around. "Me no see no adults."

Jolie leaned back in her chair with her mug at her lips. The idea sunk in. "Sweetheart, we are the adults."

***

"What is this room?"

Jolie looked around the small apartment. "This would have been where a groom or stable hand lived." She stepped into the doorway to the bathroom, which was almost the size of the living space. "I'm sure they walled in one of the horse stalls when they added the indoor plumbing back in the teens or twenties."

Dot and Fernando leaned in and looked at the tiled room. The hard surfaces echoed, but with the large south-facing window, it was cheery. The glazed tiles on each wall made a picture of early California history. The floor in front of the large claw-footed tub was a study of a Persian rug in tile.

Jolie smiled softly at the two gasps. "My grandfather was

friends with the tile maker in Pasadena. They designed the space and tiles together." She waved at the large counter with the sink. "This is Monterey and the fishing fleet. Over the tub is the story of Ramona, Santa Barbara mission is this wall, and Sutter's Mill is the small wall."

"This is like a museum." Fernando smoothed his hand over the tile. "These look like they're new, but almost a hundred-years-old."

Dot snorted. "If the tile maker be Batchelder, this is a museum. He was the best in California. His name is the big one when you talk about craftsman homes. And this be just the groom's bathroom in the barn." She hiked her hip and smiled at Jolie.

Jolie could feel the low heat around her neck. She had never shown the bathroom to anybody who knew anything about it. "Well, it's the blacksmith's bathroom now."

Dot looked at the glazed leaves and wisteria draping down into the large sink. "Oh, hell no. This is not where you wash off the black and grit. There's a tub outside for that."

Jolie rolled her eyes. "Well, if it makes you feel better, they replaced the toilet just before I got out. I guess the old one was cracked or something. Mike had the plumbing gone through house and barn. I think if I could have given him enough notice, he would have had all new electrical pulled through the house. All you need out here are a few lights. Right?"

It was Dot's turn to snort. "Not hardly. I'll need four-hundred-amp service just for my grinding room. I have one grinder rated two-twenty at thirty-amps. It's a beast, but it cuts the time for hollow grinding a sword in half. Then there is the four-axis mill. It's old and—"

Jolie held up both of her hands. "Okay, okay... I get it. I know horses... not blacksmithing. I'll call Mike and see what we can do. Jeez, who thought getting a roommate could be so complicated."

As they walked out into the barn, Jolie looked at the stall next to the bathroom. "How much space do you want for all the machines? We can wall off a couple or few of these stalls, and even cut a door straight out to the forge area. And then have them add lights out there in case you need to work past beer time."

"You sure I'm not taking up too much room?"

Jolie hung her head to one side and fluttered her right eyelid. "Did your mother drop you as a kid?" She raised her arms and slowly turned. "Does this look like a tiny back shed? My grandfather built this to house up to eighty horses or more. In those days, wagons and buggies were still in common use. Horses were important. Now, they are more of an affection or hobby for people who can afford them—or think they can."

She turned and pointed down along the one wall of stalls. "Even if I fill up all those with boarding, it's over fifty beasts. Throw in a couple of goats, and there is more work than even two people can do." Her voice softened into a husky note. "But man, it will smell like heaven."

Fernando peeked under the tarpaulin covering the trailer. "Which one is Christmas?"

"The trailer be the small grinders and belt sanders. The back of the truck be the extra gear and coal. Dat go outside."

Jolie walked toward the east end. "Why don't you pull up here. Park the trailer for later, and then you can pull the truck around to the forge area. I'll call Mike and ask what we can get done for your workroom. Maybe they can plumb a washbasin outside next to the outhouse." The two laughed at Dot's expense but received a couple of punches to shoulders.

34

SNAFFLE

Snaffle rings are the rings at the side of a horse's mouth. They're attached to the bit in its mouth and to the bridle about their head. This gives more of a spread pressure to guide the horse where you want them to go.

The sun was barely up when the two men stepped away from the group and up onto the porch. The older one, in the green khaki uniform and armored vest with the word SHERIFF stenciled on the back, rang the doorbell. The younger brunet in the sunglasses, pencil-thin mustache, and a blue windbreaker with the three yellow block letters of FBI, stood to one side. His right hand rested on his weapon while his left was ready to fish out his identification from his left rear pocket.

The agent looked up at the size of the house, and then back at the twenty uniformed deputies and agents. He wondered if they had brought enough manpower.

The door handle clicked. All nine feet of the wide door opened. The man filled most of the door. He took in the armed uniforms and vehicles lining his driveway and then turned to the deputy sheriff.

"What the hell, Larson. Why are you and your stormtroopers invading the last quarter of decency on this early Sunday morning?"

The FBI agent stepped forward. "James Castle, we have a warrant to search your home and offices." He held out the blue wrapped legal paper.

James ignored the man and continued to wait for an answer from the deputy he had known for decades. The man was the subordinate in the search-and-seizure and waited.

"Mister Castle, we——"

The grizzled white-haired head snapped around. "I don't know who the hell you are, but I'm talking to the only person I know. So get the fuck off my porch before I throw you off."

"Sir, we have tried this the easy way. So now we will resort to the hard way. Mister Castle, please turn around and place your hands on your head. You are under arrest for obstructing officers of the law in an ongoing investigation."

The man leaned in. "Fuck you." And as he stepped back to close the door, the agent stepped aside and waved his left hand.

The deputy standing at the bottom of the steps pulled the trigger on his green shotgun. The beanbag deployed at three hundred feet a second. In less than a hundredth of a second, the bag struck the large man in the chest and pushed him backward —to slide for twenty feet on the polished marble floor.

Deputy Larson waved at the deputy for the gun. "You shot him, son. Now go field dress him. Don't forget to read him his rights."

"Yes, sir."

Larson pointed to two other deputies. "Big Red is called big for a reason. Go help Danker get him up off the floor and into his car." The officers smiled and waved from the top of their heads.

The FBI agent turned around. "You've all been paired and know where you're deployed." He smiled and waved his hand in a sweeping motion as the teams invaded the house.

As the squad hauled the large homeowner out the front door, he smiled and held up his hand for them to stop. "Mister Castle, just so you know. This is the United States of America. We are a nation of laws. Just about everyone you bought off, bribed, or blackmailed—we have people even more powerful. After we find what we are looking for, we will start going after them. And when we are finished, you won't have to worry about knowing anybody to hang out with in prison; you're going to know plenty of old friends. They just might not want to talk to you."

He looked at the deputy and snarled. "Get him out of here."

———

THE NEIGHBORHOOD WAS QUIET. THE MEN IN HELMETS AND BODY armor waited crouched behind the wall. The garage door across the street opened with a silence only money can buy. The silver Mercedes Benz sat next to the Lincoln Navigator. To the discerning eye, the vehicles were a matched set. The licenses were SAL3S 1 and SAL3S 2. One of the deputies smirked. Anyone who had any mild dealings in real estate would recognize the cars and their license plates. The two were the most competitive agents in the Santa Ynez Valley. Both were brokers with their own agencies. Their competitiveness had brought them together. Lust had sealed the deal.

The two pink-tinted toy poodles strolled out of the dark depth of the garage. They were followed by the middle-aged man in a satin bathrobe open almost to indecent. Nine pairs of swat deputies couldn't miss the pink rhinestone encrusted high-heeled cowboy shoes or the mass of pin-curlers covering the man's head.

The lead dog yelped once. A heartbeat later, the man realized what he had mistaken for green foliage across the street. His coffee sloshed. "Oh my." His fingers snapped at the two dogs as he tried to draw his robe closed. The coffee slopped all over his front. "Shit. Bitsy, Sheena… get the fuck in here." He retreated with or without his dogs. The dogs only rushed to the safety of the house when they saw the garage door coming down.

The muted snickering along the wall was covered by the soft sound of the hive radio. "We have a visual of a single male seated in the dining room, and we have a thermal in the back bedroom on the southeast corner."

Two clicks acknowledged the information.

"Thermal moving."

"Heat signature obscured. Suspect shower. Still in southeast corner of building."

Two clicks.

"Units one and two, brace front door."

The two four-person teams took their positions.

The deputy in body armor and the FBI agent walked up the walkway. Their earbuds mumbled with an update on the two occupants of the house.

A white truck, with tinted windows, drove slowly past the house and SWAT team. Nobody looked—the focus was on the house. Nobody noticed the decal on the truck driving by matched the decal on the truck in the driveway. The truck reached the end of the block and turned left for the highway.

The deputy waved his hand at the doorbell. The FBI agent smiled and pushed the button. They could hear the scrape of a chair on a tile floor. The lack of the sound of footfalls might have been because of it being early on a Sunday morning.

The door swung open. The barefoot man was in his mid-thirties. His stringy hair hung from a hairline of plugs circumnavigating his head. The left septum of his nose was collapsing. The deputy and agent both suspected, from experience, cocaine, and he was left-handed. Thickening of the skin in the web of his hand from the industrial-strength acetone and ether would bare them out. The pupils of the man's green eyes were blown and only semi-focused.

"May I help you, officers.?"

"Mister Colt? Timothy Colt?"

The man weaved slightly and flared his eyes to focus on what was going on. "Nah, he went up... up... he went somewhere yesterday... I think."

The agent held up the search warrant. "May we come in and see for ourselves."

The man took a half step back. His attempt at waving them in resulted in him stumbling back against the wall. Unfortunately, only half of his back landed against the solid wall. The other half landed in the open air of the kitchen doorway, and he stumbled until he landed on the kitchen floor.

The deputy closed his eyes and then opened only one to look at the agent. Sometimes busts are what you expect, and other times, you just need to bite your tongue and laugh about it later. Professionalism, some days, could be a bitch.

The deputy looked over at team two as the agent stepped into the house. "Gonzales, Tucker, there's a guy on the floor in here. Take care of him until we see what we find."

"Sir."

The two started in.

"And Gonzales..."

The deputy turned. "Sarg?"

"Try not to get vomit all over your armor."

The partner smirked as the deputy rolled his eyes. Some things you never live down. He hoped only until retirement.

The sergeant looked at the mess in the kitchen and smiled at the agent. "Shall we see what we have in the shower?"

The two were halfway down the hallway when they heard the shower turn off. They stopped to listen. There was no sound of a shower curtain or door.

Suddenly, a tall blonde with silicone boobs the size of volleyballs bounced around the corner. Her head and shoulders were tipped as she focused on drying her long hair. Her voice was more of a whine than little girl sexy. "Baby, you're all out of cream rinse. Can you… oh." She stopped and stared at the two men. Her eyes were blinking in confusion about every half-second.

The agent jerked his thumb over his shoulder. "Baby is kind of indisposed at the moment. Maybe we can get one of the nice deputy sheriffs to go get you some cream rinse."

Her hip jacked out to one side—twisting the tiny thin exclamation mark of blonde into a loose S. Her smile did more to expose her goofy IQ. "Really? Would they really do that for me? I would really like it." Her eyes continued to blink.

The deputy cleared his throat. "Is there anyone back here with you?"

She sparkled at finally knowing an answer. "You two."

"Um, do you have any clothes you can put on? The doors are going to be open, and it's going to get a bit chilly."

They followed her into the bedroom to oversee anything she might touch or try to conceal. The room looked like the bed had thrown up everything, and nothing seemed logical. They guessed at a wild drug-fueled night. The woman opened a drawer, pulled out a few square inches of pink see-through cloth connected with string, and stepped into the thong. She adjusted it until it covered just enough. Next, she rummaged around until she found a matching bra.

She bent over, struggling to capture the twin volleyballs. The bra was destined to cover less than the thong.

Finally, standing up, she adjusted the straps until they sunk into the channels over her shoulders. She looked up as she snapped the straps with her thumbs. "Is this enough?"

"You did take evidence photos, didn't you?"

The three deputies gave the agent a glaring look of boredom. Sometimes the joint interagency investigations took strange or tedious turns and twists. "Every last pack, baggie, and mirror lined with coke, meth, or sharpie mark."

The young agent ignored his lecherous joke question. At the end of a very long day, sometimes the humor fails to rise to such an opportunity. "What about weapons?"

"Three handguns and a .223 semi-auto. There were clips for an MK-15, and even 100-shot clips for AR-15s and AK-47s. But no 30-30."

"Yeah, we were bust also. A shit load of shotguns and hunting rifles, a BAR, a Korean War bazooka, enough handguns to arm the west coast, and even 30-30 shells… but no rifle."

"Did he have shells for the bazooka?"

"Nah. One of the guys checked it out. The firing mechanism had been DOD decommissioned."

"How did he know it was DOD?"

"It had been shot with a hammer and cold punch. The tip of the punch had a D on it."

One of the deputy's phone rang. He looked at the caller and answered. The conversation was short. He hung up. "The dogs are done for now. There was so much powder scattered on the rugs they had to take them outside, vacuum, and start the dogs over. They found twenty more pounds of coke and over forty of what they think is meth hidden under the floor and in a wall stash." He looked at the agent.

The man shrugged. "One would think, if you have millions, you would keep the illegal side of your business away from your home. The old man only had a couple of pounds at the home—party candy. But his offices yielded major distribution. Our teams will expand and be busy for weeks. Tomorrow they will get an expanded set of warrants to go after his banks and see what he had in boxes and accounts. They figure it will all lead offshore, and we're not talking Santa Catalina."

35

HEAT

When a horse or bull shows exceptional bucking or spinning,
making them less to be ridden, but producing high scores to those who do,
they are said to have 'heat.' Sometimes, heat is good, but other times,
too much can be deadly.

The late night of a rodeo was always a mix of good and bad. The temperature was cooler, and Thunder liked it. He stood cool and collected in the chute. Her bare hand ran along his neck. The skin twitched—more in connection than irritated. The lights in the arena were dancing and wavering. There was a wind up in the grandstands they couldn't feel down in the chutes.

The roustabouts were struggling with the calf in the other chute. Jolie could hear their muted, angry voices. She couldn't figure out how or why they had removed the gang chute which would have held six or ten calves all lined up. Occasionally, there was the rare time a second calf snuck through into the chute, and it threw off the rider. Expecting to find one target when they break out and find two can be confusing for the rider and also the horse.

The hot breath was in her face. Launchpad was eager to go. The barn wasn't right. Something… She checked her slippers. The pink one on the left didn't match the fuzzy sheepskin on the other—but it never did. Launchpad's breath smelt like elk burgers. She needed to brush his teeth so they would look nice when Punchy jumped… jumped… ju… jumped out of…?

Pink wasn't playing games. She pushed Jolie out of bed with her nose and shoulder.

The strange moving light was the same. Jolie looked at the window. It was outside. The angry voices were too.

She stood and edged to the side of the window. A man was lighting something in the other man's hand. It flared, and he threw it at the house. The bottle shattered, and the firelight flared brighter. *Molotov cocktails.*

She backed away from the window and stayed low. She grabbed at her clothes. "Pink. Go wake up Dot. Go get Dot." The dog stayed. "Shit."

They slid out into the hall. She called out quietly. "Dot. Wake up."

Hopping her way into her jeans, she made it to the doorway. She rolled around the doorjamb. The bed was empty. "Dot?" She looked in the dark bathroom.

"Sssst. I'm down here."

Jolie and Pink turned and raced to the stairs. As they hit the landing, Jolie glanced at the windows. The entire front porch was engulfed in flames. Dot was standing at the bottom.

"I was having a hard time sleeping. I was reading in the back and heard them come in. I locked the kitchen door, but I didn't know how to lock the front door." Jolie could tell by her fidgeting she was scared but solid.

Something hit a window. It might as well have been some small gravel on a windshield. "Just so you know, the windows are good up to a Sharps fifty-caliber at fifty-yards. I think that would also cover anything these yahoos brought with them. Inside the wood of the door is a steel door. It also is basically assault proof. My father had every window on this floor replaced. So, for penetration, we're good." She turned toward the front door.

Reaching up, she gripped the small set of antlers from a California red antelope mounted on a board—and turned the whole clockwise. The sound of heavy metal rods clunked from around the door. The rack returned to its upright position. "It's not smooth or easy, but you can hang a coat or two here, and nothing will happen. To open the locks, turn it the other way." She pointed around the door. There are six rods on each side and four top and bottom. They just set an inch into solid steel all around. I don't think even a tank could come through this door."

Dot's face darted back and forth from the front windows to where the door was by the kitchen. The flames were just as bad through the window over the sink. "Okay. So, they can't come through the windows or doors… but how do we get out? There's no fire out back…"

Jolie leaned in. "Do you see me panicking?"

"No."

"Then stop panicking until I tell you to panic." She waved her hand at the dark windows along the back of the living room and library. "They didn't light up the back because that is where the man with a rifle is. If you could open one of those windows, you would be back lite by these. Then bam, they push your body back in, and you burn up with everything else."

"So what now?"

Jolie sat on the edge of the couch and reached into her boots. Pulling a sock out of each, she put them on and slid her feet into the boots. Her smile was slow and evil. "We go hunting."

Jolie turned the knob on the large buffet. The top lifted a fraction of an inch in the front. She pulled it upright. Reaching into a compartment in the back, she pulled out a harness of leather. She pulled it on over her bra and then pulled on her black T-shirt. Looking at Dot, she evaluated the dark brown shirt with a blacksmith on the front with the words: Pound Iron. It would be dark enough. She looked down at the woman's boots and pointed. "Knives?"

"Four."

"Anything else you might want from in here?"

The woman shook her head.

Jolie wiggled her eyebrows and smiled. "Then let's go underground."

She stepped to the front door.

"I thought you said underground..."

Jolie looked back as her right hand triggered a catch. The board running up as high as the plate rail swung out. She reached in and pulled out a lever-action 30-30. The barrel was slick with no sights. It had been her grandfathers. Stooping, she pulled out a belt with a box of bullets inserted in loops. She closed the secret door.

Then she turned. "Just in case we need it."

She strode to the pantry door in the kitchen. Opening it, she stepped in. "Come in, but I want to close the door before I turn on the light."

The back wall revealed a stairway going down. "There's another stairway hidden in the office off the library. I think my grandfather took Indian attacks seriously."

As they passed the cold cellar, Jolie opened the door. Dot looked in. Just the tour attitude was having a calming effect on her. "I think we can pack and store a year's supply of food in there. There is stuff in there now, but until someone tells me it's still good, I'm not going to eat anything more dangerous than prison food." She waved. "Come on. We have work to do."

As they walked, she pulled her phone out of her hip pocket. Glancing over, she explained. "One thing bad about all the steel they built into the house is the satellite can't see my phone. But under here, we only have dirt over us."

She pushed the one and held it down. The phone beeped, and she drew her thumb off.

"Punchy, there are about four or five men here. They torched the front and side of the house and are waiting for us to run out. They all had rifles when I looked… No. Dot and I are fine. I'll explain later, but we're in the barn. We're going to sneak out around and find out who is behind the house. Pink might get fed some extra meat tonight." She leaned and tousled the dog's head and ears.

"I think so. It's up to you. If you trust him, get him. Call me when you guys are here. I don't want to shoot a clown in the confusion. It would just feel funny." She hesitated. "Yeah, you too." She snapped the antenna down and stowed the phone as they got to the stairs leading up.

The barn was dark, with only slits of yellow light. Dot's truck and trailer hulked dark in the middle. Dot leaned in and whispered, "We can just drive out of here…"

Jolie shook her head. "They're not here to scare us off. They're here to kill me. I know who they are. Well, at least I know who two of them are. The rest are mixed up in it, but they aren't going away. This ends here. Now."

Dot grabbed at her arm and looked her in the eyes. "I've only had one other close friend who was like a sister to me. I'm not going to lose another."

Jolie nodded as she wound her long blond hair into a knot in the back. "We need some grease or something…" She looked at Dot, and her chest shuffled a chuckle. "Okay… I need something to darken my face and arms."

Dot smirked. "Over here."

Five minutes later, Jolie was as dark as Dot. Both greased up, but Dot's was in jagged lines on her face and arms. Camouflage was camouflage.

"The main doors here rollback. But the one on this side is narrower. After you showed me the other small doors, I looked around over here." They squeezed between piles of cast-off ranch equipment. Reaching the wall, Jolie reached high. The soft clunk of wood on wood allowed the narrow door to swing out. Jolie slipped out and held her hand toward Dot to stay. She snapped her fingers for Pink. The last thing she wanted was for the dog to run around front and straight into the barrel of a rifle.

A moment later, she waved through the door to Dot. She motioned with her hand a curve around and up the hill behind the house. Dot nodded. The three moved in the dark like shadows. As they walked up the hill, Dot stopped Jolie and pointed at the ground. Her voice was barely more than a breeze. "Is this a lawn?"

Jolie rolled her eyes but realized the mindset of city versus someone living in a forest where fire was a real danger. "No. But I have run the rake and mower through here for three hundred yards out from the house and barn. It makes it hard to burn, and for us now, no twigs to snap." She turned and then turned back, burying her mouth near Dot's ear. "It also makes it easier to walk in the dark. No small bushes to stumble over."

They stayed on the backside of the small ridge. They could hear the angry voices carry in the night. Occasionally, one of the men would shoot at the windows. Jolie hoped no one thought to shoot at the second-floor windows, which were not bulletproof.

At a point, Jolie pointed up at the ridge. She passed her right hand, like a knife, up and over her left arm to signal they would be crossing over. She stopped two fingers at the top of her arm and then pointed at her eyes.

Dot smiled and talked low. "That good signing and all, but they can't hear us."

Jolie shrugged. "It's good practice."

Dot frowned and looked at the ridge. "How come the house don't burn?"

Jolie smiled. "Every year or two, Dad would spray down the wood with a mix of zinc and borax or something. The feed store has it. It soaks in, and over the years, the wood becomes extremely hard to burn. It's not fireproof... or at least I don't think, but it is hard to burn."

Dot's smile glowed in the night. They crouched low as they crested the hill. Jolie lay down and looked for a shape on the hillside that was not a tree. The secret was to keep your eyes moving and not focus on where you were looking. The dark lump of a man became obvious, and she pointed. As they slowly moved closer, even Pink crawled on her belly. She liked the new game.

There was just enough light in the night for the man's hat and pants to stand out. Jolie thought about the hat and more about the tall-turned cuffs on the man's jeans.

She knew the uniqueness of the English snap-cap should jog her memory, but it didn't... and then the image was clear. Not recently, but before she went to prison... someone else was recently out of prison.

The man had been leaning into the bar. His one foot in the low boot-shoe was shot against the foot rail. Jolie had seen men turn their cuffs so high around the rodeo. They called then washboards. When a cowboy works in high chaparral brush, the extra layer of protection provided by buying the longest leg you could buy and turning the extra up in a long cuff, kept the thorns from sticking your legs above your boots. The stiff, prickly brush would wash on by.

She had seen a few men wearing the shoes that looked more like the lowers on a cowboy boot, but without the height. They were slip-on, more like loafers. This man's shoes were battered and worn. They were the perfect mirror for the sweat stains creeping an inch or more up the band of the cap. Dirt encrusted the cap, which probably hadn't been washed for years—if ever.

Celeste had leaned over and drunkenly whispered in a loud croak. "It's Francis MacFarland. He got released last week."

Jolie jumped as she heard Celeste's voice again, bringing her back to the present. She looked around the ridge and then realized it was coming from the lookout's radio. The man raised the walkie-talkie to his head. "No sign backa hair." The brogue of the Irishman sealed the memory.

Jolie slowly made her way down behind the man. She could see him working something out of his shirt pocket. His attention was on the back of the house, its windows, and his cigarette.

His lighter chimed as he opened the top. His thumb was on the wheel as the cold steel of the barrel snuggled down against his head where it met his sweat-stained collar. The hat sat cocked low against his damaged right ear. He froze and listened to the voice.

"Those cancer sticks will be the death of you, Francis. How about just dropping the lighter as you slowly raise both of your hands."

As she stepped around, his face moved from scared to anger to just downright mean. "You funkin' twat. You be dead and cold by morning."

"Ah, Francis, you see, there is where you're wrong. I'm very much alive, and I will be in the morning when the sun is up. But you... well, that depends on how you answer. How many did Celeste and Tim Colt bring?"

"Fook you." He tried to spit, but the thick python of a dark arm snuck around his neck and sucked him into Dot's chest. The man tried to stand or push with his legs. His shoes only moved the loose dirt. Dot rolled forward, and the boney hands slapped and grabbed uselessly at her arm. His eyes grew big and then rolled as his body turned limp.

"How long is he good for?"

"Not long enough. Get his pants off." Dot reached to her boot and drew up a small knife. Pushing the man face down on the ground, she quickly stripped the back of the shirt into four wide pieces of cloth.

Jolie handed her the jeans. They both looked at the tattered, rotting, and not-so whitey tighties. Dot smiled as she cut the jeans from the large seam knot to the fly. She fed the one leg of the jeans over the man's two arms. She drew it all up and buttoned the waist around his neck and then buckled his belt to hold it in place. Taking the second leg, she made one pass around the front of the neck and brought it back to the other leg. Taking one of the ties from the shirt, she poked a hole in both legs and then fed the tie in and tied them together. She reached for the other three ties when Jolie stopped her.

"Oh, no. I'm the professional here." Jolie wrapped and tied the ankles of the man with one tie, and then using the two others, she sat on his legs and tied the calf-tie to one of the legs.

Thinking, Jolie cut the front of the shirt and tied a gag in the man's mouth. She stood and held up her hand. It might have taken more than a single digit of seconds, but it was an award-winning tie-down.

Jolie chuckled as she picked up the small walkie-talkie. "Let's go find another calf to tie."

Her back pocket vibrated. She switched hands and thumbed up the antenna. "Yeah."

"We're down on the west side. It looks like four in the wagon yard. The porch is aflame but not burning. Why?"

"Long story. Do you see Celeste?"

"Yeah."

"Can you record with your phone?"

"Sure."

"Good, I'll call you back in a few minutes. I need to go stir up the hornets."

"Oh jeez—"

She cut him off. Slipping the phone in her back pocket, she turned to Dot. "Let's go get to a better vantage point."

Dot smiled and tousled Pinks head. "And stir up some shit."

36

BARN

Usually, a large wood structure containing all the magical hopes and dreams of a young girl. No matter what her age.

They slipped back into the back of the barn. When the walkie-talkie squawked, Jolie turned it down. She figured when Francis stopped responding to calls, the others would go searching. The man had turned out to be lighter than they figured. The last place the others would look was behind the barn. Laying him in the old rotting wood watering trough had just been a bonus point.

Jolie turned to Pink at the bottom of the ladder. "Gado."

The dog sat facing the noise coming through the front barn doors. The thick board laid in the four flatiron hands, effectively locking the barn doors. Just in case someone got the idea to check the barn.

In the hayloft, Jolie showed Dot the large door where hay could be loaded in or out. Over the door was an extension of the ridge beam with a pully on it. The rope usually hanging in the pully had long rotted away. The door would be only a diversion.

"When I give you the word, I want you to swing the doors out. Not hard, but just enough so they're wide open, but don't bang against the barn." Dot nodded. Jolie walked her a short few steps over to one side. "When they open, I need you to get down behind his wall. The barn siding is only an inch thick. This is at least four inches and over to one side. If they have AR-15s, at least this will give you some protection. Those bullets are made to go through things. Are we clear?"

"Where you gonna be?"

Jolie pointed into the gloom. "Over there is a secret room. There is a small door they will never see. I only need a couple of shots from there, and then I'll be out. Okay?"

Dot put her fist out. They connected.

Jolie lay down in the small room and crawled to the front wall. She felt for the small access she had left as she piled steel plates against the front wall. The plates she was lying on were cold but reassuring. She opened the small door, no more than the width of her palm, and peeked out. Celeste and a man were standing next to a white truck. The other two had probably gone around back to look for the missing Francis.

The flames on the porch had mostly died down. Several places were smoldering, but nothing a fire extinguisher wouldn't take care of. Jolie made a mental note to get more of the magic juice from the feed store and spray the barn and house. She didn't know if Mike knew about the magic juice or not.

She half jacked the lever on the rifle. She felt in the chamber with her left thumb. There was a shell there. Even though she had loaded the rifle only a couple of weeks before, touching was believing. She rested the end two inches in the tiny window. "Open up, Dot."

She could hear Dot move and snuggle into the reinforced hide hole. "Poke away."

The front wheel of the truck disappeared behind the curve of the barrel. Jolie took a breath and let it out. At the count of three, she eased her finger on the trigger. The top of the tire moved, and the whole went flat. The next bullet went through the side window, and she hoped to hit the steering column. She knew the soft slug would do nothing to stop the engine, but if she could stop the truck from being steered.

The hornets stirred as predicted. Both aimed at the swinging doors of the hayloft. Jolie could hear the semi-automatic slugs passing through the tin roof. She was fine with replacing the tin, as long as they stayed away from Dot.

The end of the barrel eased up to just over the man's arm and rifle. Jolie wanted to take him out of the action and only leave Celeste. She knew what a 30-30 slug could do to an arm or shoulder.

The bullet rode along the top of the rifle until it dug into the plastic of the stock. The expanding lead took several of the shards with it, into the shoulder. Jolie wasn't sure about what she saw. It could have been just the shirt getting pulled out, or it could be she had just removed the rotator of his shoulder. Either way, the man spun down face first into the side of the truck.

Celeste, sensing danger, ran toward the only spot safe from the rifle in the barn. The barn doors. To shoot down, she would have to expose herself in the hayloft door.

Good plan… until her walkie-talkie squawked.

Punchy's phone rang, and he started the recorder.

"Good try, Celeste, but I'm done shooting."

"Fuck you, Jolie. You're dead as soon as I find you."

"Dead like when you killed my mother? Or dead like how you felt when you found out Randy still loved me more than you?"

"Fuck you. I laughed when I stuck your fucking pigsticker in her chest."

"She was my mother, asshole."

"She was in the way. And she was old."

"She was only seventy-one. On your best days, you weren't a third the woman she was on her sick days."

Jolie slipped out of the small room. She left the rifle. She closed the secret door, hiding the room forever.

Holding the phone and the walkie-talkie in her one hand, she motioned to Dot to follow. She could hear the large doors being rattled. Celeste screamed with frustration at being locked out.

"You thought you could burn me out in the house?"

"Fuck you. You were supposed to die in prison, you fucking princess."

"Princess? Who the fuck had to have all the rhinestones on her jacket? Did it make it feel better when you found out people died making those fucked up jackets? You never cared about anybody but you."

The doors rattled, and Celeste screamed. "Come out here and fight me fair and square. You ain't shit without a horse. Miss High-and-Mighty, everyone had to suck your asshole and give you everything. You never shared. It was all just for you."

"You never wanted what I had, Celeste. I had barns to clean, horseshit to shovel, horses to feed so they could just shit again. But all you wanted was to ride a horse you didn't understand or love—just so you would look like you fit in. If you don't do the work, you don't get the job."

"Fuck you. I worked… I worked harder than you'll ever know. You never waited tables. Snotty city shits looking down their noses because I was just a farm girl. Try dealing with drunks at five in the afternoon."

"I have. It was you. Only you were usually plowed by fifth period."

"Fuck you… What would you know? By fifth period, you'd had four guys hands up your skirt or down your jeans under the bleachers." She kicked at the barn doors. "Come on out, you chicken."

"So you and the Colt thought you could kill my mother, send me to prison, and steal my land?"

"You were supposed to die in there."

"Yeah, that's where you went wrong. I made friends, instead."

"You don't have any friends. Just like now… alone."

Jolie stood by the small door. In the gloom, she could see a thin shaft of light where Dot was standing next to the other door.

"Was that how it was when you killed my mother? You were alone? Because your boyfriend couldn't bring himself to kill an old woman in her sleep? So you had to be alone. Is that what your problem is? You hate having to do things alone? Killing my mother, and now you are going to try to kill me, but your boyfriend is over there dying in the dirt because you have bad taste in men. Or did I miss something about Randy?"

"Colt was fine. He just didn't have the balls to stab her, so I did. I had the balls. I took your high-and-mighty pigsticker and stuck it through her heart. It was so considerate of you to leave it when you thought you were going hunting up north. What a fucking joke. That was so easy."

Dot opened the door an inch and slammed it shut. Celeste spun, looking for what had made the noise.

Jolie slipped out the other door. Her bare feet were almost silent. As she got close, she growled, and Celeste spun around. Straight into Jolie's right foot to her chest. As she fell back, the rifle flew from her hands. Dot raced past, picking up the rifle by the end of the barrel in her gloved hand.

Jolie stood relaxed, half facing Celeste. The brunette rubbed at her chest. "You always did fight dirty, just like a filthy greaser." She slowly got back up and looked around for the rifle.

"It's gone."

Celeste frowned in anger. "What is."

"All of it. Everything you have worked for. Everything you lied for. Everything you cheated for. It's gone." She held up the phone and walkie-talkie. "It's all recorded by an officer of the law. Your confession to trying to steal my land, cheating on Randy, and killing my mother. All of it. I'll even let you slide for shooting me in the shoulder."

"Fuck you. Shooting you was the best part. But then we didn't find your body. I would have buried you ten feet deep in ten different holes. Nobody would have missed you. You're nothing but a drunk and a whore. You got everything you opened your legs for."

"It was Tim Colt up on the cliff with you the day you shot me."

"Yeah, a lot of good he was… it turned out he really doesn't have the stomach for killing."

"As I said, you suck at men. The only one who was good, honest, hardworking, and faithful was the one you shit all over and cheated on."

Celeste growled and charged. Jolie sidestepped and slapped her face three times, with the last being a punch to the jaw. As the brunette turned back around, dazed, Jolie spun and kicked her jaw, continuing the turn. The woman sprawled face down in the dirt. Jolie kicked her in the ass and crotch. The body jumped two feet further, scraping the face and forearms along the way.

Jolie stepped over her to stand over her spread-legged. As Celeste rolled over, Jolie dropped—bouncing her knees on the chest and then spreading to pin both arms. She dropped the walkie-talkie and phone as her right hand flashed up under the back of her T-shirt. Grabbing the handle, she drew out the large knife in a fast arch. Celeste's eyes pinned open in horror. Jolie's hand spun the blade, and she dropped it to the woman's throat. Her hand gripped the handle backward, the sharp edge alongside her forearm. The rounded edge of the back of the blade rested safely on the woman's throat.

Jolie leaned into the wild, scared eyes. "Now you will know what it is like to die like the pig you are. This blade was built to cut through your throat all the way to your spine. At first, all you will feel is the fire of the cut. And then, you will begin to choke on your own blood. When the blood stops cooling your brain, you will feel what is called brain fire. It is your brain overheating and cooking itself in your skull. By that time, your heart will have pumped all the rest of your blood out into the dirt where it belongs. Then your muscles start to convulse because they don't have any blood or oxygen. The finale is when your body goes into grand mal seizures, and you will piss and shit your pants. But unlike the epileptic girl you made fun of in the seventh grade, your brain will be wide-awake. The last thing you will experience is your body acting like every spastic you ever made fun of. It will be soiling like every kid who had an accident in school, and you made fun of. Yes, you are about to become all the people you ever made fun of or hated."

Punchy and Norm stepped up. Punchy wasn't sure of Jolie's game plan. "Don't do it, Rocket. Killing her isn't worth the time you'd have to spend back in prison."

Norm finally saw the large knife and panicked. "Jolie, don't. She will go to prison for what she did. Don't throw it all away."

Jolie's eyes took on a maniacal swirl as she leaned closer and pushed the dull edge deeper against the neck. "All because you hated me so much, you became my best friend. And then you killed my mother—the only woman whoever treated you decently. The only woman who ever loved you unconditionally, who would have taken you in if you asked, who would have given you anything you asked for, but instead, you killed her. And for that… I'll pay the price." Jolie jerked her hand.

The smell was instant. The humiliation from the shit and pee took a second longer.

The bullet sped past just over Jolie's head. Punchy hit the ground. Norm was a little slow, the red blossoming low on his white shirt.

Jolie fell flat on Celeste as she called at Pink. "Boko. Boko banzai."

The black shadow became wind in the night. The man didn't know what hit him. A moment later, the man's throat was missing. Jolie watched. The body didn't move. "Tatsi. Hiza."

The dog returned to her side. She reached out and stroked the head once. "Go find the other one. Boko." She turned to Punchy. "There's another one out there… up behind the house. Or was. Pink will find them and disarm them. But this time, she won't kill them. There is also another one hog-tied behind the barn in the old wood watering trough."

"I'll take care of them." He turned and tried to find where Pink had disappeared in the dark.

Jolie looked down at the angry face of Celeste. She looked up. "Hey, Punch?"

"Yeah."

"Leave me your cuffs. I need to help Norm."

She looked at the man on the ground holding his side. He waved. "Yeah… no. I'm good. Just leave that toad sticker somewhere away from me."

Jolie stood up and flashed the knife in the air, and then hid it back under her shirt in its magnetic scabbard. As she stood, she kicked at Celeste's side. "Roll over, stinky." She cuffed the hands and then used the zip-ties on the ankles. She looked at the two extra ties and smiled.

She knelt next to Norm. "Let me see." She lifted the shirt and saw the two holes leaking. Norm was only applying pressure to the front. She pushed gently on his shoulder. "Lie on your side. I'll be right back."

She rushed around the side of the barn. She felt for the two switches Fernando had installed a few weeks before. The lights came on in the forge area as well as the large floods at the peak of the barn. She listened at the forge. The air was forcing the low coal to become red-hot. The steel rod Dot seemed to always leave in the coal was red as Jolie took it out. She thought about the hole in Norms back. Grabbing a hammer, she pounded the end with a three-count. Dot came around the corner. "What the hell? This no time to be playing around."

Jolie brushed the angry red end down with the wire brush. The metal looked as clean as it was going to get. As she passed Dot, she spun her with her empty hand. "Come on. I need you to hold Norm."

Holding the steel rod where he could see it, she fished his back pocket for his wallet. "Here, bite down on this. You're going to need it."

"What the—?"

"Bite." She looked at Dot. "Straddle his shoulder."

The man sounded like a bull in a squeeze chute, getting a new brand. Jolie jammed the end an inch deep. She wasn't sure what all was bleeding, but she wanted to stop the leak. She pushed on Dot and then stepped on his hip to turn him. She repeated the probe in the front hole, but deeper.

Somewhere during the slow three-count, Norm passed out. Dot grabbed the wallet with her free hand and held it in place.

Both women looked up at the lights strobing through the trees. Neither had heard the sirens.

The squad cars parked in defensive positions. The deputies hit their doors and pulled their weapons. "Drop the gun."

Dot didn't move. Her hand was at the end of the barrel. In the light, it was obvious she was holding the rifle, but not to use it. "Bring an evidence bag, and I drop it in."

"Drop. The. Weapon."

"Stand down." The bark came from the dark side of the barn. All eyes watched as a man stumbled out. His face and clothes were torn. His wrists were zip-tied behind. He was missing one shoe, and the sock was almost off.

A uniformed Punchy strode out of the shadow with a rifle over his shoulder. His hand held it by the barrel. "I said stand down. She's holding the 30-30 we've been looking for." He planted his boot on the back of the butt of the man and pushed. The man stumbled and nose-dived the dirt.

The sound of collective weapons being holstered almost sounded like rain falling.

A young deputy raced around his car door and approached Punchy. Punchy held out the rifle. "Hold it here on the end to preserve the prints. If nothing more, we can get him for vandalism and arson. Bag it and get him in a car." He turned to two other deputies. "Behind the barn, there is an old wood watering trough. There's a guy lying in it. You're going to need a knife to untie him. I don't know where his weapon is, but maybe one of the girls can tell you."

He turned to look at Norm. "We're going to need at least one ambulance."

"On its way. We heard the gunshot over the radio and figured someone would be leaking."

Punchy looked at his old partner. "Thanks, Gabe. Good to have you here. There's a body over by the white truck. He is the Colt guy they've been looking for. Check and see if the DA gets a shot, or it's case closed." The man saluted.

As he walked over to the huddle of people at the barn, he snickered. The night was a usual rodeo—all the fast riding and noise, and him watching in the barrel. The memory of old times felt warm and good. He glanced back at the sound of a single-pull siren. Ambulance. The warble of the Buellton's fire department EMT was right behind.

"Other than Norm, everybody okay?"

Jolie glanced back at the for once silent body of Celeste. She sighed and settled into Punchy's side embrace. "Just glad it's over."

Punchy glanced back at Celeste. "No regrets. You never lost

what you never had." He nudged his chin toward Dot. "But you gained so much more."

Dot snorted. "If this is the kind of nights you have on Tuesdays, I'm moving out before I have to experience a Friday."

Punchy chuffed. "At least stick around for the wedding."

3 7

FLANK

To be on another's side. When driving cattle, the stock hand riding along the side of the herd is a 'flanker' or 'riding flank.'

The early morning sun warmed the stone patio. As long as Mike could remember, he had been coming here. His father or grandfather had brought him as a young boy. The view had captivated him and still did. The surf pounded the point. There was never any accommodating surf, just a hard-sweeping crash. The spray was gentle at six or eight feet. Mike had seen the pillar of water reach up and then out to drench or capture tourists standing a hundred feet away. Nobody who knew the point would go near the jetty on a violent storm day.

"Remembering surfing?"

His face lifted on one side in amusement. "Out there? Never." His thumb and middle fingers rotated the mug. "Nah… just thinking about coming here when I was four or five. I don't remember if it was my dad or grandfather who brought me. I think both of them were as in love with this spot as I am."

Jolie rolled her head on her neck. The sun felt good and loosened her shoulder. "Kind of like the blue oak on the cliff. I think I want my ashes spread there with Mom, Dad, and his parents."

Mike raised the one eyebrow and looked out of the side of his dark glasses. "They're all up there?"

She rolled her lower lip into her teeth and nodded as she stared at her low coffee. "Them and a lot of dogs." She leaned back with a soft smile. Her right elbow hooked the back of the chair. "Not to mention a few burros."

The wave hit the point hard, and the spray caught his attention. The curl of spray sparkled with a momentary rainbow. The water died and ran back over the rocks and out to the sea. He looked to find the waiter and motioned with his finger. The young man grabbed the carafe and brought it over. As he poured, Mike turned his attention to Jolie. The lace over lace sundress left nothing of Rocket. This was all surfer girl on the beach. If he looked, he didn't even think he would be surprised to see her toenails painted a shell pink.

Her smile grew slowly. "You know, when you look at me that way, you almost look like some old lecher."

He laughed. His top teeth and bottom lip caught at the tip of his tongue. He had laughed easy like he had the last few months when he was around her. "I'm not old, just…"

"Yeah, I know… wine."

"I was thinking about how you are two very different people. There is the horse or Rocket, and then there is the surf Betty. If I didn't know about you and horses, and only saw this side of you, I would think you never got further than a mile from the ocean."

"Surfer not a sailor?"

"Ocean." His tone was safe and noncommittal.

She smiled. "And here you are preparing to become horse."

His smile was all silent laugh. He leaned back. "You have to admit it—I'm going to be living in the best of the two worlds."

"It's going to be a nice house. If nothing more, the view will get you up in the morning."

He leaned into the table and sipped on his coffee. "Speaking of houses, how is the scraping coming on yours?"

"Manual says he won't have to go down more than a half-inch on any of the bad stuff, but most of it was just a light char. If they need to replace anything, it will only be a few of the battens. And he'll soak those in the same borate stuff before he puts them up."

Mike wagged his head. "For years, I heard people swear by the magic juice, but I had never seen it work. While you were away, the ramrod told me to have it hosed down every other year. So, on the even years, he power washed the buildings and then sprayed them with magic." He glanced at the surf—thinking. "I'm glad we did."

They sat watching the surf, relaxing in their longtime mutual friendship. Comfortable.

Jolie sipped on her coffee. Her left hand draped to find the one ear. She was rewarded with a low musical moan. The seagulls cried as they sailed over the people walking along the narrow sand.

"So… Punchy…"

She tried to keep her smile slow and small. It wasn't in her nature. The teeth showed, and the ears stepped back to make room for her smile. A reporter had once written about her smile. He said if a horse could smile, her teeth would be what they would dream of looking like. The next rodeo, she had broken the man's nose. After the doctor set it straight, she took him out, and they never made it out of the bar. She realized, in his own way, he had pegged her inner soul as a horse, and only her smile let it show.

She nodded. "Punchy…"

Mike pulled the top of his mirrored glasses down and looked

over the top. "You have to admit, that was one strange marriage proposal."

"In a heated moment, some people get horny." Punchy, on the other hand, realized he was the kind of guy who wanted a woman who could take care of him.

"I guess you proved yourself there."

"He was afraid I was going to cut her throat. But I had never intended to kill her. I hadn't intended to hurt anyone. I just wanted her to confess, give up the other guys, and then find out just how I felt. Anything beyond is in the hands of other people."

"Are you going to the hearing?"

"No. They'll let me know when I need to be around for the trial. Other than testifying, I'm done. I have too much catching up to do."

"And a wedding to plan?"

She flattened her lips and blew a raspberry. "No planning needed. I just need to find a horse for me and a rodeo who needs a clown. The rest is easy."

He looked at her over his glasses.

"Seriously. That's it. Jinx has a horse for you and Dot. Pink here doesn't need a horse, and Fernando… Well…"

She started laughing. "It's Fernando's duty to be the best man."

"Why can't I be best man?"

She almost couldn't talk as her body shook. "Can you jump in and out of a barrel?"

Her purse sounded a bugle blowing charge. Every good rodeo started with a mass charge of every rider. She pulled the phone out and thumbed it open. "Yeah, Manual."

She leaned back in the chair. Her left leg came up as she tucked the barefoot under her right. Her seating slowly melted from proper to lounging. Mike watched her. The hard edge she had left the prison with was now softer, and she could relax. It wasn't all over, but the light at the end of the tunnel was the sunrise, not the 4:15 express from Atascadero.

He gently leaned back with his mug and thought about her parents. Her father wouldn't understand, but her mother would be proud. The troubled young woman... was becoming just a woman.

As he watched the spray at the end of the jetty, his mind was on the side of a hill an hour away. The early morning light was creeping down the western hills, reaching for the darker valley below. A pheasant lifted from the low scrub brush, flying close over the tops of the brush dotting the lower hill. It was joined by another, and then another. Soon, the flock was a wave moving to the fields in the lowlands. Early worms and bugs. The horse under him pawed at the ground. He knew it wanted breakfast. He took a last look. The twenty or so stakes had ribbons on them. The light blue was for the morning surf, the white for the foam, and the black for the night sky soon to turn orange gold as he caught the first wave. He pulled gently on the reins, and they headed to the other home for breakfast.

He was going to enjoy his new neighbor—even if he couldn't jump in and out of a barrel.

3 8

FENCED

When not allowed to run free.

The bus was cleaned occasionally. But even with the use of the most toxic cleaners, the smell of human stench —sweat, shit, and urine hung in the hot stripped-down to the metal bus. The windows didn't open, even if the bars and mesh weren't in the way.

The klaxon horn bellowed three times, followed by ringing the loud bell signaling opening the gate. The two tall gates shuddered as they crept back. The lack of speed made sitting on the bus all the more painful. Two more guards joined the two on the dry bridge over the gate.

The bus crept forward into the capture of the sally port. The gate retraced its path. The prisoners in orange county jumpsuits sat quietly in the steaming bus. The air-conditioner only blew moving air on the driver and guards. The fan at the back, designed to draw the cooler air back, had long been broken. The funds for something so uncritical had never been spent for repairs

The bus stopped at the disembark station. The engine was turned off. The key removed. The driver passed the key through the small window to a guard outside the bus. The bus was now useless for making an escape. The driver opened the door and exited.

One of the guards stood and drew out the key to the wire door separating the exit from the prisoners. "You will remain seated until called. When you are called, you will stand up in the aisle. There is to be no talking. If any of you talk, I will lock this door, and we will wait. If this is clear, nod your heads." He watched as all seven prisoners nodded their heads.

He pulled up his clipboard. "Cabot."

The prisoner slowly turned her feet into the aisle and stood. She shuffled until she was facing the guard.

"Come forward." He waved his hand.

A guard came into the bus. The deputy nodded his head. "Go with the guard."

He watched as she struggled with the shackles. The feet could only stretch so far from each other. Occasionally, a prisoner wasn't careful and fell. The deputy knew the guards weren't there to make the prisoner's lives hell, but they weren't there to make it easy either. Prison was a punishment.

As she touched the ground and the next guard came on the bus, he turned. "Franklin."

THE GANG SHOWER WITH THREE GUARDS WATCHING HAD BEEN ITS own hell of unpleasant memories from high school. The lack of a decent towel was only annoying until the haircut started. Because of lice, all new prisoner's hair was cut down to a #2 military cut. Any skin below now lay exposed.

She stood with her forearms level to the floor, holding her bedding and personals. The sand tinted khaki jumpsuit was stiff with newness. The six large stenciled numbers reeked of the acetone used in the ink. The shoes felt more like lead.

The loud buzz rattled from above the door. The door slid back.

"Forward."

She shuffled, the chain slapping like a dog's tail around her ankles. The large atrium on the right reeked like the blue plastic port-a-potties at the county fair, memories of standing on the bench, holding her shorts and panties, squatting so as not to touch skin to seat. She wasn't sure if she could squat for twenty-years, much less for the full twenty for murder, ten attempted murder, and a full twenty more for conspiring to commit murder, fraud, and land theft. Her forty-seven years of age weighed like she was already a hundred.

The wall of wire-embedded windows looked out tauntingly at the main gate and the freedom she knew she would never have again. It would have been better to have no window at all.

"Prisoner, stop. Face the door."

The guard never let his site waver. "Open cell three-one-two."

The general bell rang. The warning buzzer over the door hummed like an angry herd of hornets. The door rolled back

"Step inside the door and stop."

The one guard stooped down and unshackled her legs.

"Put the bedding on the floor."

The door buzzed and rolled back into place.

"Face the door."

The guard stepped to the small square of open air in the middle of the bars. "Clasp your hands and extend your arms through the port."

He removed the handcuffs and silently walked off.

Celeste chuffed to herself. "Talkative fella." She turned and looked at the white-haired woman standing, looking up and out the small barred window. There was a sparseness about her, but also a steely resolve.

Mary turned. Her hands clasped again in front of her crotch. "Hello, Bug. We are going to have such fun with you." Her smile was anything but light or warm.

Celeste swallowed as her eyes took in the catalog of scars on the woman's face, arms, and hands.

"Yes, such fun."

BAER CHARLTON

ABOUT THE AUTHOR

Baer Charlton graduated from UC Irvine with a degree in Social Anthropology, monkeyed around for a while, and then proceeded onward with a life of global travel, multi-disciplinary adventure, and meeting the memorable array of characters he would come to describe in his writing. He has ridden things with gears, engines, and sails, and made things with wood, leather, and metal. He has been stitched back together more times than the average hockey team; his long-suffering wife and an assortment of cats and dogs have nursed him back to health after each surgery.

Baer knows a lot about many things in this world. History flows through his veins and pours out of him at the slightest provocation. Do not ask him what you may think is a simple question unless you have the time to hear a fascinating story.

You can find more about Baer at his website.
www.baercharlton.com